Deep Fried Revenge

By Lynn Cahoon

The Farm-to-Fork Mysteries
Deep Fried Revenge
One Potato, Two Potato, Dead
Killer Green Tomatoes
Who Moved My Goat Cheese?
Novellas
Have a Deadly New Year

The Tourist Trap Mysteries
Memories and Murder
Killer Party
Hospitality and Homicide
Tea Cups and Carnage
Murder on Wheels
Killer Run
Dressed to Kill
If the Shoe Kills
Mission to Murder
Guidebook to Murder
Novellas
A Very Mummy Holiday
Mother's Day Mayhem
Corned Beef and Casualties
Santa Puppy
A Deadly Brew
Rockets' Dead Glare

The Cat Latimer Mysteries
A Field Guide to Homicide
Sconed to Death
Slay in Character
Of Murder and Men
Fatality by Firelight
A Story to Kill

Deep Fried Revenge

A Farm-to-Fork Mystery

Lynn Cahoon

LYRICAL UNDERGROUND
Kensington Publishing Corp.
www.kensingtonbooks.com

To the extent that the image or images on the cover of this book depict a person or persons, such person or persons are merely models, and are not intended to portray any character or characters featured in the book.

This book is a work of fiction. Names, characters, places, and incidents either are products of the author's imagination or are used fictitiously. Any resemblance to actual events or locales or persons living or dead is entirely coincidental.

LYRICAL UNDERGROUND BOOKS are published by

Kensington Publishing Corp.
119 West 40th Street
New York, NY 10018

Copyright © 2020 by Lynn Cahoon

All rights reserved. No part of this book may be reproduced in any form or by any means without the prior written consent of the Publisher, excepting brief quotes used in reviews.

All Kensington titles, imprints, and distributed lines are available at special quantity discounts for bulk purchases for sales promotion, premiums, fund-raising, educational, or institutional use.

Special book excerpts or customized printings can also be created to fit specific needs. For details, write or phone the office of the Kensington Sales Manager: Kensington Publishing Corp., 119 West 40th Street, New York, NY 10018. Attn. Sales Department. Phone: 1-800-221-2647.

Lyrical Underground and Lyrical Underground logo Reg. US Pat. & TM Off.

First Electronic Edition: April 2020
ISBN-13: 978-1-5161-0989-0 (ebook)
ISBN-10: 1-5161-0989-9 (ebook)

First Print Edition: April 2020
ISBN-13: 978-1-5161-0990-6
ISBN-10: 1-5161-0990-2

Printed in the United States of America

To my boys, you are missed.

Acknowledgments

As I was starting this book, we lost our old man, Demon. He lived a long, happy life with us—nineteen years. He had congestive heart issues and with our other dog, Homer, leaving three weeks earlier, I think his heart just broke. And so did ours. The house was way too quiet although Thor (our cat) tried to fill the void. We took the plunge into puppy land. We have two new family members. Dexter and Quinn are Keeshond puppies. They are smart and active, and they make the house full and happy again. Even if I don't get a lot of sleep.

Big thanks to my Kensington family for the love and care they gave me during this time. And to my agent, Jill Marsal, who just happened to call the same day I lost Demon. She said all the right things and listened to my sobs. Not the most professional I've been on calls, but she virtually held my hand as I dealt with the news. Jill, you rock.

Chapter 1

Angie Turner tucked the smiling teddy bear into her backpack as she walked around the carnival with her boyfriend, Ian McNeal. Idaho's largest fair had just started that morning, and they were enjoying the fun. The sun had just dipped behind the mountains, and the heat of the summer Friday had started to ease. August was typically hot and sticky, and today's weather hadn't disappointed.

Ian pointed to an ATM set up on the grass by the funnel cake booth. "I need to stop and get some more cash."

"How much did you wind up spending on Picasso?" She wiggled the bear's dark-blue face that she'd left sticking out of the top of the backpack.

"I really don't want to talk about it. I thought I was better at throwing a baseball than that. If anyone finds out, I'll have to give up my spot on the church league." He took out his wallet and pulled out his debit card.

Angie glanced around the carnival grounds. The grass, which had probably been green and fresh before the traveling carnival had set up earlier that week, now looked like a crowd of elephants had trampled through the field. The lights for the rides and the games were brightening as the natural light dimmed. Happy they'd gotten out tonight before the restaurant challenge started tomorrow, she walked over to the treat trailer while she waited.

A redheaded man glared at her as she started to speak, then he walked away from the window. Angie could hear him mutter to a young girl, "Go do your job."

The pretty girl blinked at the harsh tone, then walked over to the window and smiled down at Angie. "What can I help you with, honey?"

"Cotton candy please."

"Pink or blue?" The young woman leaned down so she could see Angie's face. "I bet you're a blue girl. Kind of a rebel, right?"

"She's definitely a rebel." Ian held out a twenty to the girl. Then turned to Angie, "So, blue?"

"Now I want to say pink, just to be contrary." Angie glanced at the two bags. "Okay, give me the blue."

As they walked away, Ian stuffed the change into his wallet. "I might have to go get more cash depending on where we eat dinner."

"You don't have to buy everything tonight. I have money too." Angie took a big bite of the fluffy candy that melted immediately in her mouth and tasted like freshly picked blueberries. "Yum."

"I am not letting my favorite girl go Dutch treat on our first date night to the fair." He held his hands up in the air, taking in the lights and sounds of the crowds. "This is what memories are made of, and I don't want you telling our grandchildren that their papa was always cheap."

Angie took another bite of the blue fluff. It gave her a moment to gauge her feelings about Ian's comment. Sometimes the thought of settling down with one man, in one place, scared her just a bit. Today, though, it felt okay. Probably due to the sugar high she was getting from the junk food. She decided to ignore the comment and turn the conversation back to dinner.

"I thought we'd hit the United Methodist Women's tent, at least for dessert. Felicia's volunteering there tonight. But first, we have to visit Estebe at the Basque Center tent. They're both working the restaurant this weekend." Angie stepped over a large power line in the path in front of her and ignored the catcalls from the carnies in the fishpond booth. "Next weekend, we'll really be short staffed. I need Felicia with me on Friday and Estebe for the final night."

"Do you really think you'll have customers during Fair Week?" Ian glanced around the carnival. "We've only been here two hours, and I think I've seen half the population of River View."

"Fairs are big business, especially in an agricultural area. Reservations are down, but not low enough we need to close." She pointed to the haunted house ride. "Let's do that before we eat."

"Only if you'll do my favorite too." Ian stopped at the ticket booth. "Are we doing more than the two? The armband is probably the best buy if we decide to ride four or more."

Always calculating the costs. She wondered if he'd glance at the County Seat books. Maybe there was a way to cut some costs there. Produce had been killing her budget this summer, but everything was so fresh and clean.

She wanted to buy all the food. She filed the idea away. Tonight was date night. Not let's-talk-business night.

"We're still early for dinner." She took in the sparkling rides and lights. "Let's do the wristbands and pretend we're teenagers."

Ian chuckled as he ordered the wristbands from the totally bored teen in the booth. He took the blue band and clicked it on her wrist. Then he leaned down and kissed her.

"What was that for?" she asked as they came up for air.

His eyes twinkled in the now-bright lights of the carnival. "You said you wanted to act like teenagers. It's been a while since I've stolen a kiss."

As they climbed into a small, metal car to enter the haunted house, Angie grinned at Ian. That probably wouldn't be the only stolen kiss this evening.

* * * *

Angie's legs still felt wobbly from what she hoped was the final ride of the night. She'd been flipped and turned and jerked every way possible. It was called Satan, and the picture of the bucking bull on the entrance should have warned her of the ferocious ride ahead. Ian appeared fine as they sauntered toward the food court.

He turned and saw her lagging behind him. "Hey, are you all right?"

"You are going to tell me you don't even feel a bit different after that last ride?" She took his offered hand and fell in step with him, dodging the crowd going toward the section of the fairgrounds where the carnival sat.

"Feel what? You mean the ride?" He grinned at her like the teenager she had wanted to pretend to be. "I thought it was gnarly. You want to go again before we eat?"

"Yeah, no. I have to be creative in the morning, and right now, it feels like my brain has turned into scrambled eggs." She pointed to a table in the Basque Community Center booth. "I'll sit there, you can order dinner."

"What do you want?" He glanced at the wooden menu hung over the line of grills at the front of the booth.

"Estebe will know what to make me." Angie laid her head on her arms, trying to fend off a migraine. "And a lemon-lime soda. Please."

She heard Ian's footsteps leave her as she took in the smells of the tent. Seasoned lamb, onions, some type of rice, and if she was right, a flatbread that Estebe liked to make for family meals to go with soup, especially on chilly fall days. The restaurant had been open a little over a year, and her employees had turned from strangers to family. Angie hadn't been able to make that kind of connection at her first restaurant. At el Pescado, she'd always been hiring. One month, she'd replaced the entire kitchen staff only to have her sous chef quit a week later. Jobs were plentiful there, and there was always somewhere willing to pay a little more to get trained staff. And Angie believed in training.

Here, the wages she paid were higher than most of the other restaurants in the area, but she kept a stable staff both in the kitchen and the front of the house. If that meant she and Felicia took home a little less profit at the end of the year, that didn't matter. She loved the way the business was developing.

"Angie, why are you looking like you got into the wine early?"

She looked up and into Estebe's big brown eyes. Her sous chef appeared concerned. She sighed and pointed toward the end of the table. "Ian just tried to kill me."

Estebe set a bowl of soup and a piece of warm flatbread in front of her, and Ian set the soda nearby. "I'm sure that is not true. Ian is a good man."

"Rides and Angie just don't get along." Ian slapped Estebe on the arm. "How have you been?"

"I have been well." As the men continued talking, going back to the makeshift kitchen for more food, Angie dug in to the soup.

Warmth and taste filled her mouth, and immediately her brain stopped spinning. She broke off a piece of the still-warm bread and dipped it in the soup. Heaven.

Felicia slipped onto the bench next to her. She grabbed a piece of the flatbread and beelined it to Angie's soup. "Yum, let me try."

Angie wanted to wrap her arms around the bowl and tell her friend to go get her own, but then her better nature prevailed. She watched as Felicia delicately dipped the bread into the bowl.

"Oh, my. We really need to add this to the menu. Maybe in October, when the chill hits the valley?" Felicia pushed a pile of papers toward Angie, then stood. "I'm getting something. I'm on a break from the booth, and I need real food before I eat another slice of pie."

Angie glanced at the papers. "What are these?"

"The rules to the contest. We get our first challenge tomorrow." Felicia ordered at the front of the line, then paid. While she waited for the food, she moved back to Angie's table to continue her conversation. "They gave us a theme for the first day. I guess what we'll prepare will be announced tomorrow and we'll have time to go grab additional food from the store if we didn't prepare right."

Angie studied the pages. Tomorrow was an appetizer round. And she had just the right idea. She'd send Matt shopping tonight and store everything at the County Seat. Matt Young was one of the line cooks and always looking for more hours. Then they'd move everything to the food storage locker on-site first thing in the morning. If she guessed wrong, they would recalculate and Matt would go back to the store. With Hope Anderson, the culinary student-slash-dishwasher as their third, the work would go fast.

"You got the rules, then." Estebe set a plate of some sort of rice dish in front of her. He held out a hand for what she'd already read, then scanned the pages. "You'll have to do a hundred servings in less than three hours. Are you sure you don't want me to help instead of Matt?"

"Matt and Hope will be fine. Besides, from what Felicia said, we have a full seating at the restaurant. Especially since we closed up tonight. You know there will be some walk-ins." She picked up a fork and took a bite. "This is wonderful."

"Of course. I am chef tonight. Tomorrow night, my brother is cooking. You may want to eat elsewhere." He set the pages down. "I appreciate you letting me have tonight off. I know it must have cost a lot to close the restaurant."

"You weren't the only one who wanted a night at the fair." Angie smiled as Felicia sat down, her plate filled. "Besides, this way we can pick up any gossip about the contest. Do we know who's entered?"

Felicia listed off the different chefs in the area who were gunning to win Boise's version of *Restaurant Wars*.

Angie set her fork down. "Whoa. That's a who's who list of everyone who has any chef cred at all in the valley. Competition's going to be steep."

"David Nubbins is the front-runner." Estebe sipped on his beer. "At least that's what we've heard here."

David Nubbins was head chef at the Sandpiper, the premier upscale restaurant in Boise. He had started the restaurant long before Angie had even thought about being a chef. She'd eaten there several times before she'd moved away. Mostly to see what a real chef did with local cuisine. "He has a lot of experience."

"And Sarah Fenny is coming up on his heels," Felicia added, her plate almost empty. "She owns Fenny's Pies over in Nampa. Since she opened, she's been the go-to place for main-dish pies and desserts."

"Copper Creek has entered too." Angie shook her head, feeling a little overwhelmed. She hadn't expected the big dogs to play in this contest at the fair. "I guess we might just get four nights of showing people what we do."

Felicia glanced at Estebe, who shook his head.

"What's going on, guys?" Angie stared from one to another. No one was talking. "Guys?"

Felicia picked up the papers and thumbed through them. When she found the page she was looking for, she pulled it out and pointed to the middle of the page. "There's been an addition to the rules. Three teams will be eliminated each night. We have to stay out of the bottom to stay in the competition. Are you sure you don't want Estebe and me to work with you all four nights?"

Angie read the section of the rules Felicia had pointed out. Then she straightened the pile of pages and put them in her backpack. "Nope. We win or we lose together. From what I can see, we'll do an appetizer, then a frozen drink—virgin and fully loaded. Then next weekend it's the main course and dessert. I'll need Estebe on Friday and you on Saturday. We might want to bring Jeorge in tomorrow night to help plan out Sunday's drink. But I think Matt and Hope will help me mix on Sunday. We're only as strong as our weakest link."

"But you might not make it to next weekend if you don't pull one of us in to help." Felicia put her hand on Angie's shoulder. "How bad do you want to win?"

"Not bad enough to make either Matt or Hope feel like they're less of a team member. We've already scheduled them to work the fair booth." Angie sipped her soda. "Look, I know the two of you are better. We'd totally kick butt with all three of us, but I've got to put my faith in all my kitchen staff. Not just the superstars."

"You are a good boss, Angie Turner." Estebe glanced at the line, frowning. "I need to go figure out what they're doing back there. People should not have to wait for their food."

When Estebe left, Felicia glanced at her watch. "I'm expected back soon. Look, I'm off shift at ten. Do you want to go over to the booth where we'll be cooking and check it out? I'd feel better if we knew there weren't any issues going into tomorrow."

"Sounds great. Ian and I will head over to the main building and wander around until then. I want to go through the exhibits and see what people sent in for judging."

Felicia took her plate along with Angie's. "Just don't tell me if they already have the ribbons out. I haven't gone over to check my entries. I'm a nervous wreck about it. Especially my banana bread. I'm worried my tweaks were too much for the judges."

It was official. Felicia had fallen in love with the rural lifestyle. When she'd found out she could enter the baking competition at the fair as a professional, she'd spent the last three weeks baking and perfecting her recipes.

"I'm sure they won't announce until tomorrow. You coming by before service?" Angie sipped on her soda. The heat of the day had wiped her out. She threw away the almost-finished bottle, then stepped over to the counter and bought three bottles of water. She handed the extras to Ian and Felicia before opening her own. "Remind me to put water on the shopping list. I'm sure that booth is going to be scorching hot by midday."

"I'll be here until about noon. You can send me for extra groceries then so you all can keep prepping." Felicia stared out into the darkness in the direction of the main exhibit hall. "I have made a decision, though."

"Oh, yeah?"

Felicia drained half of her water, then reclosed the bottle. She started walking toward the exit and back to her own booth. "Next year I'm entering the canning competition. You've canned before, right? You can teach me."

"The ag extension office has classes going now. Do you want me to get you a schedule?" Ian called after her.

Felicia paused at the doorway. "That would be lovely. I've had a little too much time on my hands since Taylor and I broke up. This is just the project I need."

Angie watched her friend disappear into the crowd. Even though the River Vista United Methodist Women's booth was only a few feet away, it seemed like Felicia disappeared into a crowd of people moving down the street, looking for the perfect place to eat dinner. "She loves living here. Someday she's going to walk in and tell me she's married a local farmer and is going to raise goats and chickens."

Ian put an arm around her waist as they made their way into the crowd to find the path to the exhibit hall. "Yeah, but she won't quit the County Seat. That girl has too much energy to stay home. She likes having her to-do list a couple pages long."

"She reminds me of you. How did the board meeting go?" Angie settled into the pace the crowd was moving. Not too fast, and she had to swerve to avoid traffic when the people in front of her stopped to read a menu board. The smells of fried onions, grilled burgers, and deep fat–fried everything made her stomach growl again, even though she knew there was no way she could be hungry after the meal they'd just eaten.

"We'll come back for pie after checking out the competition site." Ian chuckled as he turned her toward the new path and out of the crowd. "Let's not talk about the board meeting. I swear, those guys think there should be absolutely no cost in setting up a booth. Even when I show them the numbers, they don't get it."

Ian had been fighting with the board for months now. The budget was calling for a slight raise in booth prices, but the majority votes on the board were farmers and didn't want to increase costs. Which she understood, but electricity, advertising, and space rental weren't free, either.

They cut through the back alley between the two main walkways. Ian pointed to a row of empty booths in the center of a large path of grass. A large sign over the Western-style entrance said *Restaurant Wars*. "I guess that's where you're working tomorrow."

Angie stepped closer to the roped off entry. "There's our booth. Right next to Copper Creek. I'm so glad. I haven't talked to Sydney since the last time we had dinner there."

"Should be fun." Ian took her arm. "Come on, you're on a date. I already spent dinner talking about work. Let's go see what they have for sale."

"Same old, same old. I don't want a new phone service or my vents cleaned, but I might find the fudge shop." She grinned as she stepped back onto the path. A crash sounded behind her. "Is someone there?"

She saw a dark figure running out of the area. She glanced at Ian, who was already on his phone. "I'm calling fair security."

Angie paused, looking at him. "You have the number on your phone?"

"The farmers' market has a booth in the exhibit hall. I was going to surprise you when we arrived. I've got volunteers manning it tonight, but I'll be here most of the week. So we can hang out again tomorrow after your event. I hear they have bands at the dance hall every night." He held up a finger. "This is Ian McNeal, and I'm over at the Restaurant Wars section. I think someone was inside and either broke or stole something."

Angie shined her phone flashlight over the area, trying to see what the guy had been after. When Ian finished his call, she pointed to the Sandpiper display. "Does it look like the sign's been torn down?"

"Maybe." He pushed her arm down and took the phone. "We're just standing here waiting for the security people to come secure the scene, then we're out of here."

Angie smiled up at him. "You worried I'm going to go investigating?"

"I'm worried that you're going to find a dead body and ruin our date. Let's pretend the security personnel have this in hand and just have a good time tonight, okay? Tomorrow we can start figuring out the whys and hows." He put his arm around her and turned her away from the setup. "Look, there's the small animal barn. You want to go see a thousand guinea pigs?"

"I'm sure there's not that many." She leaned up and kissed his jaw. "I'm not that bad about investigating, am I?"

"Oh, honey, there's no way in the world I'm answering that question." He pointed to the golf cart speeding its way toward them. Or at least as fast as the crowd would let the driver go. "There's the officials. I think our date is almost back on schedule."

Chapter 2

Ian had been about thirty minutes off on his planning. By the time the security guys had "secured the scene" and taken their statement, it was almost eight thirty. He glanced at her. "Still up for the exhibit hall?"

"Of course. I'd love to see your booth." What Angie really wanted to know was what the guards had found, but they'd been closemouthed about what they'd seen in the Sandpiper booth. It was David's booth, and Angie wondered if one of the other contestants was trying to set up some early sabotage.

"You're almost a good liar." Ian took her arm in his, and they made their way to the large building. "Hopefully it was just a kid playing around the site."

"Yeah, I'm sure that's it." Angie pushed aside the doubt that maybe there was something more to the ruckus. "Let's find that fudge shop before they sell out."

"It's the first day of the fair. I'm sure they will have plenty." He paused at the hot tub display. "They have a fair order special. Do you think Dom would stay out of it if we bought one for your backyard?"

"I think he'd think it was a big bathtub. And you know how much he loves his baths." Angie smiled as she thought about her Saint Bernard. At a year old, he wasn't a puppy anymore, but still, he was clumsy in his growing body. "And Mabel would think it was a drinking pond. We'd have to keep a cover on it at all times."

"Of course. I'm sure they come with covers." He ran his hand through the water. "You could soak after closing up the County Seat at night."

"I'd fall asleep, and your uncle would find my body the next evening when I didn't come in to work." Angie dipped her hand into the warm water. It was a lovely thought, though.

"Leave it to you to go dark on me." He took her by the waist and moved her through the crowds. Booths of beauty products, multilevel marketing opportunities, and party sales lined the aisles. Finally, they stopped in front of a booth manned by a couple of teenagers she thought she recognized.

"Hey, Ty and Dru, how are things going tonight? Any interest in the market?" Ian picked up the sign-up sheet for their newsletter.

"Hey, Mr. McNeal. We've got two sheets of sign-ups already. Although I think they're signing up for the chance to win dinner at Ms. Turner's place. That's a great giveaway." Ty grinned at Angie. "My folks went there last month and said it was the best dinner they've had in town ever."

Ian held up the plastic frame showing the giveaway. "Felicia helped me with the setup. I take it from the look on your face she didn't talk to you about it."

"She handles the marketing. I'm sure it would have come up in our next meeting." Angie wasn't worried about the cost of the actual giveaway. Having a signage and, she noticed now, postcards with a picture of the County Seat on the front, along with their reservation phone number, didn't hurt promotion. She should have thought about this. She picked up a postcard and turned it over.

One of her Nona's recipes for potato soup was on the back of the card. She tucked one into her backpack.

"We've almost gone through the first box of those." The girl spoke up now, pointing to the postcard. "Everyone smiles when they see the recipe."

That made Angie smile as well. "Everyone loves potato soup, right? At least if you're from Idaho. It's like a law or something."

The girl laughed. "Definitely."

"Well, just tuck everything under the table when you leave tonight. Thanks for volunteering. Did you get your free passes for tomorrow?"

"We sure did. Thanks a lot." Ty patted his jeans. "I'm coming as soon as they open. I had enough saved to buy a weeklong pass for the rides. I'm signed up to work Monday too so I get another pass."

"A man with a plan." Ian tapped the table. "You're doing great work. Thank you."

As they walked away, Angie glanced back at the two, who were already pulling in another couple to the booth. "I think you should hire them full-time. They have the sales part down pat."

"It's easy when you're giving something away. I just hope the receipts and attendance to the market increase after this. The board didn't like shelling out for the booth rental." Ian sighed as they made their way through the crowd. "Where's the fudge booth? I think I need a sugar hit."

"We only have a few minutes left before we're supposed to meet Felicia at the Restaurant Wars site. I hope they let us in." Angie pointed to the wall where the candy shop was set up. "There we go."

After buying three pieces of fudge, just in case Felicia was hungry too, they made their way back to the empty booths across from the animal barns. Ian nudged Angie. "Looks like Felicia's already there and interrogating the guard."

"I'm sure she just knows him from one of her adventures. I swear, she knows more people here than I ever did. And she's only been living here a few months." Angie cut diagonally across the wave of people. Most were heading toward the exits, worn out by the fun and, probably, the heat.

"She's a people person."

She shot a dark glare at him. "What are you saying? I'm not good with people?"

He shrugged. "You're better with recipes. You get lost in your head sometimes and forget others are around. Felicia wants to know everything about everybody. You didn't even ask the kids where they went to school."

"I assumed River Vista. Is that wrong?" She paused at the side of the walkway. What was Ian trying to tell her? Was she a bad girlfriend? Didn't she notice things about him?

"They are both homeschooled by a local farmer. I about had to promise the mom I'd make sure they weren't abducted from the fair just to get them time to come and play like the rest of the kids."

"I didn't realize..."

Ian held up a hand. "Stop blaming yourself. All I'm saying is Felicia is better than you are with people. No blame, no shame, just a fact. You're better with food than anyone I've ever met. Including Felicia and Estebe. It's your strength."

"So we're okay?"

He reached out and pulled her into a hug. "I'm sorry it came across the way it did. I'm frustrated with the board and taking it out on you. I'm a bad, bad boyfriend."

"You know that's a popular trope in the romance world." She took a deep breath to settle herself. She knew she had overreacted as well. Probably nervous because of the news Estebe and Felicia had broken to her at dinner. "Let's go see what Felicia has negotiated for us."

When they walked up, the security guard nodded, then swept his hand for them to keep moving. When they stopped, he frowned and put a hand on his flashlight. "Look, there's nothing to see here..."

Felicia giggled. "Roger, they're with me. This is my partner, Angie Turner, and the River Vista Farmers' Market manager, Ian McNeal. We're just coming to see what we have to work with tomorrow."

"I'm not sure I should let you all in. There's been a break-in, after all." He sighed and smiled at Felicia. "Go ahead. I'll be out here if you need anything. Just don't go into the Sandpiper booth. It's the one with the crime-scene tape."

"Did they steal appliances?" Angie wondered what exactly someone would do with a large microwave. With as many people coming through the fair, whatever was taken had to be small enough to be tucked into someone's pocket to avoid the thief being seen.

"Mostly just trashed the place. We're thinking teenagers. Don't worry, your competition's trailer will be up and functional long before your contest starts tomorrow." Roger moved the wooden barrier that had blocked people from entering the area.

As they walked to the booth with County Seat's banner on the top, Angie stared at the damaged booth. "David must be really unlucky to have his trailer be the only one messed with tonight."

Ian held the door open as they climbed in the back of the booth and into a well-supplied and set-up kitchen. "Who said it was just bad luck?"

Angie ignored the comment, and they spent the next twenty minutes planning out her appetizer. When they were done, she had a lengthy shopping list that she handed to Felicia. "Check out the supply area at County Seat. We'll have a lot of that. And it looks like I should have the equipment I need. As long as they don't throw another curveball into the picture."

Felicia glanced at the list. "You sure about this? I'm thinking most of the other guys are going a little fancier with their dishes."

"Good food wins, no matter what. And if it doesn't, well, then, I'll be back working at the restaurant tomorrow instead of figuring out tomorrow's recipe." Angie glanced at her watch. "It's still early. Do you want to join Ian and me for a drink?"

"One. Then I'm heading home." Felicia paused at the door. "You didn't go get pie."

She handed off the piece of fudge they'd bought for Felicia. "I've got something better."

As they walked to the beer garden to sit and talk, Felicia pointed out all the fun things they hadn't gotten to do yet. "Tomorrow, after I drop off the supplies, I'm heading into the animal barns. I know I can't get anything strange for a pet, but I am thinking of looking around for a kitten." She glanced at Angie. "If my landlord says it's all right."

Angie shrugged, her mind on tomorrow's competition. "You own half the building. I guess you need to ask yourself what you want."

"I would like a kitten. I haven't had one since I lived at home." Felicia looked wistful.

"Where did you grow up, Felicia? Obviously, not here. You constantly look like you're exploring a new country." Ian studied her.

"Takes one to know one, huh?" Felicia said, referring to Ian's English upbringing. She glanced at Angie. "I don't think I ever mentioned it, but I'm from Boston."

"Really? And you specialized in pastry, not seafood?" Angie studied her friend. Even in college, she hadn't sounded like she'd come from New England.

"I've been worried about telling you this for years, and all you can think about is my food specialty?" Felicia hugged Angie, causing the crowd to swirl around them as they paused in front of the beer garden.

"Why would you be worried?" Angie eyed her suspiciously. "Do you have skeletons in your closet?"

"Probably some at the family home, but me? I'm as pure as the driven snow." Felicia held up her hand. "And, with that, I'm buying the first round. Especially since I'm horning in on your date night."

"You're perfectly welcome to tag along anytime." Ian motioned to a table. "Especially when you buy the drinks."

The beer garden was crowded, as any alcohol consumed on the fairgrounds had to stay in the area. Guards stood at the entrances and exits keeping people inside if they tried to leave with a glass in hand and checking identification for customers who looked younger than the drinking age. Angie pointed to the entrance. "I'm surprised they're letting us have leaded frozen cocktails tomorrow in the main area."

"I think I heard the guard saying that you have to have a wristband to buy. Maybe that's what they'll do at the contest?" Ian pointed to Felicia. "She had to go to a different table and get tickets to buy the drinks."

Just then, Felicia waved Ian over. When Angie started to stand, she shook her head. Ian laughed. "So much for her buying. I think they need two people's ID for three drinks. Stay here and guard the table. Others are watching us closely."

"I'll guard the castle." Angie leaned over the table, her arms outstretched, making Ian laugh.

He kissed her quickly. "We'll be right back with refreshments."

Angie leaned back in her seat and started thinking about the competition tomorrow. Twelve teams, and then there would be nine. Just like that. All they had to do was survive from day to day. The hair on the back of her neck bristled, and she got a chill. Was someone watching her? She scanned the crowded bar area and finally found the source of the ill will.

A man sat near the bar, beer in hand, staring at her. When she met his gaze, his eyes narrowed, and he lifted his bottle to her in some sort of salute. Angie glanced over to where Ian and Felicia stood. Had they given off the wrong impression? Did the creepy man think she was here single and looking for a hookup?

Felicia and Ian walked back to the table. Ian set a beer in front of Angie. He studied her face. "What's wrong? Did someone bother you?"

Angie shook her head, feeling silly. "No. Someone was just watching me. It's nothing."

Ian scanned the area. "Who? Do I need to go defend your honor?"

She giggled, which was probably what Ian had intended. "No. Just a guy. He's over there."

But when she pointed, the seat where the man had been sitting was empty. And as she scanned the area, he was gone.

"He must have gotten the message," Felicia said, then she took a piece of paper out of her back pocket. "I was thinking… If you want to deep fat–fry tomorrow, you could set the team up this way…"

Chapter 3

The group gathered promptly at nine to hear the judges' decision on just what type of appetizer they'd be making. Matt, Hope, and Felicia all stood next to her, in front of the booth. Next door, the chefs from Copper Creek were gathering too. Sydney waved at Angie, then counted out her staff.

"You know you have one too many cooks in the kitchen, right?"

Angie stepped closer. "Felicia's just here to see us off. Then she's going to go play for the day. How have you been? I haven't seen you since you guys came to chef table at the County Seat a few months ago."

"Busy, as usual. I'm trying to get everything set up before I go off on maternity leave." Sydney patted her belly. "It seems like we've been planning for this forever, but now that it's close, there's so much I need to get done."

"Congratulations. When are you due?"

"October seventh. But who knows with babies? I'm planning on a natural childbirth." She went on about all the things she was expecting when the baby came. In too much detail.

When the head judge called for quiet, Angie gratefully slipped back over to her team, promising to finish the conversation later.

She hoped she'd be too busy to keep that promise.

"I'm so glad to greet you all this beautiful summer morning." Ann Cole, the mayor of Garden City, where the fairgrounds were located, spoke clearly into the microphone. Even though most of the contestants were in tanks and jeans, Ms. Cole was dressed in a bright coral linen suit that made her look more like she was going to tea in New York than judging a cooking contest in Southwestern Idaho. All five of the judges were in suits, and Angie wondered how many were like Ms. Cole, politicians on the next voting ballot.

But then again, she'd always been cynical. At least that's what Felicia said. Angie realized that the woman was done welcoming them to the small city being swallowed up by metropolitan Boise and was now talking about the rules.

"Tomorrow morning, we'll meet here again to announce tomorrow's challenge, along with the nine teams that will continue on in the competition. The winner will also get an advantage, which we'll announce tonight after judging at six p.m."

Angie glanced over to Felicia and saw the man from the beer garden last night standing by one of the restaurant booths. He must be another chef. She glanced up at the signage. Bien Viveres. He saw her look and smirked at her. So, he wanted to play, did he? Angie kept herself from rolling her eyes and turned back to Ms. Cole, who seemed to be winding down. The woman glanced at the oversized digital clock. "You have four hours to shop, cook, and be ready to serve a hundred invited guests at twelve thirty. Your challenge? Make us the best corn dog we've ever had."

Groans came from several groups, but Hope bounced up and grabbed Angie's arm. "You guessed it."

Anger flashed over the Bien Viveres chef's face, but just as soon as Angie saw his expression, it was gone. She leaned in to Felicia and nodded to the guy, who was now circled together with his team, barking orders. "We're going to have to watch that one."

"Miquel? Why? He seemed nice when he came to eat at the County Seat last week." Felicia frowned as she studied the group.

"He came to eat at the restaurant?" Had he studied the competition? Or was this just a coincidence? Either way, she didn't have time to deal with anything but the task at hand. "Okay, Felicia? Take off. Hope and Matt? Let's get planning."

"Good luck, guys." Felicia waved as the three disappeared into the booth.

"I take it we're making our own sausage for the corn dog?" Matt stood at the end of the booth, glancing around at the options. "Is there a meat grinder?"

"Over there in the cabinet. They stocked us for most anything." Angie waved them toward the refrigerator storage bin. "I had Felicia get the ingredients for the sausage that Estebe made for family meal last month. You helped him with that, right, Matt?"

"I did." He took out a large bin and started grabbing meat. "I'll start cutting up the meat if you all want to get the veggies started."

And just like at the restaurant, things started falling together. Angie had chosen correctly. Her two least-experienced cooks had been trained well by Estebe. And they knew how to move quickly.

They finished up a trial batch of the sausage in just under an hour. Angie stuck one in the freezer and then they grilled several. She'd already made up a batch of the cornmeal batter and Hope was busy working on a sauce for dipping, even though Angie was considering using a locally made ground mustard. Maybe they should have both?

They made up three samples. One grilled, then dipped. One frozen, then dipped. And one just chilled from the fridge. First they sampled a grilled sausage without the batter.

"Perfect mix. Spicy, but not crazy hot." Angie's praise had Matt blushing.

He nodded. "Make sure you mention that to Estebe. I changed the mixture on the peppers. His were a little too aggressive, if I remember the comments from the team at family meal."

"I'm sure he'll be open to changes." Hope laughed. "Well, maybe in an alternate universe."

"Either way, it's a good change up, and yes, when we add it to the menu, we'll use your tweak." Angie smiled as Matt did a quick fist pump.

"Can I call him now?" He glanced at the clock. "I'm sure he's going to want to know this sooner than later."

"No. We're on a mission. We don't have to win, but we do have to stay alive in the competition." Angie studied the actual corn dogs that they'd made. "I like the color of the batter. But make sure you judge the batter too. We need a touch of sweetness to complement the sausage."

They sampled the three, and all agreed the batter worked. Then it was the issue of the technique. Finally, they made their choice, then set up a station to get all the sausage done first. Angie made the batter mix, keeping the wet ingredients separate and putting finishing the mix on her timeline. It was like a dance. Do one thing too soon, and the rest wouldn't get done. A big part of the challenge was time management. If no one could taste your food because you missed the deadline, you were out.

She hung the schedule on a wall where she could see it. Then she set a timer for the next step. Finally, she went to join Matt and Hope in making sausages.

Matt had brought his boom box and a mix of country, pop, and classic rock music flowed through the trailer as they worked. An hour into the schedule, a knock sounded at the door. Angie washed her hands, then grabbed a towel before answering. A woman with a microphone and a clipboard stood outside, with a man with a video camera. Time for the dog and pony show. Now she really wished she'd pulled Felicia in on the first day of the competition. She took a deep breath and went to slay the dragons.

"Good morning, you must be Angie Taylor from the County Seat." The woman who was in her late fifties beamed up at her. "I'm Dee Samson from the local NBC affiliate. Do you have a few minutes to answer some questions?"

Angie dried her hands, then stepped out of the kitchen. "Just a few. And it's Angie Turner, not Taylor."

The woman scribbled on a notebook. "Great catch. Sometimes I can't read my producers' handwriting. So, I won't keep you long. Do you mind standing over here by the front so the viewers can see your trailer sign?"

"Works for me." Angie moved to the front and self-consciously ran her fingers through her hair. Felicia would have loved doing this interview.

"Ready, Terry." When the man with the camera nodded, the reporter did a quick intro and then turned to Angie. "I understand that you're a hometown favorite here. You grew up on your grandparents' farm in River Vista?"

The woman had done her research. Or the producer had. "My Nona raised me after my parents died in a car crash. I went to high school in River Vista, then got my culinary degree here at Boise State. So yeah, I'm a hometown girl. My partner, Felicia Williams, grew up back East, but we met at BSU."

"You moved here after closing your San Diego Mexican restaurant, correct?"

Angie nodded. This interview was getting personal really fast. "Yes. We were priced out of the up-and-coming neighborhood. But we'd always wanted to do a farm-to-fork concept, and River Vista looked like the right place at the right time."

"Farm to fork, what does that mean?" Dee asked.

Angie knew the woman understood the concept but figured she was asking for her viewers. "I buy directly from local farmers for most of my supplies. Sourcing so close to the field where produce and meat were raised keeps the product fresh and helps the local community."

Dee smiled, and for a second, Angie didn't think she was going to like the next question. "I hear you found more than just fresh corn and lettuce at the farmers' market. Is it true you're dating the manager?"

Angie glanced at her watch. "Oh, my, look at the time. Thanks for stopping by this morning. You know the event is timed, so I'd better get in and help out my crew."

Dee kept filming as Angie escaped. "Well, I guess that question is just going to have to be answered at another time. Thanks to Angie Turner for taking time out of her day to chat. If you're in River Vista, be sure to stop by her quaint restaurant, the County Seat, and check out the new farm-to-fork dining rage."

Angie banged the door shut, hoping it didn't look like she was running away after the interview. Because that's exactly how it had felt.

"Hey, boss, how'd the promo go?" Matt watched her carefully. Sometimes Angie felt like she had no secrets from this group of people she worked with. Which was probably true.

"Fine." She glanced at the schedule. "How are we on sausages?"

Hope and Matt shared a look. Then Hope took out a five from her pocket and tucked it into Matt's jeans pocket.

"Don't tell me you bet on how the interview would go?" Angie walked over to the sink and washed her hands. "You know I hate those things."

"Matt said you wouldn't talk about it. I disagreed, but no matter. I hope the interview went better than you think." Hope walked over to the veggie chopping station, pulling on her gloves as she walked. "I'm chopping the onions too."

"You really need to stop betting. It seems like you're always on the losing end of the game." Angie counted up the already-made sausages. They had many more to go, and she needed time to get them grilled, cooled, to finally be ready for dipping into the cornmeal mixture.

They worked side by side for another hour or so, until finally it was close to time for service. Angie glanced out the front window. People were milling around the area, drinks in hand, and as Ian had predicted, armbands showed if they were of legal drinking age. The man knew his stuff.

"We start serving in fifteen minutes. We need at least five minutes to get ten plates ready, then we'll just repeat. Are we putting the sauce in cups or just to the side of the corn dog?"

The three of them tried a few different combinations, then decided on a plating plan. Then they started cooking the first set of dogs.

When a bell went off, Angie went to the front to start working with the customers. She couldn't tell from her angle how the other booths were doing, but customers seemed to love their version of a corn dog. Matt brought out a tray with the last ten dogs. "Did the judges come by?"

"I think so. I mean, I talked to a few of them, but they didn't come in a group." Angie smiled as she handed a basket with the corn dog and sauces to a woman carrying a baby on one hip. "Basque-style sausage with a cream sauce and a mustard sauce. Enjoy."

Matt shook his head. "I knew I should have written out your script. Do you mind if I handle that tomorrow? You don't sell the food enough."

Angie was too tired to argue. Besides, marketing had never been her strong suit. Felicia and Estebe always rewrote her menu descriptions before they sent them to the printer. "You can do it for as long as we're in the competition. Are you scheduled to work all the nights?"

"Yep. And I appreciate the extra hours. I'm so close to having a down payment on one of Estebe's rentals." Matt grinned as he handed out one of the baskets, waxing eloquent about the subtle spicing in the sausage and the sweetness of the corn batter covering. "I don't think he really thought I could come up with twenty percent, at least not for a while. But I'm determined to get this deal done before he gets a new renter in there and I have to wait for another opening."

Estebe had invested his chef's wages smartly. He owned several rentals, and Angie thought that if he didn't want to cook anymore, the guy could probably retire. A bell went off just as Matt handed off the last basket. Hope had joined them.

"The kitchen is clean, and the dishes are done. We'll be ready for tomorrow's start just as soon as we get instructions on what we're serving." She leaned on the bar in the front of the booth, watching people gather near the judges' station. The winner would be announced tonight, and only that team would have the advantage of knowing exactly the item they were supposed to make tomorrow. Angie had a suspicion it would be a milkshake type of drink.

But they had an hour before they'd find out who won. And the three losers would come back tomorrow, ready for battle, just to be sent home. Angie glanced at her watch. "I'll buy dinner over at one of the booths if we can get food and be back before six."

"Sold." Matt headed back to the kitchen. "Let me lock this place up. Anyone need anything?"

Both Hope and Angie shook their heads. "Meet us just outside the Restaurant Wars entrance. Then find us somewhere we can sit and eat. My feet are killing me."

As they walked by Bien Viveres, the man from last night called out to her. "How'd you do over there? Looked like you were struggling a bit to get customers."

"Not at all." Angie didn't like this negative banter, so she decided not to fall to his level. "Good luck tonight."

"Darling, I don't need luck. I'm the best chef here," Miquel called after them.

Hope waited until they were out of earshot. "That guy is certainly full of himself. Kind of what Estebe would be if he didn't have such a kind soul."

Angie pressed her lips together. Estebe did have a kind soul and a hardened exterior, but Hope was also his favorite student in the County Seat kitchen. The guy would do anything for the woman he called his "little sister." Luckily Matt joined them, so Angie didn't have to respond.

"Who wants fried chicken? If we hurry, we might even get somewhere to sit." He put his arms around the two women and aimed them in the direction of Food Row. Angie listened as the two young people talked about their fair memories.

"After tonight's announcement, why don't you two go have some fun? I'll do the shopping," Angie said as they sat down at the table. They'd already ordered, and she'd paid for the meal. Now they were just waiting to eat.

"I thought I was shopping." Matt frowned. "Don't you have something to do?"

"If I go back to River Vista, I'll stop at the restaurant and get in the way. You know how Estebe gets when he's 'in charge.' I'll do the shopping tonight. You can make up the hours during prep next Friday." Angie wanted to get out of the crush of people and walk the aisles, surrounded by food. Besides, she hadn't quite decided on what she was doing tomorrow. Or at least her Plan A until they told her the actual item they'd be preparing. Maybe walking through the grocery store would spark some ideas.

"I don't know. I've been studying for pastry class in the evenings," Hope commented.

Matt and Angie stared at her.

"What?" Her face reddened under the LED lights.

"School doesn't start until next week. You need to have some fun. Working all the time makes Jill a dull girl." Angie moved her arms so the server could drop off their dinner. Angie had ordered fried chicken, potato salad, and corn on the cob. The corn was on a stick and drenched in butter and salt. Her mouth watered.

"Besides, we have all those access passes to the rides the fair guys gave us." Matt held up his wrist. "This puppy isn't coming off until the carnival leaves next Monday."

"I don't know..."

Matt picked up a piece of chicken and pointed to it. "That's what you are."

"I don't get it." Hope took a bite of a leg.

"*Bawk, bawk, bawk...*" Matt said through a mouth full. "You're scared. You're a chicken."

"I can outride you with my eyes blindfolded."

Matt shrugged, apparently disinterested now in Hope's involvement in his plan. "Whatever."

"Fine, I'll go ride with you. But not on weekdays. Only on weekends." Hope shook her head and focused on Angie. "It's really sad. He doesn't have any friends but me."

"That's so not true. You're just the one I see all the time." He tipped his head toward his plate and started chowing down. "This is really good," he said through a mouthful of potato salad. They'd just finished eating when Angie's timer on her phone went off. "We have five minutes to get back." She took a deep breath. "I'm so nervous. I know I said all I wanted was to stay in the competition, but maybe…"

"Our corn dog was the ultimate best." Hope took the plates and trash off the table. "But if they can't see that, they're idiots. It's not a reflection on us or our food."

"Okay, Sally Sunshine, let's go see who won." Matt stood up to guide them out of the tent and back to the Restaurant Wars site. The area was overflowing, but Matt grabbed both women's hands and moved them through the crowd. The judges climbed to the stage just as they arrived in front of their trailers. The area was blocked off by a velvet rope. Matt pointed to the trailer, and the man standing guard at the entrance let them inside.

Hope grabbed Angie's hand, jumping up and down a little. "Sorry, nervous energy."

Angie smiled and glanced around the area at the other trailers. Miquel stood in front of his trailer, signing autographs for the teens who crowded around his area. Angie turned away, not wanting him to see her. Then she glanced the other way. All the booths had people in front of them, but the Sandpiper booth only had two people. Maybe Mr. Nubbins was still off getting dinner and had sent representatives to the meeting.

Finally, Ann Cole tapped on the microphone. After a few seconds, everyone quieted. Then she began to thank everyone who had even considered being part of the competition. Angie felt Hope's hand relax and finally, she dropped her hand to her side. The nerves must have been bored away.

When Ann Cole finally handed the microphone over to a second judge, he held up an envelope.

"Our winner is…" He grinned, then opened the envelope. "David Nubbins, from the Sandpiper."

The crowd cheered, and the two prep chefs looked at each other. Finally, one held up his hand. "I think David must be in the trailer taking a nap. Sheila will go get him."

That got a chuckle from the group. But when Sheila opened the door to the trailer, she froze. Then she started screaming.

All Angie could hear was her sobs.

"David, oh, no, David…"

Chapter 4

Security quickly started ushering people out of the area. Angie saw what was happening, and she and Hope went into their trailer and grabbed their purses and Matt's backpack. He stood guard at the door. Luckily, they had enough time to make sure they had their keys before they were escorted out of the area.

The chefs were all moved to a small security office in the middle of the fairgrounds. Sydney pointed at Angie's purse. "You were smart. I just have my phone. I didn't even think to grab my keys. Do you think they'll let us back in to get our things? Brandon's working the dinner shift. He can't leave to come get me."

"If they don't, I'll take you home," Angie promised.

Ann Cole walked into the room. "I'm sorry to inform you that David Nubbins is dead. The police aren't releasing any more information than that, but his trailer is being moved off-site so it can be examined. Of course, his winning status will stand, but I'm afraid the Sandpiper has declined our offer of replacing the trailer and continuing in the competition. Therefore, only two booths will be eliminated tonight."

She glanced over at the other judges. "And, due to the special circumstances, tonight and tonight only, we are giving you all the information for tomorrow's contest." She opened an envelope and listed off two restaurants. "I'm sorry, your entry just wasn't as good as the rest of the groups."

"Pack your knives and leave," Miquel called out, and nervous chuckles came from some of the other contestants.

"Rudely said, but yes." Ann Cole opened another envelope. "For the rest of you, your challenge tomorrow is to make a milkshake to die for."

A quiet fell over the room.

Ann's face burned bright red. "Sorry, that was an insensitive way to put it, but these challenges were made weeks before the fair even opened. The dairy commission is sponsoring this event, and not only will the winning team earn immortal glory, but five thousand dollars as well. Remember, your milkshake needs to be able to be served with or without liquor."

Angie had been right again. She'd planned on shopping tonight, but if she had to drive Sydney home, it would have to wait until tomorrow. She glanced at Hope and Matt. "Any ideas?"

"Tons." Matt glanced around the room. "But are you sure this is the best place to talk about them?"

"Good point."

When the security officer came into the room, Angie's plans were changed anyway. "I'm Harry Bodley, and I'm head of security here. Ladies and gentlemen, if you need to get into your trailers, please line up by the door. I'll have officers ready to escort you to gather anything you need to take home. The rest of you are free to leave. Your event will be delayed until ten tomorrow, so don't bother coming early. You won't be able to get inside the area."

Sydney smiled at her as she made her way to the line. "You're off the hook. I just texted Brandon and told him what happened. He sent me straight home and up to bed. I guess he's sending over dinner tonight. The good thing about living with another chef, right? Someone always wants to cook."

Angie hugged her. "If you're sure you're okay. You're not feeling dizzy or anything?"

"I'm pregnant, not sick. And I feel a lot better than poor David. Can you believe he's dead?"

Angie twisted that question around all the way home. She could have gone shopping, but she really didn't feel like it. All she wanted right now was to check on Precious and Mabel and then go inside and cuddle up to Dom.

When she got home, the lights were on in the house, and Ian's wagon was parked in the driveway. She didn't make it into the house before he'd opened the door and pulled her into his arms. "Are you all right?"

"I'm fine. It's just a shock. We didn't know anything had happened until they announced that the Sandpiper had won the contest." She stayed in his arms for a minute longer, then felt the gentle nudge on her leg. She moved into the house before sitting down and pulling Dom into a hug. "Hey, big boy. Did you get a visitor today?"

"We went out and fed the zoo, and Dom even let Precious sniff his nose before he barked and sent her scurrying." He shut the door behind them. "I told her you'd see her in the morning."

"I should go out to see her." Angie picked up the glass of water Ian had set in front of her. "I just don't have the strength."

"Well, you'll be glad to know I cooked. Felicia sent me here with takeout, but I added a fresh salad and garlic bread. It kept me too busy to worry." He nodded to the water. "You want some wine before dinner?"

"Sure. There's an open bottle of white zin in the fridge." She closed her eyes, but then reopened them. "Wait, how did you know something happened? Who called you?"

"Who didn't? But I knew because I was at Allen's house when they called him in to help out. I guess they're trying to be open about jurisdiction, probably because Garden City's police force got slashed last year due to budget cuts." He poured two glasses of wine. "Then Felicia called to see if I could stay with you since she was stuck at the restaurant. She bribed me with food."

"Well, at least we know your weak spot." Angie sipped the wine. "Did your uncle let slip any information about how David died? All I know is his pastry chef went into the trailer and started screaming."

"I probably shouldn't tell you this, but they're suspecting poison. At first, the EMTs thought it was a heart attack, but he had foam coming out of his mouth when they turned him over." Ian studied her. "Are you sure you're all right?"

"I didn't accept any gifts of poisoned apples today, so I'm thinking I'm fine. Why would someone take him out during the competition? I mean, the guy had already won this round. And seriously, the prize money isn't large enough to kill for, right?" Angie closed her eyes, reliving the scene. Sheila's happy face leaving the front of the trailer, then her horrified screams later. It seemed like a bad movie, not a low-key game at the fair.

"You never know. Some people want to win at all costs, no matter what it takes." Ian took a bowl of salad out of the fridge and set it on the table. He continued setting up dinner while he talked. "Besides, we don't know that it was someone from the competition. Maybe he owed the mob money and couldn't pay."

Angie narrowed her eyes at Ian as he took a plate out of the microwave. "Does Boise even have a mob?"

"Organized crime is everywhere. We're too close to Nevada and real gambling for me to assume we're outside their influence." He put a second plate into the microwave to warm and carried the first over to the table. "Go ahead and eat. I'll grab the second plate."

The smell of meat loaf with garlic mashed potatoes made her stomach rumble. Glancing at the plate, it looked like Estebe had made a demi-glace to go with it and some butternut squash puree for the base. She took a small bite, wanting to taste all the flavors in the glaze as well as the puree. "Just what I needed after a long day at the fair."

"Felicia's good like that. I don't even order anymore when I go in. I let her pick my meal."

Angie decided not to nitpick the plate; instead, she decided to just enjoy dinner. For once. "She knows what's coming out of the kitchen."

"She knows what the diners need. I see her do this all the time. People will ask her suggestions, and she will give them exactly what they need. She can read people. Barb says she's got a bit of the gift." When the bell dinged, he grabbed the plate and took it to the table. Sitting down, he started eating, only then realizing that Angie was watching him. "What?"

"I can't believe you think there's actually something supernatural going on with her." Anger seethed through her body. And with that one over-the-top emotion, she knew she was too tired for company.

"I don't think she's different. I'm just saying she knows, somehow." He shook his head. "But that's not what you're upset about, are you?"

Somehow he could always read her. Always sense when she glossed past a problem or a feeling. She started to tell him, but then realized she didn't have a clue what was really bothering her. "I don't know."

"Eat. You're tired. You've had a huge shock. You didn't need me showing up tonight when all you really wanted to do was cuddle on the couch with Dom and watch cooking shows." He took a bite of the meat loaf. "Man, this is good. Estebe is a good substitute when you can't be in the kitchen."

"And he knows it." Angie smiled, and this time, the emotion really felt right. "I don't want you to leave, but let's not talk about anything. Not the competition, not the fair, not even our jobs."

"Perfect. I'm just going to be here eating if you need me."

Angie laughed as she watched him focus on his dinner. Eating food, it was the perfect healing activity. Especially for her. As she continued to eat, she started feeling calmer, more in control. By the time she finished her dinner and had poured another glass of wine, she felt almost human. "How do you feel about a film version of a Broadway musical?"

"*Les Miz*? Or *Phantom*?" He started clearing away the dishes as he made a pot of coffee.

She set her plate in the sink. "I was thinking about *Hair*."

* * * *

The Sunday morning sun flowed into the bedroom as she woke. She didn't remember going to bed, but apparently Ian had carried her from where she'd fallen asleep on the couch to her bedroom, and threw a quilt over her. A bottle of water and a bottle of over-the-counter painkillers sat on her end table.

Dom stood at the side of the bed, watching her.

"Hey, boy, I guess I slept through my alarm." Or, she thought as she threw her legs over the bed and rubbed the top of his head, Ian had probably turned it off. She checked her phone, and as she had suspected, the five o'clock alarm had been turned off. She thought about turning it back on right away, but Monday was one of her sleep-in days. She'd fix it tomorrow night. "Give me a few minutes, and we can go outside and feed Precious."

Dom whined in protest and lay down at the bottom of the bed. He hated visiting the barn, mostly because he hated the black goat. Maybe she was putting too many human thoughts into the dog's head, but she could read his emotions better than she could read most people. Like that crazy Miquel. What had that been about?

She showered and got ready for her day. She'd need to be out of here soon since she still needed to stop at the grocery store for supplies, but she thought she'd be done and waiting at the site for Restaurant Wars to open. Now that she wasn't so tired and emotionally drained from the excitement, she could play with the idea of the milkshake. She wanted to go local, and hopefully, her supplier would still have huckleberries. That would be the perfect base.

Humming and holding a cup of coffee in her hand, she crossed over the yard to the barn to feed the animals. Mabel was already up and outside. She gave Angie a sideways glance, but didn't follow until she had filled the cup with chicken feed and poured it on the ground near her watering bowl. She smiled down at the hen. "You're welcome."

Then she went farther inside to greet Precious, who waited at her gate. During the summer, Angie left the back of her pen open to the outside so she could go grazing as she wanted. But the goat always seemed to know when Angie was coming to feed and would meet her at the front of her stall.

Today Precious wanted her head scratched behind her ears. Ian did that every time he saw the goat, and apparently, she'd come to expect it from all her visitors. Angie grabbed the short wooden milking stool she'd found in the barn when she'd moved back home and decided to spend some quality time with the goat. Besides, Precious was a very good listener. Angie laid out the events of yesterday, including the fact that the winner had been the one to die. She wondered if that had been the point. But if that was true, the killer had to have access to the judges' results, if not the discussion. She thought about the five judges. They were all local politicians. Would any of them have had a problem with David? Angie made a mental note to call Felicia on the way to the fairgrounds. She had at least an hour-long drive, but with it being Sunday, she might get lucky and shave some time off the commute. She needed to make a shopping list. Felicia could help with that as well.

When she'd finished her coffee and her talk with Precious, she had a plan. First off was to grab some breakfast and write out her shopping list. It was going to be a long day, and she needed fuel.

As she cooked some eggs and sausage, her phone rang. She answered, putting it on speaker.

"Hey, Angie? How are you?" Felicia's warm voice filled the room. Dom's tail pounded on the floor, and he glanced around, expecting his friend to walk through the door any minute. Angie smiled and turned off the burner since the eggs had finished. She plated them and stirred the sausage.

"I'm fine. Thanks for sending Ian over with dinner last night."

A short laugh came over the phone. "I figured you were either going to thank me or kill me for that. I hope I didn't guess wrong."

"Actually, I had both feelings. I was so tired, but he was thoughtful. What am I saying, it's Ian. He's always thoughtful. Which makes me a royal jerk for being a witch to him." Angie went to the fridge to get the jar of fresh salsa she'd made a few days earlier. She sprinkled shredded cheese on the eggs, then a dollop of the salsa.

"You're perfect for each other. You balance each other out." Felicia paused. "Anyway, I didn't get to talk to Jeorge about the mixer today. He's not answering. I doubt if I'll get him to pick up before noon."

"That's okay. I'm going to pick up both rum and vodka and do a taste test. If you reach him, ask him what goes best with milkshakes." Angie set the sausage patties on the plate and turned off the last burner. Then she put the pan in the sink and sat with the plate at the table. Dom stared up at her, his mouth drooling—one of the bad things about owning a food-sensitive Saint Bernard.

"You're actually doing a shake?" Felicia sounded surprised. "I would have thought an iced blend would be easier."

"Go big or go home." Angie glanced at her food. "Look, I'm going to eat now. Can I call you when I'm driving to the store?"

They made plans. After she hung up, Angie looked at Dom. "I don't think she believes in my vision."

Dom woofed. Which could have meant, *I believe in you*. Or, more likely it meant, *If you're not eating that breakfast, I will.*

Angie pulled out a notebook and started making a list while she ate. She had the radio playing in the background, and the music made her happy. For a minute, she paused. Maybe she shouldn't feel happy. Someone had died yesterday.

She shook her head. She was sad David had been killed, but it shouldn't affect her life. She hadn't killed him. She glanced at Dom. Then up at the clock. If she hurried, they could go for a quick run down at Celebration Park. She ran upstairs and changed into running clothes. The extra hour the contest judges had given her would be put to good use.

A little over an hour later, she was showered and back on the road, this time without Dom. He'd enjoyed his run, but now he was sleeping on his bed in the kitchen. He had learned to work around her schedule. Keeping a Saint Bernard busy was almost a full-time job.

She ordered her phone to call Felicia and got her voice mail. Leaving a quick message, she hung up and turned up the music. She spent the rest of her time planning through the day.

When she got out of the car at the grocery store, she saw Felicia leaning against her car and working on her phone. Angie walked up and stood in front of her. "What are you doing here?"

"I decided I was heading to the fairgrounds anyway. I wanted to show you something." She handed Angie her phone.

A picture of a loaf of banana bread with a blue ribbon showed on the small screen. "You won?"

"I did. And the newspaper from town is coming to take pictures and do a story on me. Which means, on us. Next year, I'm canning. Wait, I told you that already, didn't I?" Felicia was bouncing in place.

Angie smiled at her friend's excitement. "Yes, you did. But I'm so excited for you. This is amazing."

They chatted as they made their way into the store. In the produce section, Angie paused and started bagging lemons. "Check out my list and tell me what you think."

As Felicia studied the shopping list, Angie put the bag into the cart and moved toward the berry section. A tall man was working there. "Tim, I'm glad I caught you. Did you get my email?"

The short man grinned, showing a too-bright smile. He was addicted to bleaching his teeth. Sometimes when she stopped into the store, his smile was so bright it hurt her eyes. "Good morning, Ms. Turner. I did get your email. And you are in luck. I have the crate in the back. One of my small suppliers had brought in a couple of flats just yesterday. Last berries of the season."

"I'm so glad." Angie knew that the start of the huckleberry season had been slowed by a hard winter and a late spring in the mountains. If the growers couldn't get into the remote valleys to pick, the berries overripened and were ruined.

"I'll be right back." He tipped his hat at Felicia as he went to the back.

Felicia handed the paper back. "One thing, I'd add some pineapple. I know your lemon will add some acid, but the milk is going to offset that quickly."

"There's a reason I keep you around." Angie smiled at her friend. "Not just for your award-winning banana bread."

A woman in denim capris and a *Perfect Pies for Any Meal* T-shirt pushed her cart toward the area where Angie was standing. "I couldn't help overhearing. You're the one who won the banana bread category? I usually have that ribbon in my pocket, so imagine my surprise when I found I'd lost to someone." She shoved her hand out to Felicia. "Sarah Fenny. I own Fenny's Pies in downtown Nampa."

"I've eaten there." Felicia smiled and shook her hand. "Felicia Williams, and this is my partner from the County Seat, Angie Turner."

Sarah studied Angie as they finished the greetings. "I have to admit, the County Seat has been on my list to check out for a few months now. Ever since you all got that great write-up in the *Statesman*."

"You're always welcome. We can do a chef table for you. Just let us know when you're coming." Angie considered the woman in front of her. She looked like someone's maiden aunt. The one who seems to be surrounded by chaos, but yet you always have the best time at her house. "I'm afraid I haven't visited your shop yet. Felicia gets around more than I do."

An alarm went off on Sarah's watch. "Well, that's my cue, I've got a ton of stuff to do before we start today. Good luck at the contest."

Before she could move her cart, another one blocked her from advancing. "Looks like you two are collaborating on your dishes."

"We're talking, Miquel." Felicia pushed his cart away for Sarah to have room to leave. "Why are you being such a jerk this weekend?"

He ignored her question, his eyes narrowing his gaze on Angie. "You should watch out. Maybe you don't want to win. You saw what happened to the last guy who did."

"Are you saying you killed David? I have a cell, so you can call the police and confess." Angie pulled her phone out of her purse. "Do you want to use it?"

"Whatever. That's not what I said, but if I were you, I wouldn't try so hard. You all think you're so special, moving here from California, trying to steal our business."

Angie was almost able to keep the comment from coming out, but the smirk on his face made it impossible. "No one can take away your customers. You must be sending them away with a bad taste in their mouth."

"Now you've crossed the line." Miquel stepped closer, but right then Tim came out of the back, a box on his shoulder.

He frowned at the group. The emotion must have been overwhelming for him to read the situation that quickly. "What's going on? Everything okay here?"

"You watch yourself," Miquel hissed as he pushed his cart out of the area.

Tim put the box on Angie's cart. "Maybe I should help you shop. I would hate for you to run into him again without some backup."

Angie watched Miquel storm down the long aisle in the back of the store. "I wouldn't turn down the help."

Chapter 5

River Vista Sheriff Allen Brown sat outside on one of the folding chairs the contest organizers had set out by each trailer. Two folding chairs and a table. Most of the restaurants had ashtrays set out as well, but none of Angie's staff smoked. At least none who had confessed. She'd brought out two large glasses of iced tea so that Ian's uncle wouldn't have heatstroke as he interviewed her about the scene at the store.

"Look, I told Ian, it wasn't a big deal. The guy was just posturing, trying to get in our heads to mess up our performance today. I don't think he's a killer. But if he is, he's dumb as a bag of rocks for tipping his hand." Angie sipped her tea. It felt good to sit still for a minute. She'd been working full-bore since they'd been let into their trailers. The staff had moved the Sandpiper trailer off-site as well as the two "losers" from yesterday's competition.

"Can you let me do my job?" He mopped at his forehead with his handkerchief. "At least this time? I'm about done working with the hodgepodge of people over in that security trailer. Everyone thinks they're a big dog, and the territory marking is getting a little out of hand."

Angie felt her lips curve into a smile. She'd wondered how the joint task force would be working, and Sheriff Brown had just answered her question. "Anyway, Miquel's just a jerk."

"So, it was you and Felicia and who else?"

Angie sighed. The sheriff wasn't giving up. "Sarah Fenny. So, you all don't have any leads as to who killed David?"

His head popped up from focusing on his notebook. "Who said he was killed?"

"He's dead. And everyone and their dogs are here investigating. That wouldn't have happened if it was just a heart attack." She sipped her tea, considering her next words. "Besides, I talked to Ian."

"That boy. He needs to learn not to run his mouth."

Angie was about to tell Sheriff Brown if he hadn't told Ian in the first place, she wouldn't have learned anything. But she thought better of it. "Poison is a scary way to die."

"Maybe the killer just wants to scare people off. Please don't spread this rumor. I'm sure you don't want people panicking and not being able to have a good time."

"Maybe that's what the killer wants."

He ran a hand over his head. "I don't understand. What does he want?"

"For people to be scared. Maybe someone doesn't want the fair contest to continue. Or at least not here." Angie glanced around at the prime development land surrounding her. She wouldn't put it past some shady developer to want the land, come hell or high water. "You might want to look into developers who are interested in buying the land. If Garden City had to lay off police officers, maybe they're looking for a way to raise some capital."

He stared at her, then wrote something down. "Tell me again why you went into cooking rather than law enforcement?"

The backhanded compliment made her smile. "I'm good with details. And wondering why."

Matt stuck his head out of the trailer. "We're ready to taste-test if you are."

Sheriff Brown waved her away. "We're done for now. Just be careful. Don't take any shiny apples from old women."

"I would almost think you cared." Angie stood, taking her iced tea with her.

"My nephew likes having you around. I love my nephew. You do the math." He finished off the tea and handed her the glass. "I'm going to hang out here for a few minutes and make some calls."

"Works for me." Angie paused at the stairs leading into the trailer. "I will be careful. Not only for me, but for those two in there. I kind of like having them around."

"Well, let's just hope this is an isolated incident. The easiest answer is that David Nubbins had an enemy who decided to get him out of the picture."

* * * *

After the competition, which Angie felt they nailed, she found Ian sitting at the table where she'd left his uncle hours ago. "What are you doing here?"

"I came to make sure you were okay. And to get another corn dog. Man, those things are addictive. And you can't get a good one except during this one week." He stood, nodding to Matt and Hope. "How did it go?"

"Great!" Hope rolled her shoulders. "The milkshake was amazing, and with the alcohol, it just had a power punch. I know we're going to win."

"That's exactly what you said last night," Matt reminded her.

She shook her head. "No, last night I said our corn dogs were awesome. We didn't make corn dogs today."

"That's not what I meant, and you know—"

Angie interrupted the two. If there was only one piece of evidence that showed she'd turned the kitchen staff into a kitchen family, it was the way these two fought like brother and sister. "Now, children, Mama loves you both. Let's go grab something to eat. I'm buying."

They found an empty table at the Baptist Church's tent, where they were frying onions to go on top of hamburgers. Ian and Matt stood in line waiting for food while Hope and Angie saved a table.

Hope yawned. "I can't believe how much work this is. I thought going to school and working a night shift was brutal. This is crazy, and it's fewer hours."

"It's the heat. Even with the air-conditioning on high, we need to keep hydrating ourselves. Make sure you keep your water bottle full." Angie leaned back in her chair. "You're doing great. When do you graduate?"

"Next May." Hope smiled, looking off in the distance like she could see the finish line. "And the week after that, my folks are taking me on a cruise. Can you believe it? We're flying to Florida, getting on a boat, and relaxing for seven days."

"Sounds like heaven." Angie rubbed the top of her shoulder.

Hope frowned. "I mean, if I can get the time off. I don't want you to think I won't still want my job."

"Of course you can have the time off. But I think your job will be over as soon as you graduate."

Fear filled her eyes. Then she nodded. "I understand. You'll probably want to hire another student for the dishwasher job."

Angie could see the wheels turning in Hope's head. "Darn right. I mean, I can't have you doing dishes when you're supposed to be a chef, right? I think, though, we'll get a freshman so the kitchen doesn't get filled up with trained chefs too fast."

"Filled up?"

"If I hire you as a line cook, and then the next student does as well as you do, I'll have to hire them too. Then we'll have way too many cooks in the kitchen. And you know what they say about that."

Hope took a deep breath and closed her eyes for a minute. "I thought you would fire me, not promote me."

"Why would I do that?" Angie leaned back as Ian set a plate filled with a too-large burger and a matching pile of crispy fries.

"Because she's totally annoying and needs to go out into the world to find out that things aren't really as cushy as they are working for you." Matt set Hope's plate down and then shoved five or more fries in his mouth. He made wavy movements at her. "Fly little bird. Fly."

"Stop being mean." Hope took a big bite of the burger, then leaned over and breathed on Matt's face. "Here's onion breath for you."

"Cooties...girl cooties..."

Ian glanced over at Angie. "I take it you've had to deal with this all day?"

"Yeah, typically I have Estebe to put down the hammer, but these two aren't afraid of me. So, they sniped at each other all during prep and service." Angie dipped a fry into the "special sauce," which appeared to be Thousand Island dressing. "Maybe I should fire one of them. I need to up my street cred."

"You have no street cred, and you wouldn't fire either of them anyway. Especially since when they aren't talking all the time, they do a great job." Ian glanced over at the other two, who had stopped eating and were watching the exchange. "What? You think we don't talk about you behind your back too?"

"Harsh, man." Matt glanced at his watch. "Fifteen minutes before the next winner is announced. Hopefully we'll have a quiet night. I don't care if we win at this point. I just don't want to lose—or have someone on the team poisoned."

"We locked up the trailer, right?" When Matt nodded, she relaxed a little. "Just do me a favor, and if there is an open container or an unfamiliar snack that shows up, don't eat it."

"What if the bottle says 'Drink Me' on the side?" Hope took another fry and pointed it at Angie. "Or maybe there's a note?"

Ian glanced at Angie. "Is she for real?"

"She's teasing. But just to be safe, throw away anything that looks suspicious. I'd hate to have my employer rates go up because I had to pay out a death claim on our life insurance." Angie dug into her burger. This was too good to let go to waste.

"Wouldn't that be workman's comp?" Ian asked conversationally.

Angie wiped her mouth with a napkin. "I guess you're right."

Hope and Matt exchanged worried glances.

"What do you two know that we don't?" Matt asked, his fries gone and his hamburger forgotten for the moment.

"Oh, so much—but I think you're talking about more recent events." Ian looked up from dipping his last fry. "Just listen to your boss, and don't be stupid. David Nubbins is dead from a suspected poisoning. You don't want to follow in his footsteps."

By the time they got back to the Restaurant Wars section, the area was crowded with people. Apparently a suspected murder had increased interest in the local competition. Angie was having trouble making her way through the crowd. Matt pulled the two women behind him. They were making good progress when she bumped into someone and lost hold of Matt's hand.

She realized she'd dropped her bag in the shuffle, but when she peered down at the ground, in between a mass of feet and legs, she spied it a few inches to her left. She reached down, but a male hand dropped down and picked it up. She lifted her head and came face-to-face with the guy who had sold her the cotton candy on Friday night.

"Well, if it isn't the blue girl." He smiled. A missing tooth on the left side of his mouth made his smile seem a little sinister. He held out her bag. "You dropped this."

"Thanks. It's a big crowd."

He glanced around, nodding. His gray hair was pulled back into a ponytail. His faded blue eyes seemed to scan the crowd and then return to meet hers, confirming her statement. "People like competitions. Makes them feel important."

"And they like trying new restaurants too." Angie wasn't sure where the conversation was going, but he seemed to have a negative bent on humankind. Which was odd for a man who worked in a fun customer service career. She moved toward her trailer. "Sorry, I need to be in place when the announcement is made."

"You're one of the competitors?" He looked surprised at her statement.

"The County Seat. Stop by if you have time before you head out of town. We're in River Vista."

As she started to walk away, she heard his response. "I just might do that." For some reason, it chilled her.

When she finally got to the trailer, Ian was watching for her. She handed her bag to Hope and asked her to put it away inside.

"What kept you? I was about to go looking, but in this crowd, I would have probably been better off standing on top of the stage to give me some height." Ian put his arm around her. "You're shaking. What happened?"

"Remember the guy at the cotton candy booth the other night?" Angie shook her head when Ann Cole tapped on the microphone. "Never mind. I'll tell you later."

Although he didn't ask any follow-up questions, she saw him scan the crowd looking for the guy from the carnival. Angie wondered if he was even still here. He'd been strange—but he worked at a traveling carnival for weeks or months on end. Maybe he just didn't have social skills. She pushed her concern out of her head and focused on what Ann was telling the crowd.

More stuff about the upcoming election and voter registration tonight. Did she really think this discourse was earning her more votes? Angie leaned into Ian, and he swung his arms around her. She felt safe. Loved. And warm in the gentle summer evening. Her life was good. No, her life was great.

Someone must have talked to Ann Cole about her over-the-top campaigning the previous night because her intro remarks focused more about the joy of childhood visits to the fair. And she kept it short. She pulled out the envelope. "We enjoyed all the frozen delights, but there can only be one winner. And that team is—Copper Creek."

Sydney squealed and jumped a little too enthusiastically for a pregnant woman, at least from Angie's perspective. But she was happy for her friend. Now she had to wait for the bad news. Had they made the cut to the next round?

Ann Cole tapped on the microphone. "Since our next contest isn't scheduled until Friday, we decided we'd cut the waiting time for at least the three losing teams."

Hope grabbed Angie's hand again. Man, the girl had a death grip.

When Ann Cole read off the names, Hope glanced up at Angie. "She didn't call our name."

"That's a good thing, peanut." Matt squeezed Hope's shoulders. "It means we're going on to the next round."

"Main courses on the run. Or what can you put on a stick." Angie shook her head. "This is going to be rough. But if anyone can figure out something, Estebe can. Matt? You're going to be helping Felicia at the restaurant Friday, and then Estebe on Saturday. Hope? You're staying on with me."

Hope stuck her tongue out at Matt. "Shows you who's more important to her."

"Yeah, the guy who's indispensable at the County Seat." Matt made an Ironman pose, flexing his biceps.

"Children..." Angie warned.

"Anyway, let's go play. We didn't get to ride everything last night, and you're going to be a wet blanket tomorrow and stay home." Matt slapped Ian on the back. "See you later, farm guy."

After they left, Angie and Ian sat at the small table near the trailer. They sipped on a couple of beers that they'd stashed in the trailer's refrigerator. Ian pulled the label on the bottle. "Do you need me to help clean up?"

"Hope's already taken care of everything. All I want to do is relax and maybe walk through the animal barns tonight. Do you want to continue our fair date?" She sipped her beer, happy that they'd made it through another round. "If you're lucky, I'll let you win me another stuffed bear."

"Maybe I'll just buy you a diamond necklace. I'm sure it will be cheaper and will last longer." Ian rubbed his shoulder.

"You have a game tomorrow night?"

Ian nodded. "We're playing the Meridian Baptist team. They've been impossible to live with since they won the league last year. Every team is trying to kick butt against them."

Angie hid her smile behind her beer bottle. "I thought winning wasn't everything."

"It's not. But payback is amazingly satisfying. I'm thinking I'm going to have to spend some time in prayer if we win to try to get my overwhelmingly strong need to go TP their church lawn in celebration under control." He finished his beer and stood up. "So, if we don't have to clean up, let's go play for a couple of hours. I want a caramel apple."

"Let me lock up. I'm going to leave my backpack here until we're done, so don't let me forget or I'll be out of the gates without my keys." She paused at the door. "And I can't really stay out that late. Dom hasn't been fed since this morning."

"Actually, I ran out to your place to check on everyone before I came into town." He grinned. "Yes, I am the best boyfriend in the world. Dom, Precious, and Mabel are all fed and watered for the night."

Angie turned off the lights and locked the door, slipping the trailer key into her pocket. "Well, I wouldn't say 'in the world,' but you do have your moments."

"What? You're holding out for a prince? I don't think Dom or Mabel would like living in a castle."

"Precious would love it." Angie put her arm in his and they made their way back into the stream of people and toward the animal barns. "And I'd leave the others in your capable hands."

"I'm afraid you have thought this all out." He leaned down and kissed her head. "Is my English accent wearing on you?"

"More like fading. You sound more and more like the rest of us." She hugged his arm. She loved their banter.

As they walked past the carnival entrance, someone grabbed her arm. She turned to see a wild-eyed Matt standing next to her. "What's going on?"

"Come quick. Hope, she just collapsed. She's in the carnival area." He pulled on her arm.

Ian came around to the other side. "Slow down, Matt. Did you call the medical team?"

"Yes. They're with her now. I don't know the answers to the questions they're asking. I never asked her about her folks. Can you come and talk to them?"

"Of course." She put a hand on his shoulder. "She's going to be fine."

Matt shook his head. "What if she's not? What if she's been poisoned like Chef Nubbins?"

Chapter 6

A wall of people surrounded the area near the balloon dart game. Ian and Matt pushed their way through. And Ian pulled her after him, not letting go. A pale, unconscious Hope lay on a stretcher.

"Come on, folks, move along. Nothing here to see." A security officer tried to move Ian and Matt away from the scene.

"We're her friends." Ian pushed Angie to the front of the group. "She works for Angie."

The security guard looked unimpressed, but then one of the EMTs called out to him, "Let them in. The kid was with her when she went down. We have a few questions."

Angie recognized one of the guys from last night. "It's been a crazy few days here."

"You're not wrong." He studied her. "You guys are from the Restaurant Wars contest."

"Angie Turner. And this is Hope Anderson. She and Matt work for me. What happened?"

The EMT nodded at Matt. "According to her boyfriend over there, they'd just gotten off the Dust Storm and she stopped and went down."

Angie pushed out the one question she didn't want to ask. "Has she been poisoned?"

The EMT shook his head. "I don't think so. More likely it's heatstroke. Those trailers have air-conditioning, right? Was she hydrating enough?"

Angie thought about the day. She could remember Matt getting out bottles of water, but Hope? She hadn't been near the fridge. "Matt? Was she drinking water today?"

He shook his head. "I gave her a bottle first thing when we started working, but I don't think she even finished that."

The other two EMTs were starting to move her toward the back of the carnival area.

"Where are they going?" Matt demanded.

Angie put a hand on his arm. "Let them do their job."

The EMT who'd been talking to them stood in front of Matt to block his forward movement. "We have an ambulance at the access road behind the tents. We're taking her to St. Luke's on Cole. Can you call her next of kin? If she's not eighteen, someone will have to approve treatment."

"She's twenty. Almost twenty-one," Matt said.

Angie nodded. "We'll call her parents on the way and will meet you at the hospital."

"I'm sure it's just heatstroke. Don't worry. She's in good hands." The EMT nodded at the group and then left to follow his teammates.

Ian took Angie and Matt by the arms and led them away from the area and toward the exit. "I'll drive to the hospital. We can stop by here and get your cars later."

Angie shook off his grasp. "I'm fine. I'm going to go grab my bag and check the trailer one more time. I'll meet you at the hospital."

When Ian paused, she put a hand on his arm.

"Really, I'm fine to drive. I need my car, and I don't want you running everyone around." She kissed him on the cheek. "Sorry about missing our impromptu date."

"There will be other times." He nodded to Matt, who looked like he was about to sprint to the hospital. "I'll see you soon."

Angie watched as they power walked through the food court aisle. She turned back toward the Restaurant Wars section, taking her phone out of her pocket. Dinner service had just started, so she called the landline. A hostess answered, and a few minutes later, Felicia was on the line.

"Don't tell me you won?" Excitement flowed over the speaker.

"No. Copper Creek took the win today. Look, I need you to do me a favor and not freak out. Are you in my office?"

"No, but I can be. Let me put you on hold." Felicia's tone went from excitement to professional in seconds.

Angie listened to the upbeat music track they'd chosen for their hold music. "Positive energy,"

Felicia had said when she vetoed Angie's idea of a country music track. And as usual, she'd been right. As she was waiting, she walked through the gate, nodding at the same security guy who had been stationed there yesterday. She unlocked the trailer, grabbed her backpack, and had already locked things back up when Felicia came back on the line.

"What happened?"

Angie sank into one of the chairs, the adrenaline rush she'd felt a few minutes ago leaving her. "Hope fainted. At least that's what the EMTs think. We asked about poison but they don't believe that's the problem. I just hope they're right."

"Oh, no. Where is she?"

"On her way to St. Luke's Emergency Center on Cole. I hate to ask, but would you call her parents and have them meet us there? Ian and Matt are already on their way to the hospital." Angie closed her eyes and tried to settle herself. Heatstroke. Not a big deal. Especially for someone as young and healthy as Hope.

"Wait, they left you alone? What were they thinking?"

"I'm an adult. I can make it to the car and to the hospital by myself." Angie felt her lips curve at Felicia's worry. "I wanted to check on the trailer and grab my bag before I took off. Things have been weird here."

"It's a freaking fair. It should be all fun and play, not running to the hospital."

"True, but you deal with the cards you're dealt. Look, just call Hope's parents. Tell them as little as possible, but lean toward heatstroke, okay? We don't need to freak them out too."

Felicia expelled a breath. "I think telling them is going to be easier than telling your team. You know Estebe's going to want to take off."

"The service comes first. Remind him of that, and tell him I'll be there with her. Maybe that will help."

"Just keep us in the loop. As soon as you hear that she's okay, call please."

"Definitely." Angie stood. "I've got to get going. Thanks."

"No problem."

She tucked the phone into her backpack and took out her keys, a safety habit she'd picked up in California. She never dug for her keys in a parking lot. Boise might not be San Francisco, but she continued the habit, mostly because it calmed her. And she needed the calm today. She started to walk out and saw the door to Copper Creek's trailer open. She looked to the security guard, but he was out of sight.

"What else could go wrong today?" Angie stepped over and called out, "Sydney, are you in there?"

When there was no answer, she looked for the guard again. He was across the street, talking to a young woman in a golf cart. They were laughing over something. Apparently flirting with the fair personnel was more important than staying at his post. Whatever.

She decided she'd just step over and shut and lock the door. She would never forgive herself if something happened to their trailer if she could have stopped it.

Stepping up the stairs, she had the doorknob in hand, ready to turn the lock and slam the door. She glanced inside to make sure no one was there or to see if she needed to shut off the lights, and gasped.

The inside of the trailer had been ransacked. Pots, pans, and supplies were all over the floor. She backed down the stairs and ran over to the security guard. "Someone's trashed Sydney's trailer."

He stared down at her, obviously annoyed at being interrupted. "What are you talking about?"

Angie slowed her words down. But her heart was still pounding in her chest. Thank God she'd locked up her trailer before heading out to play, or it could have been her stuff scattered all around and who knows what they would have taken. "The trailer next to mine has been broken in to. You need to call the police."

Now his eyes widened, and he ran toward the area, already on his walkie-talkie. The girl in the golf cart stared after him. "Maybe I should go too." She didn't wait for an answer, but instead started the cart up and took off down the food court lane.

"So much for security." She wondered if she needed to stay, but then thought of Ian and Matt waiting for her.

She dug her phone out of her pocket and called the number she now knew by heart. Sheriff Brown answered on the first ring.

"What can I help you with, Ms. Turner?" His tone was brisk, and Angie wondered if she'd caught him at dinner.

When she told him about the break-in, he swore. "Stay there. It will take me about an hour to get back."

"I can't." Angie explained that she'd be at the hospital with Hope.

She could hear rustling on the other side of the phone, and she realized he was already getting ready to leave.

"I'm sorry about that. I hope she's all right. I'll talk to you later, then."

And the phone went dead. She'd done all she could here. Now it was time to go wait for news about Hope. And talk to Hope's parents. And hope they didn't blame her.

Ian and Matt were in the waiting room when she got there. When Ian looked questioningly at her, she shook her head. Not the time to talk about another issue. "How is she?"

"They won't tell us anything." Matt had his head in his hand. "This is my fault. I pushed her into going and riding the rides. She said she wasn't feeling well before we got on that last roller coaster, but I called her a chicken."

"It's not your fault, Matt." Angie sat next to him and rubbed his back. "She's a big girl. You can't make her do anything she doesn't want to do."

"You must be talking about my daughter." An older man with gray hair stood in front of them in jeans and a T-shirt with a picture of Smokey Bear. Somehow the bear even seemed to look accusingly at Angie. "I'm Bill Anderson. My wife, Gayle, has already gone back to the exam room with the nurses, but they tell us that you followed her in. I'm assuming you're her work family?"

Ian stood and shook hands. "I'm Ian McNeal. This is Angie Turner and Matt Young. How is she?"

"They tell us she was dehydrated." He held out his arms to welcome a newcomer to the conversation.

A woman came and hugged him. "She's awake. They have an IV in for fluids, but they say she's going to be fine."

Angie waited for the hug to break before she stood and introduced herself to Hope's mom. "I'm Angie Turner, Hope's boss. I'm so glad she's better. And if there's anything you need, please feel free to call."

"We appreciate all you've done for her. All she can talk about is the County Seat. Not many chefs get to work at such a wonderful restaurant just starting out." Gayle hugged her. "Our girl is going to be fine. This is just another lesson for her life plan."

As Bill and Gayle walked back to the exam room to be with Hope, Angie stood up. "I'm grabbing a few bottles of water for us and then heading home. I need some Dom time."

When she found the break room, a sobbing Sydney was there, sitting on one of the plastic folding chairs. "Oh, my God, what happened? Are you in labor?"

Sydney looked up at Angie, her face tearstained. "Oh, Angie. I'm so glad to see you."

She stood and pulled Angie into a hug and cried some more.

Angie let her get it out, then went over to the vending machine. "What do you want to drink?"

"Water's fine." Sydney sniffled into her tissue. "My sister's with Brandon while they move him to a room. I needed some air. I don't like to cry in front of him."

"What happened to Brandon? Heatstroke?" Angie wondered how many people the EMTs had transported out of the fairgrounds this weekend.

"What? No, they think he got food poisoning." She shook her head. "I told him not to eat those nachos that the contest sponsors gave us."

"What nachos?" Angie figured it wasn't a good time to mention the break-in at the trailer. Sydney might just go over the deep end. Let her find out later, once Brandon was better.

She looked up at her quizzically. "The ones that were in our trailer after the competition this afternoon. Well, maybe they just gave it to the winning trailer. I can't believe I won and now we're here at the hospital rather than celebrating at the restaurant."

Her phone buzzed with a text. She stood and hugged Angie. "I've got to go. They've got him moved. The doctors say he'll be fine by the morning, but pregnant me is tied up in knots with worry."

Angie waited for her to leave, then set the extra bottles of water down. And for the second time that night, she called Sheriff Brown.

Ian frowned when she came back to the waiting room. "I almost went looking for you. What happened?"

"I ran into a friend." Angie decided she'd tell him the whole story later, not in front of an already upset Matt. "Are we ready to go?"

"I went to the room and said good-bye to Hope. She's embarrassed, but at least she has color in her cheeks. I told her she owed me a carnival night soon." Matt glanced up at Angie. "That was the right thing to say, right? I didn't want her to know how crazy with worry I was."

Angie glanced at Ian, who shrugged. Yep, he'd seen it too. There was a workplace crush happening here. "It was perfect. Ian will take you to your car. Go home and get some sleep."

"Give us a minute," Ian said to Matt, and then took Angie by the arm. "Okay, what happened that you're not telling me?"

"Call me once you get Matt back to his car. I've got a few things to catch you up on." Angie rolled her shoulders. "Maybe participating in this Restaurant Wars competition was a bad idea."

"But you've made it through two rounds. Hope's heatstroke wasn't your fault."

Angie knew he was right, but she was afraid that she'd just put another bull's-eye on her and her team's back. One that didn't end well for Chef Nubbins nor for the Copper Creek gang. She stretched up on her toes and kissed him. "Just call me."

Chapter 7

Monday morning started out with not just Ian in the kitchen for breakfast, but Felicia and Estebe there as well. Estebe had volunteered to cook omelets, so he was chopping meat and vegetables to mix into the eggs. Felicia was baking a couple loaves of quick breads to share. Angie sat at the table drinking coffee.

"So, you really think that the nachos were poisoned?" Ian asked as he rubbed Dom's head. "I've talked to Allen, and he said they didn't find any trace of nachos in Sydney's trailer."

"The trailer that was ransacked, remember?" Angie had a notebook out taking notes and writing down questions. "I'm just concerned that someone, probably someone in the contest, is trying to narrow down the field even more than the actual contest is doing."

"And you think it's Miquel. That's jumping to conclusions, isn't it?" Felicia popped up when the timer went off for the breads. She'd made a banana loaf and a dried cranberry and orange bread while Angie fed the zoo in the barns. Satisfied the breads were done, she grabbed hot pads and set the loaf pans on the counter to cool. Then she turned off the oven and picked up the coffeepot to refill everyone's cups before sitting back down. "He's not that bad of a guy."

Estebe rolled his eyes at Felicia's statement, which made Angie laugh. The two of them had been dating for several months, and from what she'd seen, the pairing worked. Even though Estebe didn't like it when Felicia brought up other men. Like now.

"I knew him. I didn't date him. Calm down, hot stuff." She laughed as she paused by Estebe and kissed him on the cheek.

"I didn't say anything," Estebe protested.

"Whatever." Angie drew a box around Miquel's name. "All I know is he's been acting weird. He all but threatened us at the market. Sarah agrees with me that he's a problem."

"Sheriff Brown talked to him and didn't find any reason to think he's a serial killer." Felicia sat back at the table and sipped her coffee. "So, who else has a reason to knock off the competition?"

"Rumor has it that your friend Sarah is losing her business. The building she owns is needing too many repairs." Estebe washed his hands and then sat down at the table with the rest of them. "I looked at buying that building five years ago to open my own restaurant, and it was falling down into itself even then."

It always surprised Angie when Estebe talked about his financial situation. The guy was a shrewd investor of his money, and he worked his butt off. She knew he didn't need to work, which made the fact he had taken on the job at the County Seat so much more impressive. "I'll put her on the list, but even if she wins, the money's not going to be enough to fix a building."

"But it might get her enough to start over." Ian nodded. "I've heard rumblings that she might be looking at other locations."

"I've written her down. Who else?" Angie looked around the table. "Okay then, I'll say it. We have a vested interest in winning to make more people aware of the County Seat."

Ian nodded. "Okay, so which one of you is the killer? Felicia in the kitchen with the club? Or Angie in the barn with the goat washer."

"Maybe it's me? I could want to take over the shop but want it to be more successful before I knock off the two owners. Did either of you put me in the will?" Estebe sipped his coffee. "Or maybe it's our sensitive Hope. She might have just pretended to get heatstroke yesterday. Did they send her home yet?"

"Her mom called last night. They sent her home with orders to rest." Angie crossed off the County Seat on her paper. "Okay, so it was a dumb idea."

"No idea is dumb, dear. Just the people who promote it." Ian smiled at her. "So we're down to six restaurant teams. Copper Creek, the County Seat, Bien Viveres, Fenny's Pies, and who are the other two?"

"The Black Angus and Tara's Tea House." Felicia supplied the answer. "Has anyone heard anything about either of them?"

The table was silent again.

"I don't even think I've been in either restaurant," Ian mused.

"Then we have our assignments. Estebe and I will go to the Black Angus tonight and see what we can find out about the chefs. You two go to Tara's Tea House." Felicia stood. "But for now, let's get breakfast going. I'm starving."

"Now, did you give us the tea shop because I'm British?" Ian stood, took out the juice from the fridge, and set it on the table.

Felicia grinned. "Actually, I just wanted a good steak dinner."

As they got ready for breakfast, Angie stood by Ian. "You know your uncle is going to be upset we're investigating."

"I think he feels like everyone's investigating, and so as long as we feed the information his way so he looks good in front of the task force, I don't think he'll care." Ian kissed Angie lightly. "This is exciting. I feel like those people on the television."

"The ones who find serial killers?" Estebe set the last omelet on the table, and everyone sat down again.

Ian shook his head. "No, the ones on *Scooby Doo.* We used to watch it when we came to the States to visit my family." Ian bowed his head and for a second, the table was quiet. When Estebe said, "Amen," everyone opened their eyes and started eating.

Once the breakfast was done, Estebe and Felicia left in his Hummer. Angie and Ian sat outside on the porch drinking iced tea. "I better get back and open the office. We don't have a board meeting for a while, but I want to go over Saturday's numbers. There's a lot of work that goes into just four hours of actual selling at the farmers' market."

"Either Estebe or Felicia will be doing the shopping this week," Angie said absently. "Or maybe Nancy. Now that she's down to only one second job, I've been trying to build her more hours at the restaurant. Do you know her ex left her in debt up to her ears? The girl's too sweet for her own good."

"Some men don't live by the right principles. We both know that." Ian might have been referencing his own friend who'd shown up a few months ago with a new profession. "Anyway, I've got to go. What's on your plate today?"

"Absolutely nothing. I'm playing with a few recipes this afternoon. But I should be ready for our dinner date at five." She stroked Dom's head. She loved these quiet moments when no one really had to talk.

"Make it five thirty. That way I can go back to the apartment and clean up before I come get you."

"I'll make the reservations for six thirty, then. The restaurant is set in one of those old houses off Warm Springs so it's near the foothills." Angie didn't want to move, but her mind was already thinking about the recipe she wanted to play with today.

"Maybe we'll take a drive afterward." He stood and kissed her. "I've got to go, as much as I don't want to."

"Leave the glass here. I'll take it inside." She stroked his cheek. "Thanks for playing detective with me. I don't want to go back to the contest next weekend without knowing if there really is something going on. I'd hate to see any of my crew hurt over a stupid competition."

"I wouldn't be helping if I didn't think you were on the right track with this. According to Allen, the rest of the task force is writing it off to an unfortunate incident. Maybe Nubbins had enemies. But they are careful not to blame the contest as the cause. Ann Cole put a lot of her own money into this to get her in front of more voters. I guess the challenger in the next election has deep pockets."

After Ian left, Angie sat with Dom for a while longer. But now, her mind wasn't on the recipe. Instead, she was thinking about local politics and a whole different angle for the killing. What if someone just wanted to upset Ann's campaign? Could it be that easy?

"People are strange creatures, Dom."

He looked up at her and rested his head on her lap, his tail wagging. She checked the thermometer on the porch. It was barn shaped and had hung there for as long as Angie could remember, but it was still accurate.

"If we leave right now, we can fit in a short walk by the river before it gets scorching hot. Want to go?" She stared into his deep brown eyes and jerked back in surprise when he woofed and went to stand by the door of the SUV.

"Well, I guess that's a yes. Let me change shoes and grab the bag and your leash." She stood, patting her leg for Dom to follow.

Reluctantly, he followed her into the house. Angie was sure he thought he'd been played, so she hurried to dump the tea glasses out and put them into the dishwasher. Then she grabbed two bottles of chilled water from the fridge, slipped on her walking shoes, and took the backpack and leash off the hook by the door. Now Dom sat at attention near the door. She glanced around her kitchen, found her keys and wallet, then opened the door again.

Dom beat her to the car before she even got the back door closed and locked. He wasn't going to let her change her mind.

Angie started the car and turned up the stereo. The worries of the last few days melted away as they made their way to the Centennial Park walking paths.

They'd just finished their mile and were on their way back to the car when Angie spied a woman sitting on the bench near the walking bridge over the river. As they got closer, she recognized her as Barb Travis, owner and manager of the Red Eye Saloon. Felicia liked to visit the country dive bar on most weekends, especially since it was less than a block from her apartment. Angie figured her friend could probably hear the band from her bedroom window on hot summer nights.

Somehow, in the light of the day, Barb looked less tired and somewhat younger than she did in the smoky bar. She glanced up at Angie from the book she'd been reading. "I thought you were off playing at the fair."

Angie pointed to the bench, and Barb nodded her invitation. Dom sat too, watching his soon-to-be new friend with interest. "I was there most of the weekend. The restaurant is still in the competition, so I'll have to go back on Friday."

"From the rumors I'm hearing, it's not safe to still be playing. Who in the world would poison people? It seems like such a cowardly way to deal with an argument or a disagreement. Give me a good old-fashioned bar brawl anytime." Barb put a bookmark into her book and closed the cover. "As long as it's not in my place. I've thrown more than one fight out into the street for them to deal with their issues. Men."

Angie smiled and stroked Dom's head. "I'm not sure, but it's got me worried. My friend's husband ate some bad nachos, but luckily, she got him to the hospital in time. They're not sure if it's the same guy or not."

"Oh, it's the same guy."

Angie looked at Barb, wondering what she knew.

Barb laughed and waved the concern away. "Don't look at me like that. I don't know who's been poisoning the chefs, I just know the type. Unless he, or she, has gotten what they wanted, it will continue."

"You're probably right."

Barb reached out and let Dom smell her fingers. The woman's hands were tiny and well-worn from all the work she'd done over the years. Angie's Nona's hands had looked the same: rough and wrinkled, but still strong enough to get the work done. When Dom approved, Barb reached up and stroked his soft fur. "Besides, I watch a lot of true crime shows. Sometimes they're overdramatic and stupid, but mostly they're good. Especially at three in the morning, when I've just gotten home from closing the bar and I can't sleep."

"You should hire a night manager."

The cackle that came out of Barb's mouth turned into a cough, and she pulled a tissue out of the long sleeve of her T-shirt. Once she'd settled back, she shook her head. "Not going to happen. If I leave, they'll rob me blind. Besides, if I can't sleep, I might as well be useful."

Angie glanced at the time. She should head home to try to work on at least one recipe before lunch. "Hey, I'm doing some experimenting today on menu items. Do you want me to bring you over some dinner when I get done? Ian's taking me out to Boise for dinner tonight so we could drop by the bar with the food about quarter to six?"

Barb looked at her quizzically. "Sure. But you know I can cook, right?"

"I know. I just hate throwing food away when I know I can feed people. It's a problem." Angie was already making up delivery boxes for Mrs. Potter and Erica anyway since she came home for the summer. Her elderly neighbor had been splitting her time between sunny California and the farm across the street.

"Well, as long as it's not a problem. But don't forget me. If I don't eat by seven, I'm a raging witch all night long." She tapped her book. "I have to admit I'm hooked on this author. She writes about Oregon and Colorado and family. The stories make me happy. I guess that's another reason I like owning the bar. I get to watch people fall in love and celebrate their milestones."

"I wouldn't have pegged you for a romantic." Angie stood, pausing as Dom reached over to allow Barb to pet him before he left. He'd made a new friend.

"If you tell anyone you saw me reading this, I'll spread rumors that you're dating that chef of yours as well as Ian," Barb threatened as she gave Dom a kiss on his nose.

"He's dating Felicia right now. No one would believe you," Angie said with a smile. Barb had a hard crust but a heart of gold.

"Which would make you look even worse. Betraying your boyfriend and your best friend. I'm sure the church ladies would be lining up at your grandmother's house to help you see the light." Barb gave Dom one more pat, then opened her book. "Besides, soon it's going to be too hot to sit out here and read anyway. I need to enjoy the time I still have."

Something about the wording made Angie take a second look at Barb, but the woman had clearly dismissed her. She was focused on reading and lost in the story. Just the way Angie felt when she was perusing new cookbooks.

"We'll see you tonight then," Angie said before turning away and heading down the path to the parking lot and home.

* * * *

Angie had already cleaned up and delivered Mrs. Potter's food when Ian pulled into the driveway. He'd brought his truck, and the way it shined, she wondered if he'd run it through the car wash before coming to get her. She glanced around the kitchen, making sure there wasn't anything out that might tempt Dom into bad behavior, then gave her dog a kiss.

"We'll be home early." She smiled at Ian as he walked inside. "Maybe your friend Ian will make popcorn tonight and stay for a movie."

"Probably not. I've got an early meeting with a new farmer who wants to meet over breakfast in Meridian." He gave Dom some love, then turned to Angie. "Are you ready?"

She nodded, handing him a box. "We've got a delivery to make before we go to Boise."

He took a long breath in. "We taking dinner to Mrs. Potter?"

"No. I've already walked her food over. That's for Barb." She grabbed her purse and took out her keys. "Be good, Dom."

As she locked the door behind them, Ian waited to walk down the stairs and to the truck with her. "You know that's like telling the wind not to blow. Dom doesn't know how to be good."

"Well, he'd better start. I'm running out of furniture with wooden legs for him to destroy." After climbing up into his truck, Angie took the box. "No one warned me that raising a Saint Bernard would be so costly."

"Excuse me? I'm pretty sure I have and I've heard Felicia tell you stories. And even Estebe talks about mistakes you've made with Dom." He shut the door, then walked around the truck, getting in at the driver's side.

"I meant before I bought him."

Ian started the engine, then glanced at her. "I thought he was an impulse buy."

"That makes my point exactly." Angie grinned. "You're supposed to read my mind and keep me out of problems like this."

"One, I didn't know you then..." Ian paused. "Are we fighting?"

"Are you upset?"

He shook his head. "No, but I don't think we've ever disagreed with each other before."

"You really think the first fight I'm going to pick will be over why you didn't stop me from buying the best dog in the world?" Angie picked up her phone and read a text. "Felicia says that they have a reservation at six tonight. They want to know if we want to meet them at the Ice Cream Palace for dessert after dinner."

Ian pulled onto the highway and toward River Vista. "Works for me. Did you bring your clues notebook, Velma?"

Angie laughed and pulled out the red spiral from her purse. "Of course, but I'm Daphne, not Velma. Get it straight, Fred."

Chapter 8

Ian parked the truck in front of the Red Eye. "I'll just wait here. I need to check my emails again to make sure that guy is actually showing up in the morning. He's had a ton of questions."

"I'll be right back out." Angie slid out of the truck and slammed the door, earning a glance from Ian, who shook his head at her. "Not my fault the guy drives a tank," she mumbled as she pushed open the heavy wooden door of the bar.

Immediately she went from a bright summer day to darkness. The beer signs around the bar glowed neon light and the pool tables all had a light bar over the top, but mostly, the light was provided by strands of white Christmas lights all around the room. She blinked, letting her eyes adjust before taking a step farther into the room. She didn't want to run into a table or trip on a step.

Soon, she was able to see the bar and the small woman standing behind it, watching her. She had a cup of coffee in her hand, and she had the same look that Ian had given her just now outside.

"Come on over. There's nothing in here that's going to hurt you." Barb called out.

"Just trying to see so I can walk. Man, you keep it dark in here." Angie moved toward the bar, the box of food held in front of her.

"That's so you women look better and better the more I drink. By the time I leave here, I'll have a beauty queen on my arm." An older man turned and drank beer out of a glass.

"Jerry, the last time you left here with a woman was so long ago you probably don't remember you married her a week later. Don't mind him,

Angie, he's confused with his role in life. He thinks he's God's gift to women."

Jerry chuckled and turned back to talk to someone to his left. Barb picked up the coffeepot and refilled her cup. She held it up to Angie. "You want some?"

"I'm good. Ian's out front and we have reservations." Angie set the box on the bar and turned to leave. "I hope you enjoy."

"Hold on a sec." Barb opened the box, took a whiff, then closed it again and set it behind her. "That smells good."

"Thank you." Angie paused, wondering if she was excused now.

Barb nodded to the stool. "Sit down a minute. You're making me nervous."

"But, Ian..." Angie stopped talking when Barb threw her a look. Nona used to have that same look at times. It meant stop talking and listen. She sat. "Yes, ma'am."

"Now, I got to thinking after you left about that contest that you're in. And I need to tell you there's at least one of your competitors that I know is up to no good. He used to work here, and although I could never prove it, I'm sure he skimmed off the top of the receipts. He's one of the reasons I don't let anyone but me handle the night's till." Barb leaned closer, her voice quiet. "He was trying to woo me. Like I'd fall for some young stud whom I could have given birth to. He'd flirt hard, but I didn't let him hook me. Then I started noticing the receipts going down. So, I'd send him on break and do a count halfway through. When my halfway count was more than the end of the night till one Saturday, I told him where the door was and not to come back."

"Did you report him?"

Barb shook her head. "He called a few days later and apologized. Said he'd pay me back, that it was a onetime slip. But I knew better than to believe his lie."

Angie thought she could guess whom Barb was talking about, but she didn't want to jump to conclusions. "Who was it?"

"Miquel Montoya. I hear he's a big-shot chef over in Boise at some Mexican restaurant." She grabbed the box and a fork and sat down on her stool. When Angie glanced at her, she shook her head. "Just watch yourself. That's all I'm going to say. Now, get out of here and go have a real date with your guy."

Angie blinked coming out of the dark and into the light. She could still smell the smoky odor mixed with stale beer. She climbed into the truck. "Sorry that took so long. Barb was chatty."

Ian nodded, finishing a note on his phone. "She usually is. At least with people she likes." He sniffed, then rolled down the window to let the breeze in.

"Do I smell that bad?" Angie lifted the top of her sundress and groaned when she took a whiff. "Maybe we should go back to the house so I can change."

"You'll be aired out by the time we get to dinner." He turned onto the road and headed the truck toward Boise. "Felicia and Estebe stopped by for a second on their way out of town. They said good luck."

"We're going to need it." Angie filled Ian in on Barb's experience with Miquel. After she was finished, Ian drove on, quiet. She waited for some kind of response, but when he didn't speak, she asked, "Are you awake?"

"I heard everything you said. I just don't understand some men. Why would you steal, and definitely why steal from an older woman who's just trying to make a living? There are ads everywhere for jobs available. Just work, save your money, and live a normal life. No one gets rich quick. And found money is like shifting sand. Not something to build a strong foundation on."

Angie smiled. Ian was solid in his beliefs that you worked your way through life and carved out your own treasure. She hadn't told him about the weirdness she'd run into with Miquel at the fair, and she didn't think she would. He hadn't done anything but be creepy. And she could handle that on her own. But she thought she might just go visit Bien Viveres tomorrow and have a talk with the guy. Putting poison in nachos was a little like shining a spotlight directly on the chef at Bien Viveres, but maybe subtlety wasn't his strong suit.

She'd take Felicia with her. Just in case.

She realized Ian was watching her as he took the entrance to the freeway. As he merged into the speeding traffic, she smiled. "I haven't been in Boise for what, a day? I like it better when I just hang out at the farm on my days off."

"I think you'd stay there forever or until you ran out of food. Have you found anyone who delivers that far out?" Ian swore under his breath as a small sedan swerved in front of him, causing him to brake quickly.

"No. So if you want a new business idea, there you go. Food delivery to rural homes. But not meat in a freezer. Those guys creep me out."

"Maybe we could rehab a semi, set up a mini store, and drive it around. The problem is, I don't think the profit margin on fresh produce is big enough to pay for the gas for the semi."

"Details." Angie pulled out her phone and found the website for Tara's Tea House and started reading. "This is something interesting on the About the Chef page—did you know Tara McKnight worked at the Sandpiper right out of culinary school? She's a local who has been in the restaurant business for over twenty years. The Tea House opened two years ago and is getting good reviews."

"Good, not great?"

Angie shrugged. "Three-star average. Mostly complaints about the food being just okay. I hate judging people on reviews, especially since you don't know what actually went down that day."

"Okay, so if our food tonight is bland, then you'll be more comfortable judging her?"

Angie laughed. "Exactly. I'm an experiential learner. I have to know what's being said is true because it happened to me."

"So you burned your hand on the stove when you were a kid."

"Take that exit to downtown." Angie pointed to the left, and Ian moved the truck into the correct lane. "I burned it twice. Once, because I thought I'd turned it off and I hadn't. And once, just to see what my mom was talking about."

"You must have been a handful as a kid." Ian took the bend off the main freeway and onto the connector. "I didn't give my mom anything to worry about until I turned a teenager. I've told you that story already. If there was a rule growing up, I followed it to a tee. I like rules."

Angie glanced around the too-clean truck cab. "You do have a plan for your life."

He reached over and squeezed her hand. "I'm glad you noticed."

When they reached the restaurant, Ian eased his truck into a larger spot at the back of the parking lot. As they got out, he glanced around the area. "I should have brought the wagon. It would have fit in these too-small spots better."

"City rules tell you how many spots you need. If you don't have the room, you make the spots as small as possible. I didn't have any parking regulations in California or in River Vista. But the rules that the City of Boise have fill a book. I'm glad I decided to take the risk on having the County Seat out so far."

"Doesn't seem to have hurt your business." They walked to the entrance, where a hostess in a black skirt and a white blouse greeted them.

"Reservation for McNeal," Ian said in his too-British accent.

Angie thought the girl was going to start panting. She saw her swallow, then study the computer.

"We have a lovely window table overlooking the garden for you." She picked up menus and led them through the dining room. It was early, and there weren't many other customers.

As they reached the table, Angie paused, pasting on a large smile as she focused on the girl. "Can you tell your chef that Angie Turner of the County Seat is dining with you tonight? I'd love to talk to Tara if she has a minute."

"Oh, yes. I'll be glad to tell her." She set the menus in front of them. "My boyfriend took me to your restaurant last month for my birthday. I'm studying hospitality management. It was such a lovely evening and a great dinner."

"So glad you enjoyed. Next time, let me know you're there and I'll come out to chat for a minute." Angie watched as the hostess skittered away toward what Angie assumed was the kitchen. "Either she'll come out and chat, or send the waitress back saying she's out of the kitchen tonight."

"But you think she's here." Ian studied the menu.

"Yeah, I do. The hostess would have told us if Tara wasn't here, right up front. So we'll see whether she lies."

They didn't have to wait long. After the waitress had provided drinks and taken their orders, an older woman in a chef's coat and a blue beret came out of the kitchen. She looked around the dining room. When her gaze landed on Angie, she put on a smile that didn't seem genuine and strolled over, holding her outstretched hand in front of her. "Well, Angie Turner. I was going to come over this weekend at the event, but we were so busy. And what a tragic event. I was shocked to hear about Nubbins."

"I know, right?" Angie stood and shook the woman's hand. "Tara, this is my boyfriend, Ian McNeal."

"Tara McKnight. So nice to meet you. Is this your first trip to the Tea House?"

"I'm trying to get around to all the restaurants and meet the chefs, but you know how it is." Angie pointed out to the patio area. "Is that an herb garden? I have one at my farmhouse, but having it this close to the kitchen would be amazing."

The two of them chatted about food and gardens and cooking for a few minutes. Then Tara glanced at her watch. "I've got to get busy. We're having a large group from the legislature coming in about seven. They'll close the place up about eleven, hopefully. I don't need a long night playing hostess."

"I hear you. I'm so glad we don't open until Wednesday. It gives me some downtime and time to play with the amazing product you all have here. I thought, leaving California, I might have to give up my obsession with using fresh, but it's just different fresh foods."

As they said their good-byes, Ian picked up his phone, answering a text. He glanced up when Angie sat back down. "Sorry, I needed to take this."

"You're on your phone a lot lately." She worried about him. His job paid little, yet he put in so many hours, basically working for free. "Anything I need to worry about?"

"Like I'm having a torrid affair with Mildred?"

"As long as she continues running the goat farm and dairy so I don't have to find a new supplier, I guess that's fine." Angie checked to make sure that Tara had really returned to the kitchen. "I don't think she's involved."

"Because she has an herb garden and likes talking about cooking?" Ian nodded. "That makes total sense."

"I know. And it's just a feeling, but she doesn't seem to need either the recognition from winning or the money. Do you know what you can charge for a group dinner and use of the room for four hours?" She tapped her spoon on her water glass. "Maybe we should block off a room for private events at the County Seat?"

Their dinners arrived, and they moved their conversation away from their jobs and the case. Ian asked if she wanted to take a drive up to Sun Valley next week. He'd take Monday off, and they could leave when Angie woke up on Sunday.

"I'll have to ask Erica or Felicia if they'd stay with Dom. He'd eat my entire house if I left him alone that long."

They turned down dessert, and when the check came, Angie reached for it. "I'll buy, since this was County Seat research."

He let her pay, then took her arm as they walked out. "I feel like a kept man."

"Does that bother you?" She looked up at his face as they made their way out of the dining room.

"Not in the least."

Felicia and Estebe were waiting outside the Ice Cream Palace on a bench when Ian pulled in to the parking lot. As they got out of the truck and walked over, Ian leaned close. "Now, I didn't see that one coming at all."

"The two of them? Honestly, I didn't either. But I kind of like it." She sighed. "On the other hand, if the breakup goes bad, I might just lose my sous chef."

Ian slipped his arm around her waist. "Well, let's just hope for a long and happy relationship, then."

They didn't talk about what they'd learned until they were seated and had their orders in. Felicia leaned in toward the others, her eyes bright with excitement. "I feel like a secret agent. Did you know I was going to go and work for the government after college in one of the investigative areas?"

"And you fell in love with cooking instead?" Ian provided the next line.

"Totally. I took a class with the boy I was dating. Some holiday cooking class, but the instructor was from the culinary department. I fell in love with him." Felicia grinned as the waitress brought her Court Jester, a peanut and chocolate parfait. Angie had ordered the same thing, knowing if she didn't, she would be jealous of her friend's treat. Estebe had two scoops of vanilla, and Ian had a banana split.

Estebe handed her a napkin. "You mean you fell in love with cooking?"

Felicia shook her head. "Nope. The instructor. He was so fine. I changed my major and dumped the boyfriend that winter break. Right after he took me to the last concert we'd planned on attending together."

"You are a cold, cold woman." Estebe took a bite of his ice cream. "Just like this treat."

"Whatever. I was young. Young people do stupid things. And besides, that decision led me here." She held Estebe's gaze, then seemed to remember something. She filled her spoon with a mix of the ice cream dessert and pointed it at Angie. "Anyway, I almost forgot. I think we found the killer."

Chapter 9

"Way to bury the lead." Ian chuckled. "At least someone got something besides a long discussion on the positives of having an herb garden on-site and larger rooms for private events."

"Wait, she has a private event room? I've been meaning to talk to you about that. My yoga group wants to rent out a space for their semiannual luncheons, and I was thinking about that other area where we talked about setting up another storage area, but it's just filled with boxes right now…?"

"I was thinking the same thing." Angie leaned closer. "I mean, if we used larger event tables that can be folded up and nice folding chairs, not the cheaper metal ones, we could rent it out for community events as well as banquet dinners."

"Um, hello? What about the killer?" Ian broke into their conversation just as Angie was pulling out a notebook to start sketching out the area and listing off what they'd need to invest to get it done.

Angie held up a finger, scribbled a couple of notes, and focused on Felicia. "We'll get together tomorrow to hash this out, but I think it's a great idea."

She nodded, her mouth filled with ice cream. When she'd finished her bite, she wiped her lips with a napkin. "Me too. Now, let me tell you about our trip to the Black Angus."

Angie ate while she listened to Felicia's story. When they got to the menu, she leaned closer. "What did you order?"

Ian put his hand on her arm. "Does it matter to the story?"

Angie grimaced, then shook her head. "Sorry, go on. You can tell me later."

"Anyway, as soon as we ordered our steaks and sides, including a version of avocado toast using sourdough and guacamole," Felicia added, her gaze on Angie, "which was freaking amazing, by the way—the chef came out, Rider James."

Estebe nodded. "That is exactly how he said it. 'I'm Rider James, thanks for coming in.' Then he drooled over Felicia and ignored my existence."

"Well, not quite, but yeah, he was a little smarmy." Felicia squeezed Estebe's shoulder. "He told us all about how he was about to hit it big. That this place was just a hole in the wall on his trip to the big leagues."

"The restaurant was very well set up. Very nice. A little steakhouse franchise that most chefs would love to manage, at least at the beginning of their career. This guy? He thinks he should be famous." Estebe shook his head and focused on his ice cream. "It's like those guys who buy a big motorcycle, when really they should be riding a scooter to learn their balance first."

"Interesting analogy, but yeah." Felicia turned back to Angie. "And get this, when he left, he told me not to get my hopes up for the contest because he had it in the bag."

"Okay, so none of that screams 'killer' to me. He's a jerk, I admit, but so is Miquel." Ian finished his ice cream. "Sorry to call this short, but I've got an early meeting tomorrow."

Angie scooped the last of the ice cream out of her dish. The chocolate had slid down and mixed with the melted ice cream, hiding a few last peanuts for a burst of salt. This was a perfect way to end the evening.

In the truck, on the way home, Angie was daydreaming about how to change the extra room they had into the banquet room she'd envisioned. The room was at the edge of the building so it had two brick walls that would add atmosphere. The city council was always looking for meeting space. The last time, they'd borrowed Ian's small conference room in the farmers' market office to meet, but that meant people had had to stand. That might have made the meeting shorter. They could volunteer the space for nonprofits and use that as a community service project.

She was so deep into the pros of building out the area that she almost didn't hear Ian when he turned down the music.

"I have something I need to ask you." His voice was tense.

She sat up, putting the new space out of her head. Worry filled her as she focused on his profile in the dark truck cab. "What's going on? Is your mom okay?"

"Mom's fine. And no, I'm not taking off for England. I told you I'd tell you the next time I needed to leave. Before getting on the plane." He took her hand and squeezed it. "This is a favor I need to ask."

"If you're worried about me getting involved in the investigation, this time it's different. My friends are in danger. What if we win on Friday? Will I or someone I love be poisoned just because we made a better dish? This is so stupid. I can't believe someone's doing this. Or that you'd ask me to just stay out of it. Sometimes your uncle can be so infuriating." Angie ranted on for several minutes, then realized Ian wasn't talking. She fell silent.

"Are you done?" he asked in the darkness. They were off the freeway and driving on the back roads toward her farmhouse now. Cars sharing the road were few and far between, even at ten thirty at night.

"I'm done. Sorry. I'm a little tired." Angie took a breath. "Let me start over. What can I do for you, Ian?"

"I need you to hire someone. She has absolutely no work experience. And I'm not sure she's ever even tried to cook before. But she needs a job and a purpose." He sighed. "I'd hire her myself, but I don't have any more funding for wages. None at all. I could give her volunteer experience, but she needs to make some money."

"Sure. Send her over and I'll tell Felicia to train her for the front of the house. If you get good experience there, you can get a job almost anywhere. It won't pay a lot, but it's a good skill. And if she's good, we'll move her up into a server position." Angie leaned on the door, watching him. "So, where did she come from?"

"She was sleeping in the alley. For goodness' sake, she must be no more than fifteen. She says she's eighteen, though. I had Allen run a check on her, and there's not a missing persons report here in Idaho. That is, if she's telling us the truth on her name." He shook his head. "She's been sleeping in the back of the office for about a week. I thought it was temporary, but now, I don't know."

"What's her name?"

"She goes by Bleak. I'm pretty sure no normal parent would name a blond-haired, blue-eyed baby girl Bleak, but she swears that's her name. If she's lying to me about that, I know there's a lot more she's lying to be about."

Angie felt conflicted. On the one hand, Ian taking care of a street kid was so his personality, but she hoped it wouldn't come back and bite him. "Is she on drugs? I can't have her working for me if she's on drugs. The crew all has to take a prehire drug test. After that, it's based on trust."

Ian sighed, and turned on the blinker. His face turned red in the flashing light, but his eyes looked sad. "I don't think so. I've told her I'd take her shopping for clothes if this works out. And I'm going to have to find a better place for her to live. Maggie says she can stay with them for a while if she gets a job. The women's group at the church is looking into low-income housing, but she's been less than forthcoming about working with social services. I think she's scared she'll be taken home or sent to a group home."

"Your aunt is a smart woman." Angie relaxed. "Let me talk to Felicia in the morning. We'll set up a doctor's appointment for a physical and the drug test. And take her shopping for some clothes. Felicia knows all the good secondhand shops that have upscale donations."

"Thank you." He turned and smiled at her. "I know taking someone in off the street isn't an ideal way to get a new employee, but I'm hoping we can turn this girl's world around. And if she sees there are good people in the world, maybe she'll open up."

Angie hoped Ian wouldn't be taken advantage of. She knew how much he cared for others. And this girl seemed like just one more project he needed to save.

Dom was ecstatic to see her, but still he left her in the house and went out to the barn with Ian to feed Mabel and Precious. Angie watched them walk through the barnyard toward the large door. Dom would look up every so often, which meant Ian was talking to him. Her dog had wrapped Ian around his paw as badly as he had Angie. She made a cup of coffee and poured it into a travel mug. It wasn't far from her farmhouse to Ian's apartment over the farmers' market office, but she'd rather he be wide awake for the drive. Then she started a pot of hot chocolate for herself. She and Dom would spend some time in the living room catching up on her DVR'd shows until she got sleepy.

She set her alarm on her phone so she'd remember to call Felicia, then smiled as she watched Ian and Dom move back toward the house. Ian picked up strays just like she did. However, her last rescue was the goat in her barn, not a troubled teen. The only thing that made her feel better about this was that Sheriff Brown and his wife were involved as well. That woman had an iron fist. She went back to stirring the pot of hot chocolate, muttering one of Nona's favorite sayings: "What will be, will be."

The next morning, she turned off the alarm and crawled out of bed. She'd been up for over an hour already anyway, tossing and turning. She didn't know what was bothering her—well, besides competing in a contest where the winners turned up dead. And Ian picking up a teenage girl to raise. And running a restaurant with a mortgage on the building. And... Dom woofed at her, interrupting her listing off of all the things that might be keeping her awake.

"You have a dog door. And I know you can't be hungry." She looked down at her dog and then flopped back on the bed. She held her arms open, and he moved in for the hug. It was a morning tradition since the time when she had been able to pick him up and give him a squeeze. Now, if he sat on one of her feet, he crushed it. Angie leaned into his head and kissed him on one of his big ears. "I love you to the moon and back."

That earned her a big, sloppy kiss on her face. Laughing, she got up and headed to the bathroom. Time to shower and get ready. She decided to call Felicia right after she'd checked on the barn crew. And made coffee.

A few minutes later, she sat at the table, her phone angled against a book as she called Felicia. Her coffee was starting to do the trick. She really needed to learn how to sleep better. Dragging through the day wasn't her best look.

"Hey, I was just about to call you." Felicia's cheerful voice filled the speaker. "When do you want to get together on the new project?"

Had she actually called Felicia last night? Or had Ian told her? Angie felt confused, then realized her friend was talking about the *other* new project, setting up a banquet/meeting room. "No time like right now. I'll drive in if you'll make breakfast."

"Sounds like a plan. Do you want anything special?"

Angie wanted a lot of things, like an open mind and assurance that Ian's rescue wasn't going to turn into a disaster for all of them. "As long as it's food, I don't care."

"Perfect. I'll see you in thirty minutes."

When Felicia clicked off, Angie looked at Dom, who wagged his tail hopefully.

"Sorry…" Angie stopped. If she was doing a favor for Ian, he could return one and watch Dom if they went into town shopping with his new project. "You're right, you should go."

Dom woofed his approval at the word "*go*" and went to sit by the door. Angie put some food into a baggie along with a bottle of water and a couple of dog toys. Then they left for their adventure.

When she reached town, she parked in the back and let Dom out of the SUV. He ran to the back door of the kitchen and watched her approach. "Just because you're faster than me doesn't mean you're the boss of me." She rubbed his head and realized, that yes, the dog had become her boss over the last few months. And she didn't care one iota.

She unlocked the door and Dom went into the kitchen, then turned right and stood at the bottom of the stairs. Somehow he knew the kitchen was off-limits here versus at home, where he spent most of his time with Angie in the kitchen.

Dogs, they were amazing creatures. Angie pointed up the stairs, letting him go first since there wasn't room for both of them. She heard Felicia open the door and praise Dom for beating her.

When she reached the landing, Angie shook her head. "The only reason he wins is because I let him go first. Not everything is a race, you know."

Felicia stepped back so they could come into the apartment. "You can't tell him that. How are you this morning?"

They talked about little things, like their dinner dates the night before, the upcoming team meeting and family meal before service on Wednesday, then Angie took a breath.

"Go ahead, tell me the bad news." Felicia turned to check on something in the oven.

"What are you talking about?" Angie saw Dom had already taken to the bed Felicia kept under her dining room table and was halfway asleep. "What bad news?"

"You don't usually come over for breakfast after just seeing me last night. Did Ian do something stupid?" Felicia closed the oven and came over to sit on a counter stool next to Angie.

"Yes and no." Angie went on to tell her about the teenage girl he'd found sleeping in the alley. When she got to the fact that the girl needed a job, Felicia perked up.

"Tell him to send her to us. I don't know how many teenagers I trained as servers at El Pescado. Remember Joey? He was homeless when he came to work for us. The shelter down the street had him walking around checking every business in the area for a job."

"Joey? The tall kid with bright red hair? He was so funny." Angie smiled at the memory. "Didn't he leave to go to college?"

"Yes. The restaurant paid for a small scholarship with the school to cover his room and board. He keeps in touch. He started a job with an engineering firm in a town north of the city." Felicia sipped her coffee. "I thought I told you this."

"Maybe." Angie thought back. She'd been dealing with the whole Todd mess at the time and probably her mind hadn't been on the business as much as it should have been. "Do we help out Hope?"

"You really don't listen, do you?" Felicia turned back to the oven and pulled the warm egg, potato, and cheese casserole out. Angie watched as Dom's head popped up when he smelled the food.

"Guilty as charged." She stood and got plates out of the cabinet while Felicia went to the fridge for freshly made salsa.

"Since Hope's living at home, we pay her tuition. As long as she gets a B average." Felicia plated a large square out of the dish along with salsa and then topped it with half of a sliced avocado. She set the plates on the counter and glanced at Felicia. "Orange juice?"

"Sure. Just a little." Angie took silverware out and then sat, taking in the dish. "Do we have this on our class menu?"

"Not yet. I wanted to see what you thought. We have the brunch class in two weeks, and it's already full, with a waiting list. I'm tempted to add more, but then, is that oversaturating the market?" Felicia poured the juice, then sat and watched Angie take a bite.

Angie took her time in responding. She could taste the fresh herbs along with the spices that the potatoes must have been fried with. The cheese was a sharp cheddar and melted into large strands as she ate. "The only thing I might add is a different cheese. Either add or replace. I'd like something that felt more umpcious."

"I don't think that's a word, but I agree with you. Maybe a layer of ricotta and egg like a lasagna in addition to the cheddar."

Angie imagined the creamy goodness that change would bring and nodded. "Yep, that's perfect. So, she's hitting her grades, right?"

"Who, Hope? Of course, she's mostly an A student. I think the classes she struggles in are the theory courses. You give her a recipe, she can cook anything. I think working with Estebe has been good for her confidence."

Angie smiled and took another bite. "So, Estebe..."

Felicia shook her head. "No, no way, and no again. I'm not talking about my relationship with Estebe with you." Felicia's cheeks brightened.

"So, it is a relationship?" Angie pressed.

Felicia set her fork down. "Okay, this I will say. I enjoy spending time with him. We have a lot in common. He gets my jokes, mostly. And I love how he opens the car door for me. I feel like a princess."

"You should feel like a princess." Angie thought about Felicia's last boyfriend, who had basically used her as a second set of hands for his nonprofit. "I just wanted to say, I'm glad for both of you, but don't screw it up and lose me a sous chef."

"Sometimes you are a little too direct for my taste." Felicia laughed. "But yeah, we know that dating someone you work with can be an issue. We've talked about it, and we both agree that if either one of us wants to call it quits, we'll part amicably."

Angie had seen Felicia break up with someone she cared about before, and it wasn't an easy break. Estebe had a reputation for being cool and overconfident in the kitchen. Maybe even brusque at times. No, a breakup between those two wouldn't be amicable. Not in the least. She just hoped the County Seat wouldn't implode with their failed relationship.

Felicia had been watching her as she processed the look she saw on Angie's face. Now she sighed. "Yeah, that's what I'm thinking too."

Chapter 10

After breakfast, they put another meeting time on their schedule to talk about the new dining area and went to meet Ian and Bleak. They were in Ian's office, drinking coffee. Ian stood and gave Angie a kiss as they walked in, then greeted Felicia. Dom came and sat on his foot until he acknowledged him.

"Bleak, this is Angie Turner, Felicia Williams, and this big guy here is Dom." He nodded to the other chairs around the thread-worn sofa. "Let's sit down and talk about what's going to happen today."

Bleak ignored the woman and focused on Dom. "Does he bite?"

"He's a big teddy bear." Angie got Dom's attention, then pointed to Bleak. "Go say hi, Dom."

Wagging his tail and eager to meet someone new, Dom complied. Bleak fell to her knees and gave him a huge hug. "You're such a beautiful boy."

"We think so." Angie watched the two interact, then met Ian's gaze. "You're babysitting him while we go to the doctor and clothes shopping."

"I'm not sick." Bleak stood and flopped back into her chair. "I don't need a doctor."

Felicia shook her head. "You do if you want to work in our restaurant. It's the law. Besides, it's free to you. Take us up on our generosity."

Bleak narrowed her eyes. "What about the shopping? Will I have to pay you back for the clothes? Because I have clothes. I don't need more. I don't have anywhere to keep them anyhow."

"Here. You don't have anywhere here. But when you move in with the Browns for a while, you'll have your own bedroom with a closet." Ian quickly glanced at Angie. "Besides, she needs a specific uniform at the restaurant, right?"

"Black pants, white shirt, and good, solid shoes. You're going to be on your feet a lot." Angie took out a job application. "While we're driving in to Boise, you can fill this out. It's a new employee packet we give all our hires. And Felicia will go over your schedule and pay. Do you need a certain schedule?"

"I don't understand. Don't you set my work hours?" Bleak took the papers and a pen from Angie.

"Yeah, but if you have appointments or want to take some classes, we can work around things like that, especially if we know up-front. It's harder to replace you after the schedule has been set. But don't worry, if you have an emergency, your team will help out."

"Just curious, Bleak." Ian leaned back in his chair, like he really wasn't interested in the answer. "Did you finish school? Because if you didn't, we can set you up with the GED people. And we'll find you a ride into Boise for the classes."

"I told you I was eighteen."

Angie could see the anger in the girl. And the fact that she was hiding something was as apparent as her fury. She thought about saying that even if she was eighteen, that didn't mean she'd graduated, but she didn't want the girl to stomp out. "Okay, then no restrictions on your work hours."

Bleak opened her mouth to say something, then closed it and leaned back into the chair, appearing bored with the whole conversation.

"Okay then, Dom, stay with Ian." Angie handed Ian the backpack. "Make sure you take him out every two hours. He's used to having his open schedule using the dog door."

Ian held up his watch. "I just set a timer."

Angie looked at Felicia. "We should be back, what, around five or six? We'll eat lunch while we're out and maybe pick up dinner for the two of you."

"We're going to the Browns' for dinner. Maggie's excited to meet Bleak." He smiled at the girl, but she turned her head.

Angie knew how she felt. She hadn't wanted to go over to the Allen house for dinner the first time Ian had taken her, either. "Well then, we'll make sure we're back no later than five thirty."

"Sounds good." Ian went back around the desk and turned on his computer. "Let me know if you need anything."

"I'll take your credit card, if you don't mind." Angie held out her hand.

"No way. I might not see any of you again until they shut down the credit line." He pulled five one-hundred-dollar bills from his wallet. "This should cover what she needs."

"I'll bring you back the change." Angie's hands clamped on the money and she started to walk away.

Ian laughed. "You'd better. I have your dog as ransom."

Angie didn't think Dom would even try a breakout to get home. And if he did, it might take him months to find his way home. He'd have to meet all the people along the way, which would take more time.

"I don't need that much stuff," Bleak protested again.

Angie pointed to the door. "Then there'll be a lot of change to give back. My SUV is out in the parking lot at the end of the alley behind the County Seat."

When everyone was out of the office except Ian and Angie, he called after her, "Good luck."

She had a feeling she was going to need it.

* * * *

Bleak was quiet during the trip to Boise. Angie asked her three times if she was done with the application, but she kept saying one more minute. Finally, she passed it forward and Felicia stuck it into her tote. "Thanks, I'll read it later. So, what's your favorite band?"

"I don't know."

"Okay, let's start with something a little easier. Favorite book you read. Or last book you read, that would be even easier." Felicia turned in the seat to watch Bleak, who had her face turned toward the window, watching the world go by.

"For school or for fun?" Bleak answered, not turning her head.

"For fun. The books they make you read in school aren't half as fun as what I read now," Felicia said.

Angie watched the interaction with interest. Felicia was good at getting information, but she hadn't watched her friend in action for a while.

"You wouldn't know it," Bleak muttered.

"Oh, I like a challenge, especially around books. Angie just reads cookbooks mostly. And some local women's fiction." Felicia pressed, "So, what was it?"

"Paranormal, I guess. It was about magicians. I found it at one of the shelters. It was a trilogy, but the shelter didn't have the other two books. And then there was this television show. I didn't get to see all of the season, but it was really, really good." Animation flowed through her voice for the first time since Angie had been introduced.

"Did you read all three books?" Felicia asked casually.

Bleak turned her head. "No, I couldn't afford to buy them. I went to the library but they kicked me out once they realized I was there too much. They thought I was a runaway and kept trying to get me to talk to their social worker. When I refused, they kicked me out. I thought libraries were supposed to be free."

"Yeah, me too." Felicia leaned back and changed the subject. "So, you like books about magic. What about werewolves or vampires?"

Bleak shrugged. "Sometimes. But there's this other book one of the kids was talking about. Something about vamps and witches and how they fall in love. I'd love to read that."

"*Twilight*?" Angie guessed and both Felicia and Bleak laughed. "What?"

"Not *Twilight*. That's too old. I probably won't find it again, since the guy who recommended it is dead." Now she turned back to the window.

Felicia was on her phone doing something, and Angie felt like a chauffeur, just driving from one place to the next one. At least she was almost at the doctor's office. She pulled into the parking lot and turned off the engine. She grabbed her tote with her notebook and looked at Felicia. "You going in with us?"

"No, I need to finish this. Give me ten minutes. I've already told the office what we need." She looked up at Bleak. "Unless you need me in the room with the doctor?"

"What do you think I am, twelve?"

Angie and Felicia watched her walk to the office door and swing it open, disappearing inside.

"I was going to say fifteen, but I don't think she wanted an actual answer to that question." Angie pulled her bag farther up on her shoulder. She handed Felicia the keys. "Just don't forget to lock it. I don't want any more drama for the day. I'll go back to the fair to get that type of abuse."

She went into the office, where someone had already called Bleak's name, so she was going into the back when Angie walked up to the counter. "Do you need me to fill out any paperwork for Bleak?" She pointed to the disappearing doctor and girl.

The woman glanced through the computer file, then shook her head. "Your partner, Felicia, faxed us everything. We're good to go."

Angie returned to the waiting area and pulled out her notebook to go through her to-do list for the next week, as well as add in new items. Like finalizing the menu for the brunch class, adding in Felicia's new recipe. She was thinking about the contest and the creepy things that had gone on so far, making notes and action steps to figure out who was messing with the valley's chefs, when Felicia came in from the car.

She dropped the keys into Angie's lap. "Sorry I'm late. Everything okay?"

"You took care of everything this morning when you made the appointment apparently." Angie dropped the keys into her purse. "You really think the guy who's running the Black Angus is kind of sketchy?"

Felicia nodded. "He just felt wrong. Maybe I was just projecting, but it's worth mentioning to Sheriff Brown. He should be interviewing everyone and anyone attached to the contest anyway. But maybe we could give him a heads-up on this guy."

"I still think Miquel needs a second look." Angie tapped her pen on the pad. "Even Barb doesn't like him, and she likes most everyone."

"Barb hates everyone." Felicia laughed, then turned red when several people in the waiting room turned to stare. She dropped her voice. "Anyway, that's how it appears to me."

"Well, she has reason to with this Miquel." Angie glanced at her list. Maybe she could fit it in tomorrow.

"Then let's go to Bien Viveres for lunch. We told Bleak we'd feed her during this visit to the city. Might as well kill two birds with one stone." Felicia picked up a gossip magazine. "I knew these two were dating, even when they denied it because they were both still married."

Angie wasn't sure she even knew who the two people were. But she grabbed her phone and made reservations for lunch. Then she made a checkmark next to Miquel's name and wrote down one more thing: Go talk to Sheriff Brown about all that they'd found out. Even though Ian might have already told him, it felt like good karma points to be up-front with the investigation. It did involve her, but more importantly, he seemed to be open to her getting involved this time. That made her pause. Why *was* he okay with her looking into things?

Before she could puzzle it out, Bleak came out of the hallway, her dark eyes flashing. Angie noticed her choppy haircut and wondered if they had time for one more stop. Bleak thrust the paperwork into Angie's hands.

"Here. He said the health department would have the lab results next week. But I looked healthy enough to him." She rolled her eyes. "Can we go now?"

Angie glanced at the receptionist, who nodded. Apparently, Felicia had dealt with the payment issues as well. She stuffed the papers in her tote and grabbed the keys. "Let's go shopping."

By one, Bleak had several pairs of new jeans, T-shirts, dress pants, and work shoes. They'd even gotten Bleak to accept one dress, which Angie felt sure the Browns would appreciate since they would probably drag their new roommate to church with them. Felicia glanced through the lists she'd made. "One more stop after lunch and we're done. You need some underthings, and we're going new but cheap on those. And we can get you a couple pairs of cute shorts and tanks for next to nothing there."

Angie expected the girl to complain, but instead, she asked, "Where are we eating?"

Shopping therapy must work on some people. For Angie, it made her grumpy. "Bien Viveres, it's an upscale Mexican restaurant near the river."

"I like Mexican. My mom used to take me to this little hole-in-the-wall. She thought they had the best food. I bet this place is even better." Bleak was leaning back and reading a paperback she'd picked out at the next-to-last resale shop they'd visited.

Angie and Felicia exchanged glances, not wanting to stop the conversation. Finally, Angie spoke. "I haven't been there, but I'm hoping it's good. It's one of the restaurants that we're competing against at the fair."

Bleak's eyes narrowed. "Ian told me about the Restaurant Wars. So, you're going as spies?"

Felicia laughed. "Checking out the competition, but not spying."

"I don't really see the difference," Bleak said, returning to her book.

Angie shrugged and made the turn into the parking lot of the restaurant. "Maybe she has a point."

When they were seated with drinks on the table and their orders in to their waitress. Angie asked the older woman if Miquel was in the kitchen.

Nodding, she grinned. "I'm thinking you want to talk to him? You all must be chefs. We've had a lot of the competition for the fair group coming in the last week or so to try out our food. I'll let him know that you are here."

Felicia waited for the woman to leave. "Okay, so why didn't we think about checking out the competition before? Apparently everyone else has."

Angie sipped her iced tea. Bleak was still reading, seemingly ignoring their conversation. "Did you notice any of them at the County Seat last week?"

"Besides Miquel? No. And I think I would have. Unless they sent other employees in like secret shoppers. No one announced themselves, not like we're doing." Felicia crossed her arms. "Somehow I feel so violated."

"Spies don't tell the enemy they're coming. It messes with the information they get. Do you think they're going to burn our tacos now that they know we're the ones eating the food?" Bleak glanced at them over the paperback. "Seriously, you all need someone to plan your strategy."

Angie wasn't worried about burnt food. She was more concerned about someone adding poison to the food, like what had happened to Brandon

Cook. She smiled at Felicia. "Again, she has a point. Maybe she should be our tactical adviser the next time we do a local competition."

"There's a food truck event in late December. We could rent a truck and enter." Felicia pulled out her phone and keyed in some information, searching for something. "Yep, it's still open for entries. Want to go play?"

Angie wasn't sure she wanted to go back to the competition she was in on Friday, let alone enter another one. One where they'd have to cook in a rental food truck, if they could even find one. She shook her head. "Let's talk to the team on Wednesday at staff meeting about the event. If they want to be part of it, we'll do it."

"You have staff meetings?" Bleak set down the book after carefully putting in a piece of paper she'd taken out of her tote to mark her place. "Do I have to come?"

"If you're not in school or working another job," Angie added the second qualifier quickly so Bleak wouldn't go ballistic on her again, "you're expected at all staff meetings. This one, you'll get to eat a few of the new menu items we'll be adding to service that night."

Felicia smiled over at her. "What she's saying is, don't eat lunch before you come to work Wednesday. And speaking of, I want you to come for a couple of hours tomorrow. I'll have Tara come in and train you on busing tables."

"Two hours to learn that?" She glanced around the room. "Clean the dirty dishes, take them to the dishwasher, come back, rinse, repeat."

"And I'll do your paperwork so we can get you on the books and set up for a paycheck." Felicia reached out to pat the girl's arm, but then thought better of it and picked up the book. "I don't think I've read this one. I have several from this author up in my apartment. I'll bring them down on Wednesday if you want them."

Bleak looked at them like the whole conversation was a setup for an elaborate practical joke. "Whatever."

"Good afternoon, ladies, I wondered when I'd see you here." Miquel stood at the front of the table, watching the interplay.

"We were in town shopping and thought we'd stop in." Angie forced her lips into a smile. *Be polite even if you don't want to* had been one of Nona's favorite sayings. Especially when they were driving home after church. "I hear you already know Felicia. This is our newest staff member, Bleak."

"Interesting name for such a lovely young woman." He nodded to Bleak, who rolled her eyes. Chuckling, he lifted his arms. "I am Miquel Montoya, head chef of Bien Viveres."

"Are you ready for the next event?" Felicia asked, sipping her tea.

He pulled a chair from an empty table next to them and turned it backward, then straddled it and leaned forward until his chin rested on the wooden back. "So ready. It's been a challenging contest so far. And yet, neither of us has won a round. I'm sure we're better than that, aren't we?"

"I don't know." Angie watched his face. "It almost seems like bad luck to win. First, Chef Nubbins dies, then Sydney Cook's husband is taken ill by eating nachos that were left for her."

"Nachos don't usually kill people." He frowned and glanced at the kitchen.

"And yet, one chef is dead. You have nachos on your menu here, right?" Bleak blurted out. Then, when she saw the look on Angie and Felicia's face, she shrugged. "What? Just asking the obvious."

Miquel stared at the young girl, then started laughing. "I like this one. She has spunk. If you get tired of working for these women, give me a call. I'll hire you."

The waitress came by with their food, and Miquel took the dishes off of the tray and set them on the table. "Enjoy, ladies. Lunch is on the house."

After he walked away, Angie threw a questioning look at Bleak. "Are you trying to get us killed?"

Chapter 11

Tuesday morning Angie decided to put the competition, the murder, and her new employee who seemed to have a death wish, behind her. Today would be about new recipes. She showered away all the bad mojo she'd felt while they ate lunch at Bien Viveres. If Miquel wasn't a killer, he was totally a jerk.

After she'd fed the zoo and was finally sitting at the table with her coffee and a warmed-up slice of the breakfast casserole Felicia had sent home with her, she glanced at her phone. Maybe she should call Ian and see what his uncle had told him? "Get behind me, Satan."

Dom glanced up from his bed, wondering if her words meant something to him, like "walk" or "eat this." When he decided that no, his master was just talking to herself again, he laid his head back down for his morning nap.

Angie pulled out her notebook and a list of holes in the menu. She'd already decided what she needed to take off this month's offerings. That was the easy part. The garden and produce supplies told her when it was time to move from summer's bounty to fall's more rustic flavors. She thought about the light soups they'd had for the season, then an image came to her. Nona's corn chowder. Corn was still readily available, as were a variety of spicy peppers. With a chunky potato added to it, the chowder would be filling as well as tasty.

She went to her fridge and pulled out some corn on the cob she'd brought home from the storehouse at the restaurant. Then she ran out to the garden to pick several varieties of peppers. Mabel had beat her to the plot and was pulling up an earthworm that seemed to be longer than the hen was tall.

Gathering the peppers, she spied a sweet onion popping out of the soil. With all of these, she went back to the kitchen to start her creating process.

It was ten o'clock when a knock came at the door. Angie had two pots of soups on the stove and was considering putting a pork roast into the pressure cooker so she could play with some sandwiches. Of course, that meant baking bread as well.

She walked over to the door, beating Dom to it, and swung it open. Sheriff Allen Brown stood on her porch, hat in hand. "Come on in. I didn't expect to see you today."

He stopped at the doorway. "Whatever you're cooking, you should make into a room spray. You'd have men drooling at your feet."

"Well, thank you, I guess. Come on in and I'll dish you up a bowl. Or two. I have Snow Chicken Chili and Last of the Summer Corn Chowder. I might have to change the name of the chili or wait to put it on the menu, though." Angie went to the cupboard and got out three bowls. "Are you game to try both?"

"I really shouldn't, but what the heck?" He came inside and shut the door behind him. "How have you been, big guy?"

Dom wiggled at his feet.

"He's happy I'm home. I've been gone a lot. Have you done any background checks on this Bleak girl who's got Ian wrapped around her little finger?"

"Now, don't you be saying stuff like that. My nephew only has one girl he's sweet on, and I'm talking to her." Sheriff Brown sat at the table, resting his hat on the chair next to him.

Angie set the two bowls in front of him and went back to get spoons. "I think that's the nicest thing you've ever said to me. But seriously, she's got to be what, fifteen?"

"Sixteen, according to a missing person's report out of Utah. Her folks are in a group that lives near the Nevada border in some sort of commune."

"Are they coming to get her?" Maybe Angie wouldn't have to train a new staff member after all.

He shook his head. "According to her father, whom I talked to this afternoon, she's made her bed. They've washed their hands of her. The social worker I called said there was a problem with jurisdiction and asked if I could hold her for a few days."

"Hold her. As in, put her in a jail cell? Why? Because her folks don't want her?" Angie brought her bowl of the corn chowder over to the table and handed him a spoon. "This just keeps getting worse."

"I'm not putting her in custody, but she is moving in with Maggie and me tonight. If you're serious about giving her a job, I want you to copy her work schedule to me. We'll make sure she gets there. And I'm going to talk to the school about education options." He took a sip of the chowder. "This almost makes up for the worst day in my career."

"How long before the state takes her?"

He shook his head. "Honestly, I don't know."

They sat, eating in silence for a while.

Finally, he set his spoon down. "Anyway, that's not why I came by. I wanted to check in and see what progress you've had in checking out the other contestants."

Angie went through what she and the rest of the crew had found out. Then she ended it with the discussion with Miquel the day before. "I'll be honest, I don't like the guy. But is he a killer? I don't know."

"I'll do some research. I'm going to pull up that report from Barb. I vaguely remember that situation. I think when he left, she dropped the charges." He scribbled in his notebook. "The guy makes me think there's some smoke there, but it may not have anything to do with the murder." He finished eating his soup.

"Do you want more?" Angie stood and held out her hand for a bowl. "Tell me which one you liked the best."

"More chowder please. The chili's good, but this is amazing." He handed her that bowl and then stood to take his other bowl to the sink. "I want you to know, if you think it's too dangerous, you don't have to go back to the fair. It's not worth the risk."

Angie sat a full bowl of chowder at his spot. She grabbed two bottles of water and brought them to the table. "I have to finish this. I don't know why, but it's important."

"Well, the idiot who's leading this task force thinks you're fine. That Nubbins's death isn't related to the contest. Of course, he's also trying to make it into an accident." Sheriff Brown stirred his soup, blowing on the spoonful before eating it.

"You don't think it was an accident." Angie took a bite of her own soup, considering the implications.

"The coroner said he ingested enough poison to kill a mountain gorilla. I don't think he would do that accidentally. And, before you ask, the food in his stomach wasn't nachos. He'd just eaten a funnel cake."

Angie thought about Brandon and his "accident." "Did they test Brandon for the toxin?"

"They weren't going to, but I pulled a few strings. I know the head of emergency over there. He ran a special tox screen, and yes, Brandon had the same stuff in his bloodstream. He's lucky he got to the hospital as fast as he did." Sheriff Brown finished his soup. "I'll deny it if you mention this to Maggie, but that's the best soup I've ever had."

"Thanks. And, Sheriff Brown?"

He paused as he rose to put his bowl in the sink. "Yes?"

"Thank you for talking to me. I know you don't like my amateur investigating." She smiled. "This feels like we're actually cooperating on something." She stood and watched him put on his hat as he walked to the door.

"Well, if we're going to be working together, maybe you should call me Allen. I know Ian would be happy if we could bury the hatchet." He nodded, then left the kitchen.

Angie watched out the open door as he drove away. She saw Mrs. Potter out in her yard, walker nearby, directing while Erica dug in the front flower beds. She turned back. Time to share what she'd made and make time for a short visit to her only neighbors.

She packaged up two containers of soup—one for today, one for later—and put that and a loaf of wheat bread she'd made and frozen a few weeks ago as well as a jar of strawberry jelly, into a basket. She shook her head at Dom. "Sorry, dude, I don't want you to think you can cross the road without me, so you need to stay home."

Shutting the door behind her, she walked down the dirt driveway and crossed the street to Mrs. Potter's house. She picked up the afternoon paper from the slot where the driver had left it a few minutes before.

Arriving at the front stoop, she set her bundles down. Mrs. Potter patted the bench next to her. "Come sit by me. I haven't seen you in a while. What have you been up to?"

"Busy as usual." She waved to Erica. Mrs. Potter's granddaughter was finishing school as well as watching out for her grandmother when she was in her Idaho home. "You're planting flowers? Isn't it late?"

"Actually, it's time for the mums to go in. I lost all of the mums last winter when I went to California to stay with the kids. This year, Erica's staying around, so she's promised to watch out for them." Mrs. Potter pointed to the left. "Move that one over about three inches before you plant. They need to be spaced evenly so we get the most blooms."

"Yes, ma'am." Erica grinned at Angie. "I think I promised too much in plant care over the winter semester. I have a black thumb."

"Don't be silly. You just need to learn what they need." Mrs. Potter smiled softly at her. "You should have seen all the flowers I killed my first year married to your grandfather. He started calling me a plant serial killer."

Erica barked out a laugh. "I think I heard him say that once."

"I hadn't killed a plant in over forty years and he still teased me. That's what happens when you marry your high school sweetheart." Mrs. Potter's eyes sparkled with humor. "I know all about Erica's love life since the boy has to drive out here to get her just to go to the movies, but what about you, dear? When are you and Ian getting busy?"

Angie choked on the breath she'd just taken. "Excuse me?"

"What do you kids call it?" Mrs. Potter tapped her fingers on her chin. "Shaking up, right? When are you shaking up?"

"You mean shacking up, Grans. Getting busy and shaking up have a whole different meaning." Erica chuckled as she planted the last mum. "Angie's about to have a coronary over there."

"I am not," Angie said, but if the heat from her face wasn't from the sun, she had to be beet red right now.

"Are too." Erica stood and brushed the dirt off her hands. "You might as well tell her, she's going to keep asking about you and Ian moving in together."

Nona would have been pushing the same buttons, although, Angie thought, she would have been saying the *m* word. Or at least an engagement. She put her hands on her cheeks, hoping it would cool her and drop the blush. "Ian and I haven't talked about taking that kind of step yet. We've only been dating a little while."

"Over a year." Mrs. Potter patted her leg. "You're not getting any younger, my dear. You'll want to have memories to warm your nights when you're old and widowed like me."

Angie bit her lip. She wasn't sure how to respond. How do you talk about your love life with an elderly neighbor? Not thinking of any response, she glanced at the stoop. "Anyway, I brought you over two types of soup—chicken chili and corn chowder—and a few other things."

"Sounds like lunch is ready, then." Mrs. Potter stood, using her walker to help pull herself up. "Erica, would you bring those in and get me some food? I'm feeling a little warm out here. I think I'll take a nap after I eat."

They watched Mrs. Potter move slowly into the house. Angie stood next to Erica. "She's so fragile lately."

"You're noticing it too? I think I need to call Mom." Erica picked up the basket and the paper. "You want to wait for the basket?"

"No, I'll pick it up tomorrow. Let me know how she's doing, okay?" Angie turned to go back across the street.

"Of course, and thanks for grabbing the paper." Erica waved as Angie walked across the two-lane blacktop and back over to her own mailbox.

Angie got out the small stack of mail and then turned to watch Erica disappear into the house. A wave of sadness filled her as the door closed. Angie hadn't been around as Nona had slowly descended into her final illness. She'd been off in California and believing her grandmother's claims that everything was fine.

When she got back to the house, Dom sat staring at the door. Somehow he knew she'd gone visiting without him. Glancing at the mess she needed to clean up in the kitchen before starting her new sandwich project, she grabbed the leash instead. "Let's go for a walk."

Immediately, Dom forgave her the insult of leaving him behind and went crazy. She slipped on walking shoes and grabbed her backpack, adding water bottles. She would work later. Right now, she needed to do something happy to ease her mind.

Her phone rang as they drove to the park. She didn't recognize the number, but it was local, so it could be a supplier. Taking a chance that it wasn't a spam robo call, she answered, "This is Angie."

"Oh, my God, Angie. Brandon was poisoned. It wasn't just food poisoning. Someone actually tried to kill him." A frantic Sydney was on the other end of the line.

"How did you find out?" Angie didn't bother pretending like she didn't know.

"A reporter came to the house and started asking questions about the break-in. I was so glad I didn't keep any of my stuff in the trailer. I sent it all back to the restaurant right after the contest finished. I guess I was lucky there. The fair has to replace everything in the trailer. Of course, they have the stuff from the eliminated contestants."

Sydney was on a roll. Angie hadn't heard her talk this fast, ever. When she took a breath, Angie interrupted. "So, this reporter told you about Brandon being poisoned?"

"Well, kind of. I mean, he asked what had happened and if anyone had told me that he was being tested for poison. I guess he could have been fishing since the police let it out that poor David was poisoned the day before. I mean, seriously, what a sad way to go for a chef. We should go out with something besides food poisoning, don't you think? In medieval times, the king had a taster. If they died, the king didn't eat. Maybe we should get testers."

Angie pulled the car into the parking lot and glanced at Dom. There was no way he was going to be good, knowing the walk was right out his window. "Hey, Sydney? Can you hold on a second? I have to transfer you to my earbuds. Dom and I just got to the walking path."

"Actually, let me call you back. My lawyer is on the phone. I called him right after I talked to that reporter. I hope this doesn't hurt the restaurant. I should be more careful about what I say."

Angie was going to try to comfort her when she realized that Sydney had already disconnected the call. Whomever Sheriff Brown—no, Allen, she corrected herself—whomever Allen had said was in charge of the task force wasn't going to be happy when *The Statesman* blasted the cause of death as poison and reported that the killer might have tried again. She could just see the headlines.

Deadly Food Kills Chef. Chef Dips into Wrong Bin. Food Strikes Back?

Okay, maybe she couldn't.

Chapter 12

She and Dom had just walked past the bridge when her phone rang again. She looked down and saw Matt's number. "Hey, I hope you're not calling off for tomorrow. I've got a killer chowder I want you to try."

"No, I'm not calling off. I just wanted to check in and see if you've heard from Hope?" Matt's voice, typically so calm, sounded tight, stressed. "I mean, I would have thought you might have called to check up on her."

Crap, I should have called to check up on her. She pushed the guilt away. Hope had been left in her parents' capable hands. But the restaurant should have sent flowers. Or did an emergency room visit warrant that? She had been working that day at the fair. She pushed the questions away and answered Matt honestly, "No, I haven't heard from her."

"But you think she's okay, right?"

Angie thought about Matt's concern. Maybe there was more going on with the two of them than she knew. "If she wasn't going to make service tomorrow, I'm sure she would have called."

"Yeah, you're right." He paused, and even over the telephone line, Angie could sense his thoughts whirling around in his head. "Maybe I should call her?"

"Yeah, maybe." Who was she? Matchmaker Melda? She took a breath and smiled. She'd read that you sounded friendlier over the phone if you smiled. "Look, Matt, Dom and I are walking right now, so I need to go."

"Okay. Tell Dom hi. And I'll see you tomorrow for staff meeting."

"Later." She hung up before Matt could ask her another time if she thought he should call Hope. Maybe he was just concerned because he'd watched her fall. That was probably it. She dialed another number. "Felicia, can we send flowers to Hope?"

"Already done. I called and talked to her mom yesterday. Hope's doing better. Her family physician cleared her to come to work tomorrow. So, no worries."

"She gave us quite a scare." Angie reined Dom in, as there was a runner coming down the trail. "Matt's worried sick."

"Is that why he's calling? I missed his last call, and now he's calling again," Felicia asked.

"Really? That's interesting." Angie spied a large dog coming their way off the leash. "Let me talk to you tomorrow. I've got a situation here."

She grabbed Dom's leash and had him sitting before the other dog arrived. The dog stepped closer, probably going to sniff Dom, but his growl made the dog step back and lie down on the other side of the trail. Angie glanced around. Did the dog belong to someone? She spotted a person farther along the trail, but he didn't seem to be even watching the unfolding scene.

When he got closer, Angie waved her arm. "Is this your dog?"

The man popped earbuds out and looked at her, confused. "What?"

"Your dog. Is this your dog? Dogs are supposed to be leashed."

He looked down at the empty leash with a collar clipped to his waistband. "Crap, sorry. Timber, come here."

The black dog got up and trotted over to his master, letting him slip the collar back over his head. He fumbled with it and tightened the fit. "Sorry, I'm not used to running with him. He was my wife's dog."

Angie's nerves settled now that she knew she wouldn't have to break up a fight between the two dogs, which both probably weighed more than she did. Or close. "It happens. I'm just glad he wasn't aggressive."

"Timber's a sweetheart. He's a labradoodle. He's just missing his mama. My wife, she passed away a few months ago. This is the first time we've gotten out to run. I guess I'm going to have to keep a better eye out for him." He tucked the earbuds into his pocket. "Listening to gratitude lectures. They're supposed to help."

Angie studied the man. In his forties, probably, and he seemed nice. "I'm sorry for your loss. Are you new to the area?"

He shook his head. "We've lived south of River Vista for the last five years. I work in Boise, though. I'm an attorney. Jon Ansley. And you met Timber."

"Angie Turner. I own the County Seat in town." She took his outstretched hand and shook it.

"I've been meaning to get over there. My wife, well, she wanted to go, but..." He sighed. "I'm sure you didn't come out here to listen to some stranger go on about their sad life. It was nice to meet you, Angie Turner. And Dom too."

Angie and Dom continued their walk, and it wasn't until she'd got back into the car an hour later that a thought hit her. She glanced back at the smiling but tired face behind her. "How did he know your name was Dom?"

When she got home, she did an internet search on *John Ansley*. Nothing local came up. Then she tried a different spelling for *John*, dropping the *h*. This time a *Jon Ansley* showed up. He was a lawyer at a Boise firm. She read his bio and mostly it matched what he'd told her, but his wife was still mentioned. Either the company hadn't updated it, or he'd lied about losing her. She wrote his name down in her notebook. *Jon Ansley*. She'd ask Felicia tomorrow if she'd ever met him.

She put the laptop away and took out mixing bowls. Time to make some bread and play with sandwich recipes. Later tonight she'd take her scribbled notes and make up recipes for what she'd created today. Tomorrow she'd see how they translated to her cooks for family meal. Nancy was also presenting a dish for possible inclusion on the menu. Wednesday would be a full day.

* * * *

Angie woke up the next morning feeling ready for the day. Not only did she have a killer corn chowder recipe to share, she'd concocted a twist on a Reuben that she thought was better than the original. She hurried through her morning routine, only spending a few minutes with Precious but promising her that after the fair was over, they'd have more quality time.

Dom lay on his bed, his gaze frozen on the leash. "Sorry, guy. You know you can't come to work on days we're opening. You'd be cooped up there way too long. I'll be home as soon as I can, and we'll watch the Food Network."

He closed his eyes and turned his head away from her. Angie walked through the downstairs one more time, just to make sure she hadn't left anything down that Dom could mistake as a chew toy. Then she gave her dog a kiss on his head and headed out the door. She locked up the house, more out of habit than expectation that someone would break in. In San Francisco, her condo had had a doorman and three locks on the door, as well as a video camera in the hallway. She'd always felt like she was locking herself inside away from the world when she threw the dead bolts after coming home from work.

Now it just felt like she was keeping Dom safe. No use inviting people to easy pickings, as Nona would have said.

She started the car, and as she pulled out onto the driveway, she noticed that Mrs. Potter had a visitor. Was this Erica's boyfriend visiting? As she passed by, the man turned and looked at her. She recognized him immediately. It was the man from the park with the loose dog, Jon Ansley.

Glancing at the clock, she knew she didn't have time to stop, so she dialed Erica's number instead. She got her voice mail, and left a message asking Erica to call her back. Why was the supposedly grieving widower visiting her neighbor?

Her concern grew as she drove away. There could be a lot of reasons he was there. Maybe he was part of Mrs. Potter's church and was visiting. Or maybe she was late on her taxes and he was trying to collect. Just as she arrived in River Vista, her phone rang.

"Hey, Angie, what's going on?" Erica's cheerful voice was a comfort.

Angie tried to sound casual. "Hey, I'm just being a nosy neighbor. You guys have company?"

"You saw him, huh? Yeah, Mr. Ansley came by to talk to Grans. He's part of the men's group at church, and they wanted to know if she needed any work done on the house. I guess the pastor sent them her name."

"He wants to help take care of the house?" Angie's radar was way off. The first thing she'd thought when she saw him there was that he was up to no good. Now she was discovering that he was just trying to help.

"Yeah, they did a complete walk around through the house. He's a sweetheart. I guess the group's going to talk about it and then decide if they can help." She paused. "Sorry, I just saw the time. I'm going to be late for my first class if I don't hurry. Did you need me to check on anything at the house?"

"No, I'm good. I've overfed Precious and Mabel, and Dom's got his own door in and out. But thanks for asking." She terminated the call, but the feeling of unease continued with her as she parked, then made her way to her office. Something was definitely up with this Jon guy. If she hadn't already been trying to figure out who had killed Chef Nubbins, she'd take the time to look into Jon's background further.

The restaurant was empty when she came in through the back door. She turned on the lights as she walked and turned up the air-conditioning. They kept the temperature higher when no one was working or on nonservice days. Even with that habit of trying to conserve, her electric bill was out-of-this-world high.

She sat in front of her computer and started her day by reviewing last week's income and expenses sheet. Felicia had hired a local CPA who came into the restaurant on Mondays to do the week's books. Then Angie did the review on Wednesday. This way neither she or Felicia had to take responsibility of the accounting. And there was a double-check verification process in place, just in case this CPA wanted to take off with their funds. She'd had a couple of classes in college in hospitality management, and she'd learned early the value of keeping things separate.

Lost in the work, she didn't notice Felicia coming into the room until she set a glass of tea in front of Angie, then plopped in her visitor's chair. She took a long sip. "Thanks, I didn't realize I was so thirsty."

"Hopefully you're at a good stopping point with that, because I really, really want to talk about this new banquet area. I couldn't sleep last night so I came down and started measuring out the space. Do you realize it would add capacity for over a hundred more people?" Felicia opened a sketch pad. "We could have the loan paid off on this place in record time."

Angie glanced at the numbers from last week. They were making a profit, but not by much. Adding in more income would make the margin wider and her anxiety level lower. She saved the final report, sent it to Felicia's email to review, then she'd do the final approval. Angie closed the file. "Extra income would be great, but what's it going to cost us to implement this? You know we don't have a lot of cash to invest."

"Unless you win Restaurant Wars," Felicia added, lost in her sketch.

"From what I see, winners don't get to stay around long to collect their prizes." She shook her head. "Let's come up with a plan where I don't put myself in the crosshairs of whoever is playing the Whack-a-Chef game."

"Whack-a-Chef, that's funny. Maybe we should do a fund-raiser where we put you guys into one of those water chairs and sell balls so they can throw them at you."

"A dunk tank."

Felicia frowned. "Really, that's what it's called? Seems like they could have come up with a better name."

"I guess 'torture chamber' was already taken." She held out her hand. "Let's see your plans."

They worked on the drawings, then did initial cost estimates for the project. Finally, Angie leaned back in her chair. "I know it looks like the right decision."

"You have a 'but' in there somewhere." Felicia glanced over the first sketch she'd drawn with a round table setup.

"We didn't figure in a sound system. Which we'd need. And this is all based on the theory that people will rent the area after we sink the money into it. What if no one comes?" Angie shook her head. "I'm not saying it's not a good idea. We need more facts, though. Ask around about the sound system. Let's get some bids. Then let's talk to some of the community groups. Who would consider renting the area, and what would they be willing to pay?"

"I can do that. I needed a project, anyway. Well, besides Bleak. Did you know she already finished that book she bought? She showed up last night asking to borrow the rest of the series." Felicia sighed. "I wish we knew where she was from."

"I forgot to tell you about my visit with Allen yesterday." Angie sipped her tea.

"Wait, when did you start calling Sheriff Brown by his first name?" Felicia studied her face. "Are you really Angie or some doppelganger?"

"He asked me to call him Allen. Yeah, it feels weird to me as well. But what's even weirder? He said I was the best thing to happen to Ian in a long time." Angie lifted her shoulders in surprise at Felicia's wide-eyed reaction. "I know! It's the strangest thing."

"Okay, so then tell me the rest of the story. Why was he at the house?"

"From what I could tell, he came over for lunch. And for an update on our secret investigation society." Angie told her about his questions about the other chefs and what they had found out. "I think the task force is trying to sweep this under the rug. And Sheriff Brown—I mean, Allen—keeps coming back with evidence that doesn't support their accident conclusion."

"They're idiots." Felicia leaned back in her chair.

"Who are idiots?" Estebe stood in the doorway. "Please don't tell me any of my staff called in today. We have things to discuss. I want to present a new cold box setup."

"What's wrong with the way the refrigerator is set up?" Angie didn't bother pointing out that the kitchen staff was *her* staff, not his. Besides, he really wouldn't believe her anyway.

He came over and stood by Felicia. Not touching, but even Angie could feel the connection between the two. "It is inefficient. We waste a lot of time looking for things."

He might have a point there. Angie decided to let it go. "Everyone's coming to work, as far as I know. Even Hope."

"Felicia told me she was feeling better." He met Felicia's gaze and smiled. "Our girl is a strong survivor. Heatstroke isn't going to keep her down."

"Yeah, but Matt's overprotectiveness might." When Estebe's eyes narrowed, Angie waved the question away. "Anyway, what do you think of our plans to open up the back room for banquets and meetings?"

"I know I can have it booked at least once a month. My men's group at the community center is looking for a room where we can have food and a bit of refreshments." Estebe leaned on the arm of Felicia's chair. "Of course, you'll have to have it on a night where I'm not on the line."

"I'm thinking we could move our classes in there too. That would get them out of the kitchen," Felicia added.

"You'd have to set up a small kitchen in the front." Angie thought there would be room, but that would cut down the number of people they could get into the room. "Cost that out for me too? You'd have to downgrade our capacity limits."

Felicia made a note and then paused. "We're really doing this, right?"

"We've opened two restaurants together. Why is opening a room so exciting all of a sudden?" Angie studied her friend.

"I love new beginnings. I was beginning to get itchy feet since we hadn't done anything new and exciting for a long time." Felicia closed her notebook and moved toward the door. "I'll have the new estimates ready next week. We can go over them on Tuesday."

Estebe and Angie watched her leave. Angie could see a touch of fear in his eyes. Was he thinking the same thing: that Felicia wouldn't ever settle down? That the lure of something new might threaten their relationship, already on weak ground? "I'm sure she meant she likes new projects, not anything about..."

Estebe held out his hand. "Don't say it. I knew who she was when we started dating. I just hope she gets over this need sooner than later."

Angie watched him walk out of the office and wondered how long it would be before Felicia broke his heart.

Chapter 13

They were in the middle of family meal when Bleak leaned over to Angie and whispered, "Do I have to eat everything? I don't really like soup."

Trying to keep the laughter inside, Angie nodded. "Well, it's a family meal, so just like in my family, you have to try a little of everything."

"But she doesn't make you clean your plate like my mom does." Hope smiled at the younger girl. She'd been the first to greet Bleak after Felicia introduced her to the team. And since they'd had a little bit of time, Hope had walked her through the restaurant. "I'm betting you'll like it, though. There hasn't been one dish that Angie's brought to the table for menu consideration that I didn't love."

"Hey now, my dish is on the table this week too." Nancy gave Hope a gentle nudge with her elbow. "I'm sure you'll love it as well."

"Of course she will," Estebe said, trying to move the conversation away from picky eaters and back to the topic at hand: his cold box rework. "I've given you all a mock-up to look at, and if you agree, I'll need a couple of people to come in for a few hours on Monday to restock."

"I need the hours." Matt lifted his hand. He looked across the table at Hope. "What about you? You aren't in school yet, are you?"

"No, but my family is going to Coeur d'Alene for the week. It's the only time all of us could get together. I've already taken the week off, right, Angie?"

"Yep. You're off the schedule. And I want you to train Bleak in running the dishwasher this week so she can cover for you." Angie and Felicia had decided earlier that they'd use the new employee to cover for Hope's vacation rather than bringing in a temp whom they'd have to train anyway.

"I thought I was just cleaning up tables?" Bleak's eyes widened as she thought of the enormity of the job.

When Bleak turned her way, Felicia added, "After Hope gets back, you'll be busing tables. By the time we have you fully trained, you may know every job in the restaurant."

"Also, I'm taking you with me to the fair on Friday and Saturday. I won't be able to have you in the trailer, but I think we can keep you busy. And you'll have time to explore the grounds when we don't need you."

"And once we're off, we'll go play on the rides!" Hope clapped her hands together, bouncing in her chair. "It will be a blast. I'll drive you home so Angie doesn't have to wait around for us."

Matt shook his head. "You weren't that excited to go on the rides with me."

"Stop being a baby. You've had your fun. Now it's girls' night," Hope said.

Bleak sank deeper into her shoulders. "I don't know. I mean, I don't have any money for rides."

"Oh, I'll pay for the wristband." Angie hoped that the other two wouldn't complain, or at least that they wouldn't do it in front of Bleak. "It's part of your benefits for the day. We do extra things like this all the time, so I just appreciate you all chipping in. And since you don't have school or anything, you're the lucky one to be scheduled."

Bleak seemed to accept that. For her being homeless a few days ago, the girl had standards. Angie couldn't understand how anyone would let her run away. Or disown her once she was found.

Angie glanced around the table. Most of the people were finished eating, so she thought she'd go over the plan for the week while they finished. "Okay then, we still need someone to work with Matt and Estebe on Monday. I'll pay for pizza to be brought in as an added incentive."

"If you show me what to do, I'll come." Bleak raised her hand a little, then dropped it when Angie looked at her. "I'll probably just be reading anyway."

"That's awesome." Angie glanced at Estebe, who nodded. "So now it's a vote on the new menu items. You aren't going to hurt anyone's feelings if you vote against an item. Except remember—I sign your paychecks."

"Hey," Nancy chimed in, "no fair. I just want to say I *will* cry and hold it against you if you don't like my dish."

Chuckling, Estebe stepped in. "I'll explain the voting for our newest team member. I'll ask for three votes for a dish. The first time I'll ask if you liked it. Raise your hands and keep them up. The second time, I'll ask if you would order it again at a restaurant. Again, keep your hands up. Then finally, I'll ask if you would recommend this dish to your grandmother if she came into the County Seat. You have to have at least three-quarters of the room's votes in the last question for the dish to go on the menu."

"That's crazy." Bleak shook her head. "What if I just don't like soup?"

"Then you don't raise your hand. Not everyone likes everything. But we only want the best for our menu." He held up a portion of the soup that had been plated and set aside on a table for the voting process. "Who liked the chowder?"

After they'd gone through all three dishes and had moved them all onto the menu for the next month, the group disbanded to get ready for service. Angie took Bleak's hand. "You'll be in the kitchen this week. Hope? Come show Bleak your prep."

As prep for the night continued, Estebe pulled her aside. "This Bleak girl, she isn't eighteen."

"I know. But she's sixteen, so she can work. Just don't have her cooking, please." Angie watched as Hope showed her how to set up the steaks for the cold box. "Her folks have washed their hands of her. I don't even understand it. She seems a little goth, but mostly she's a sweet kid."

"Who should be in school," Estebe noted.

Angie nodded. "I agree, but right now Sheriff Brown is taking over her guardian tasks. He just wants her here in a safe working environment until he can get her to go back."

"She is strong-headed. Like a yearling colt. She needs to be given some room." He nodded. "We will watch out for her."

"We need to brainstorm some ideas for a walking main dish for Friday's contest. Do you want me to come in early tomorrow, and we can play with some ideas before prep?"

Estebe set a plate up on the pass for the waitress to deliver. "That will work."

Angie checked her chef coat for stains. "I'm going to go walk the dining room. If I'm not back in ten minutes, come save me."

"You are good at the talking thing. I don't believe you'll need saved." A smile curved his lips. "Besides, it scares me out there."

"Chicken." Angie walked to the door and paused, taking a deep breath. Going out into the dining room to meet and greet the customers kind of scared her. More than what she'd admit to her second in command, or even herself.

Felicia was in the alcove watching the room. "Hey, I didn't think I'd get you out here tonight."

"I decided to be brave." She peered at a table. "Isn't that..."

Nodding, Felicia picked up a water pitcher. "Miquel decided to grace us with his presence. Or he decided we were worth worrying about. Let's go over and see how his dinner is tasting."

They walked over and stood at the table. When he looked up, the sly smile went on like a mask. "Good evening, ladies. I'm so glad to be able to come enjoy your lovely place."

"Do you like the lamb? The rancher is local, but of course, you probably know we source as much of our supplies from local markets as we can." Angie smiled at the woman sitting across from Miquel. "I'm Angie Turner, and this is my co-owner, Felicia Williams."

"Talla Evans. It's a great place. Honestly, when Miquel said he was taking me to dinner out in the country, I thought we were going to Riverside in Marsing. I didn't know this place existed." The blonde pushed back her hair before taking a sip of wine. "Everything is so lovely. I'll definitely be back."

"Talla writes for the *Sun Valley Journal*. Maybe you'll get a good write-up out of this." Miquel smiled at the woman, and for a minute, Angie thought she saw true affection. Then his face turned back into the mask. "I'm sorry, but Angie, could I speak with you outside for a short minute? I know you're probably needed in the kitchen, but this is important."

Angie glanced at Felicia, who nodded. She'd entertain Talla while Angie talked to Miquel. She thought her friend was getting the better end of the deal. When they got outside, Miquel took a pack of cigarettes out of his jacket pocket and offered her one.

"I don't smoke. And I don't have time for chitchat. What do you need, Miquel?" She stood while he took a seat on one of the benches they kept just outside the door for overflow guests.

"I want you to call off your sheriff. I didn't kill Nubbins or poison that guy. Sure, I want to win the competition, but my food's good enough to win. I don't have to eliminate the competition." He lit his cigarette, then glanced inside the window. "Talla hates it when I smoke."

"I don't control what the sheriff does. Why do you think I can keep him from looking your way for this?"

"Everyone knows you're the mystery chef. You helped your girl out of that mess a few months ago. From what I heard, she was getting ready to be fitted for an orange jumpsuit until you found the real killer." He studied his cigarette, taking a drag. "I've been a little stressed, and having someone come and interrogate me at work doesn't look good."

"*Someone* killed Nubbins." Angie studied him. He looked worn out. Not at all like the cocky jerk who'd messed with them at the grocery store.

"If I was investigating, I'd look at that Tara chick. You know she's been in jail before for her anger issues. And rumor has it, her business isn't doing the best."

That was the second time she'd heard that rumor. Was it true? Or was someone just trying to move the attention away from themselves? "I don't know if I can trust what you're telling me. From what I've heard, you have a history of being dishonest." She glanced down toward the Red Eye, where the music poured out onto the street every time someone opened the door.

He sighed. "You talked to Barb. Yeah, I skimmed. I was in a bad spot and needed rent money. I bet she didn't tell you that I gave it back a few years later." He glanced at the cigarette, considering another drag, then crushed it under his feet. "I'm not perfect. But I'm trying now. I'm trying for Talla."

He stood up, picked up what was left of the cigarette, and went back inside.

Angie leaned against the brick near the entrance. Was Miquel telling the truth? Or just his version of it? She decided tomorrow she'd go in and talk to Tara one more time. Maybe there was something there. Something she hadn't wanted to see when they'd gone to dinner at her place.

She closed her eyes for a minute, trying to calm the questions running through her mind.

"Excuse me, but do you cook here?" A man's voice broke through her thoughts.

Putting a smile on her face so she'd be polite to the potential customer, she opened her eyes. A tall man with red hair stood in front of her. He wore jeans and an older T-shirt with the *VA Is for Lovers* slogan on the front. He was probably freaking out about the possibility of a dress code at the County Seat.

"I do work here. In fact, it's my restaurant. Are you coming in for a meal? We're a farm-to-table restaurant, so all of our products are locally sourced." Felicia was so much better at the customer service and marketing part. All she wanted to talk about was the food. "We have an amazing menu with late-summer produce right now."

"Good to know. Did you know that ninety percent of restaurants close in the first five years?" He glanced in the window. "You've got a nice setup here. You must have a huge loan on this place."

Totally inappropriate comment. This was why she didn't like talking to customers. "The business does well. We're early in developing a clientele, but I'm positive it will be a success. Did you have a reservation?"

He grinned, one tooth missing from the front, making the grin look a little lopsided. "I tried, but couldn't get in. I'm only in town for a few weeks. Work keeps me busy."

Alarms went off in her head. She glanced at the door. Would anyone hear her if she screamed? She moved toward the door. "We always have open seating at the bar if you'd like to eat."

"Not tonight. I'm just out for a stroll. It was nice to meet you." And with that, he turned and crossed the street to go into the small city park.

Angie watched as he disappeared into the trees, wondering what the guy really wanted. She started to go inside, but then stopped and turned back. She'd seen the guy before, hadn't she? Most of her time was spent at the restaurant or at home. Or walking Dom. But it hadn't been any of those places.

The fair—she'd bumped into him at the fair. At the contest. He was obviously interested in the restaurant business. She shook off the unease she'd felt. It was probably because she'd seen him at Restaurant Wars.

The strains of one of her favorite songs came through the wooden door of Barb's place, and she hummed along as she made her way back into the restaurant and her kitchen. All she could do was handle her own emotions. But she had to admit, having others think she was some sort of investigator extraordinaire was pretty great too.

When dinner service was over, Felicia came to the door. "Sheriff Brown is here."

"Great, now what?" Images of the man she'd talked to earlier filled Angie's head. She started taking off her chef coat.

Felicia held up a hand, stopping her. "Actually, he's here to pick up Bleak."

The girl's face turned bright red. "I told him I could walk. It's only a few blocks to their house."

"He's overprotective. Take advantage of it. Your feet are probably going to hurt later anyway." Angie waved the girl off. "Go ahead, we can finish up here. See you tomorrow."

"Definitely." Bleak actually smiled as she put her apron in the dirty clothes hamper and grabbed her backpack. "This was fun."

"Girl, you are on crack if you think working is fun," Matt teased her as she left. She ignored the comment and went through the door with Felicia.

"Hope, come over here a minute." Angie moved to sit at the chef's table and go over her notes about the service and the menu items.

Hope pulled a chair back and sat. "If this is about my vacation, I can see if my mom will fly me back earlier if you need me to work."

"Are you crazy? Take the week. You're going to have a busy fall semester coming up. And you know we always pick up business as soon as school starts." Angie leaned back in her chair and opened the bottle of water she'd pulled out of the fridge. "I wanted to talk to you about Bleak. How did she do tonight?"

"Wow. She was great. She really caught on fast, and for a bit, I did some late prep work for Nancy and she ran the station all by herself." Hope smiled. "I think she'll be a great addition."

"If you wouldn't mind, find out when she last went to school. I'd rather she be going to school than working at her age."

Hope blushed. "She told me she wasn't eighteen yet, but that it was a secret. I didn't know how to tell you."

"I'm not looking for you to betray a confidence, just maybe lead the conversation back to how important graduating from school is. And maybe how much you love your program. Maybe we have a future chef on our hands." Angie watched as Hope took in the information.

"I can do that. Maybe we can do a field trip and she can come with me to school one day. That would get her focused. And maybe admit she needs help. I could see she was embarrassed by Sheriff Brown coming to get her. Like she was weak. She's not weak."

"We all know that. But she is a kid. And sometimes kids need looked after, even if they don't think they do." Angie tried again. "We all have Bleak's best interest at heart. She doesn't have to be alone. She looks up to you. You need to help lead her down the right path."

Hope played with a fork that had been left on the table. "I know, but sometimes being responsible is hard."

Angie nodded. "You got that right."

Angie sat at the chef's table long after most of the kitchen staff had cleaned up and left. Thinking about what might have happened to her when her folks had died if Nona hadn't been around. Or worse, hadn't wanted her. Bleak needed a brighter future. And she needed to reclaim her real name. Bleak wasn't her destiny anymore. Angie would make sure of that.

Estebe sat down next to her. "The ovens are off, the stove tops clean, and the food put away. All of your customers have gone home. When are you leaving?"

"Soon." She sipped on the coffee she'd poured into her travel mug. "Sometimes it's a hard world out there."

"Sometimes. But that's when we need to pull family closer. And trust that you don't have to hold the entire world up on your own shoulders." He took a sip of his water. "Bleak is a sweet girl once you get past the gruff exterior. I take it her family isn't in a hurry to come claim the missing member?"

"According to Sheriff Brown, they basically washed their hands of her. Who does that?" Tears stung Angie's eyes. She'd leave it to the sheriff to tell the girl that she wasn't going home but instead was on her own. "She's sixteen. She should be doing algebra and going to football games, not working to keep a roof over her head."

"The sheriff is charging her rent?" Estebe looked confused.

Angie barked out a laugh. "No, sorry, it was a bad analogy. He's trying to figure out a way to get her back into school without her bolting again. If she keeps going north, she'll wind up in Canada taking care of the moose."

"He is a caring man. He will figure out a way. And until then, we will take care of her the best we can." Estebe stood, draining his water bottle. "Go home, Angie Turner. Your dog is going to be worried."

Of course, he was right. She rose as well. Nothing got solved by worrying. Another one of Nona's favorite sayings. But it didn't stop Angie from trying to save the world. One worry at a time.

Chapter 14

Angie spent the morning looking at descriptions of different poisons and their sources. She could ask Allen what toxin was found in Nubbins's autopsy, but she hesitated to pick up the phone. She didn't want him to think she was calling about Bleak. To ask about how yesterday went. And she definitely didn't want him asking her to get her back to school. Angie wasn't good with kids. Even when she'd been one herself. She didn't understand their thought processes. She'd always been rational, even methodical, in her thinking. Which was probably why cooking appealed to her so much. If she mixed this ingredient and that, she got something she knew. It never changed, unless she changed it herself.

She glanced at the clock. She'd made an appointment to meet up with Tara for coffee at ten. She had to be at the County Seat by two to work with Estebe on Friday's planning session, and according to the computer, it would take her over an hour to get to the coffee place. She shut down the laptop and moved it closer to the middle of the table. Dom might not want to eat the metal or plastic, but if it was within reach, he'd probably try.

She packed her tote, aware of his eyes on her back. "Sorry, dude, it's a workday. We'll go walking on Sunday as long as it doesn't rain." It rarely rained in Idaho in August, so she was pretty sure she'd be able to keep her promise.

On her way to Boise, she turned up the music and was getting her driver's seat dance on when her phone rang. She punched a button for the car system to pick up the call. "Hey, Ian, what's going on?"

"We're looking for Bleak. Is she with you?"

Crap. Someone must have pushed the school button. Or the family one. With that girl, there were so many hot buttons it could have been anything.

"No. I haven't seen her since your uncle came to get her last night. When did she disappear?"

"Maggie thinks early this morning. She heard a door shut, but thought it was Allen leaving for work. He was working in his office at the back of the house." He sighed. "Maggie's a wreck. She really likes the kid."

"Did she take her stuff?" She heard Ian ask the question and waited.

He came back on the line. "Apparently not. She took her backpack and the books Felicia had left her. But a lot of her clothes are still in her room."

"Then maybe she just went out for a walk." Angie didn't want to downplay the event, but maybe the girl just needed some space. "It must be hard going from being on your own to living with the town sheriff and his wife."

"I hadn't thought of that. Just to be safe, I'm going to drive around River Vista and see if I can see her. If you hear from her, call me, okay?"

"I will." She hung up the phone and, using voice command, dialed Hope. She got her voice mail. "Hey, Hope, this is Angie. We're looking for Bleak. If you've seen her, call me and let me know she's all right, okay? She has a lot of people worried about her."

She hung up, and the music came back on. But this time, she didn't feel like a dance party. She touched the crystal that hung in her car, the one that Nona had hung in her own car for as long as Angie could remember. "Be safe. Be smart. Come home."

She considered canceling her coffee date with Tara, but thought it might be better to keep busy. Bleak would show up sooner or later. Angie was almost 99 percent sure she was talking to Hope. Their connection had been strong last night, and the girl needed support from someone she could trust.

She pulled into the parking lot of the library. It had been opened in a converted house that now held room after room of comfortable seating and floor-to-ceiling bookshelves. It was the perfect place to settle in with coffee and a bakery treat, either with friends or alone. Today she'd be talking to someone who might just be a killer. But at least the coffee would be good.

Tara was already in the shop when Angie walked inside. She stood at the counter, laughing with the barista, while he made her something foamy with whipped cream on the top.

"Hey, Angie." Chris, the barista, smiled. "The usual?"

"Works for me. Tara, thanks for meeting me halfway." She waited for Chris to finish and paid him for the overpriced mocha that she loved. "Let's go sit in the living room. It's so comfortable."

"I love this little shop, but I never have a good reason to drive all the way out here. Maybe we should make this a monthly excuse." Tara sat on the overstuffed couch while Angie chose a small upholstered chair nearby.

"Sounds great." But Angie wondered if Tara would really want to talk again after she asked her some rather pointed questions. "How's the restaurant?"

"You mean between now and Monday?" Tara sipped her coffee, watching Angie carefully. "Tell me you're not here because that sheriff thinks I'm a killer."

"Sheriff Brown didn't send me to talk to you. But someone else did. They said that your business is in trouble." Angie wiped her lip after taking a drink of the mocha. She didn't want a foam mustache to upstage the message she was trying to send. "So, how's business?"

"If it's any of your business, we've run into a little trouble making ends meet. One of our regular customers for the catering part of the business went into bankruptcy, after holding two large events at our place. It's not fair, but what can you do?" Tara set her coffee down on the table. "Who told you? If it was that weasel Miquel, I'm going to shake him silly."

"I'm not at liberty to say, but if it's all innocent, why not just tell whoever interviewed you about Chef Nubbins's death?"

"And let the world know we're hanging on by a thread? People don't make reservations for large events in the future if they don't think you're going to be in business. I've got three wedding accounts considering using us for their reception. If we get the contract, it will more than cover what we lost." She leaned back. "Did you disclose all your financial records when they interviewed you? It didn't seem that important. Do I want to win the contest? Heck, yeah, but I have plans so if we don't, we'll still be all right. Even if I have to take a second job to keep the place afloat."

"You're determined." Angie nodded. "I get it. Believe me, we've had our own challenges in running the County Seat. This is a small town. Things get mixed up. Things get jacked around and misinterpreted."

Tara stood and slung her purse over her shoulder. "Yeah, but someone who claims to want to be a friend doesn't let rumors determine what they think of someone."

"Tara, I didn't mean to upset you." Angie stood as well, hoping she could calm the woman down long enough for them to finish their coffee. What had Nona called it? Breaking bread? They needed some happy time to cover over the anger Tara felt at Angie's questioning.

"Well, we're long past that." Tara narrowed her eyes. "I can see you're just like all the others. All you want is to win."

Angie watched as the woman spun on her heel and left the room. A few minutes later, Chris came into the small room with a tray, picking up Tara's cup.

"Don't feel bad. Everyone's talking about her bankruptcy and her affair with Nubbins." He leaned against the doorway. "Apparently his wife found out before she could talk him into bailing her out. She has a history of using sugar daddies for her support."

Angie stared at him in shock. "How did you find all this out?"

He laughed. "One, I listen when people come here. The walls aren't very thick. Tara and Nubbins came in once a week, every week. Two, my friend at the motel by the freeway told me the couple had a standing reservation for Thursdays at three. And three, my wife works with Mrs. Nubbins. So we got both sides of the story. Like you said, it's a small town."

The bell on the door rang. He glanced back toward the coffee shop. "I'll be right there," he called. Then he pointed to Angie's cup. "Want a free refill? You kind of got beat up just now, and chocolate makes everything better."

Angie shook her head, wondering if Chef Nubbins thought chocolate made everything better. "I'm good. I've got to get to work. We've got a planning meeting."

"Just know I'm rooting for you. You're one of my favorite customers. And not just because you laugh at my jokes. Although that does help."

Angie stayed for a few minutes, thinking about what Chris and Tara had just told her. Of course, Tara's story had left out that she was in a relationship with the victim. Angie took out her phone and texted Sheriff Brown about what she'd found out. When the man finally responded, it was just one word.

Okay.

She waited to see if there was any follow-up statement, but after ten minutes, she gave up and took her empty cup to the dish return tub. Chris was still talking to the new customer, so she just waved and made her way out.

On her way back to River Vista and the County Seat, Angie dialed Felicia.

"Where are you? Estebe's worried that you're in a ditch somewhere," Felicia asked, her voice lowered. Estebe must be nearby.

"I'm fine. Coming back into town now. I had coffee in Meridian with Tara."

Angie heard the intake of breath. "Tea Cup Tara?"

"One and the same. Did you know she was having an affair with Chef Nubbins?"

A pause on the other end of the line answered Angie's question.

"You did know. Why didn't you say something?" Angie glanced at the speedometer and realized she was traveling more than ten miles over the posted speed. She dropped her foot off the gas. She'd get there when she got there. And she didn't need a ticket.

"I didn't know for sure. Yeah, I'd heard the rumors. But you can't trust gossip. So many people just say anything."

"Well, I think this source is credible. If they weren't having an affair, they were really, really close once a week in a town always away from where his wife worked." Angie changed lanes to go around a slow-moving tractor in front of her, thankful the road was four lanes. "Anyway, I'm on my way back. What are you doing?"

"We got back from lunch about one. Since then Estebe's been helping me move furniture in my apartment. Let's just say he's ready to be back in his chef jacket, even if he is waiting for you."

"Men just don't understand the rules of relationships." The official rules mean that you can ask them at any time to do a spot of manual labor. Like cleaning out flower beds or moving a chair from one room to another. She'd had Ian move boxes out of the attic and into her living room so she could start going through what Nona had left behind. From what she'd seen, the paper could be discarded in all the boxes, except her grandmother had a habit of writing recipes on the backs of receipts. So, every piece had to be examined before it was boxed up to burn in the fire. "Anyway, I'm coming up to the city limits now. Go tell him to start playing with whatever he wanted to present. I've got a few ideas too, but I want him to go first."

"I'll tell him. See you in a couple."

Angie disconnected the call, and music filled her car. And since it was her favorite song, she let it go as she sang along, all the way to the back parking lot. She hurried up the stairs, locking her car door as she went. The door was unlocked, and she burst into the kitchen, tossing her tote on the chef's table and going directly to the handwashing station.

"What's up first?" She stepped closer to Estebe, loving the smell of grilled onions and peppers.

"I wanted to play with the idea of a sandwich on a stick. Maybe a Philadelphia cheesesteak or even a hamburger." He showed her the hamburger grilling, wrapped around a stick.

She considered the options. "I like the idea, but I think we need to go further. Like, mashed potatoes in a tube or deconstruct something and put it on a stick."

"So, you're saying my ideas don't go far enough." He stared at the grilling hamburger.

Angie didn't want to hurt his feelings, but there was no way they'd win with a dish like the one he was describing. She was about to speak when he nodded.

"You are right. This is pedestrian. We need a wow factor. Like chicken and dumplings on a stick."

"Right idea, wrong season. Something summery. Something they're already craving because they're at the fair." She pulled up a chair and a notebook. "Let's brainstorm. I'll put down the chicken and dumplings idea."

"I thought you hated it." He looked at her, curious.

"All ideas go on the page while we're brainstorming." She tapped her pen. "Besides, I didn't hate the idea. I said it was the wrong season. So deconstructing a sandwich isn't a bad idea either. What else do we have to work with?"

They spent the next thirty minutes working through a list. Finally, they decided on two to fix and then they'd make a final choice.

"The team will be able to help us choose what would be best." Angie stretched her arms, tired from the activity. "Do you mind if I go to the office for a few minutes? I need to talk to Sheriff Brown."

"He should not be putting you in harm's way. If this man finds out what you're doing, you might be the next one killed." Estebe started mixing the batter that they'd use around the beef to mimic the bread for the first sandwich.

"Maybe it's a woman. Did you ever think of that?" Angie teased as she made her way out to the hallway.

"Women do tend to use poison more often than men." He nodded thoughtfully. When he saw Angie pause at the door, watching him, he shrugged. "What? I have been researching this situation as well."

"You always surprise me," Angie muttered as she left the kitchen. When she reached her office, she called the police station. The guy manning the phones hated her. And it didn't seem like it mattered which officer was on duty. No one wanted her talking to Allen to be an easy task. When she was told the sheriff was out on a call, she left her name and number. Ten to one, her message would be lost. But she had an ace in the hole.

She dialed Ian's number. And got his voice mail. Technology really wasn't on her side today. She left him a message, telling him what she needed to tell the sheriff. As she hung up, she hoped this game of telephone tag would get the correct message across.

She hung up the phone and noticed the plans for the banquet room sitting on her desk. Felicia must have been working down here. She took a pen and a blank piece of paper and wrote: *Make sure to get money ahead of time. The Tara Principle.* That should remind her of what she wanted to tell Felicia later.

Feeling less than accomplished, she returned to the kitchen, where Hope and Matt had already arrived. She moved closer to Hope. "Did you get ahold of Bleak?"

"We were having coffee at the diner when Sheriff Brown burst in and took her away. He was mad. He said she'd be at work at her scheduled time." Hope looked up from the knife cuts she was doing for prep. "I think he's going to be sitting outside in his car all the time she's working so she can't take off again. My dad would do something like that."

"Man, living with the police in your house must be a trip. You'd never know when you were going to be busted just for being you." Matt pondered the situation.

"She doesn't have the same problem as you do." Estebe's eyes twinkled.

"What's that?"

"She's a good kid. Not like you," Estebe said.

Angie knew he was waiting for the fallout. And he didn't have time to wait.

"I'm a good kid. I brush my teeth, say my prayers, and help set the table for family meal. What else is there?" Matt looked imploringly at Angie. "Come on, Ang, stand up for me here."

The kitchen was back to normal. The teasing had resumed.

Chapter 15

"What's jimsonweed?" Hope sat at the table reading one of her textbooks. "Has anyone heard of it?"

"Its real name is datura, but it's also called devil's snare or trumpet." Estebe glanced at the book. "Why are you studying deadly plants?"

"It's a class on foraging for food. The professor says that if you don't know what you're trying to use, you could do some real damage. So we have to be able to identify all these plants and fungi by sight. I'm really not good at memorization." She held out the book. "Besides, look at this picture. The flower is really pretty. It looks like a morning glory."

"Maybe you shouldn't eat anything you don't find at a store." Matt scrubbed the grill, the last task to closing up the kitchen.

Bleak had already come and gone, via her Sheriff Brown taxi service. She'd been quiet during shift today. When Angie had tried to start a conversation, Bleak had cut it short, blaming a headache.

"Wait a minute," Angie said, holding out her hand as Hope started to turn the book away. "Let me see that."

Angie took the book and studied the photo. There was no doubt. This was the same plant that she'd seen in Tara's herb garden on Monday. She flipped through the pages. "Where does it talk about its toxicity?"

Hope took the book back and turned a few pages. Then she handed it back to Angie. "Why do you want to know?"

"Because that plant is in Tara's herb garden." Angie sank back into her chair. "Reading the effects, it could be what was given to Chef Nubbins. I wonder if Brandon had any hallucinations."

"You don't think Tara put this in their food, do you?" Hope stared at the book. It lay open on the table, the picture of the devil's trumpet staring back at the group gathered around.

"I don't know, but I know someone who can find out." Angie wrote down all the names and side effects of the plant. It even had the names of the actual poisons that were hidden in the leaves. She gathered her stuff. "I'm heading home to check this out. Maybe we've found the killer. And taken out another one of the competitors for Friday's event."

"Way to look on the bright side." Estebe opened the door for her. "Don't mind us, we'll close up and give the keys to Felicia."

"I'll see you tomorrow." Angie knew he was kidding with her, but she felt the smallest slight from his words. "You know, once this is done, I'll have a lot more time to be with all of you."

"Promises, promises." He waved her away, toward her car. "Go play Nancy Drew. The rest of us have grown-up things to do."

She tried calling Ian again, but got his voice mail once more. Apparently, Sheriff Brown was having problems convincing Bleak that they only had her best interests at heart. Which meant Sheriff Brown wouldn't answer her call either.

Instead of talking, she relaxed and made her way home. Even if Tara wasn't the killer, she might have just identified the murder weapon. Or at least something like that. If this plant was in Tara's garden, what else did she have growing there? And who else used her small garden?

Too many questions, not enough answers. And still, not her job. It was still early by the time she got back to the house, so after she fed Precious and Mabel, she and Dom sat out on the porch, listening to the sounds of the night. Soybean crops filled the fields around her house. Besides Mrs. Potter, she didn't have a neighbor closer than a couple of miles. And she didn't know any of them. The soybean field down the side road across the street had been owned by River Vista's former veterinarian. Rumor was, he had sold the property to an out-of-state developer.

Hoping that the area was too far out from any neighboring towns for a high-end subdivision, she pushed the worry out of her head. Tomorrow was her turn to get water from the irrigation ditch behind her property. She'd set it on the pasture behind the barn, and if she knew her goat, Precious would spend the day playing in the water as it flooded the field. If she had time, she'd pump some of the water over to the garden. Tomatoes were still growing on the aging plants, and she knew she would get a ton of potatoes, onions, and garlic when the frost threatened and she had to clear out the space for the next year.

Dom nuzzled her hand and she absently petted him. She checked her phone one more time, just to make sure she hadn't missed a call, then decided to call it a day.

* * * *

The next morning, Ian was sitting on her porch when she got up to feed the barn crew. "What are you doing here?"

"Waiting for you to get up. I set your irrigation water on the pasture." He stood and kissed her. "Can I come in and get a refill? I ran out of coffee."

"You should have just called to wake me up." She glanced at the barn. "I guess you already fed the crew too."

"Yes, ma'am. I'm a full-service boyfriend." He followed her into the kitchen and went over to the coffeepot to brew a cup. "Did you sleep well?"

"Like a rock. Which is unusual with so much in my head. I take it you were at Allen's last night?"

"Yeah. Bleak's aunt called and said she wants to take her home to Utah."

"That's good news." Angie got her own cup out of the cupboard, and when his coffee finished brewing, put in a pod for herself.

"Yes and no. Bleak says if we send her back, she'll just run away again. But she wouldn't tell us why. I think she's afraid that since he's a police officer, he'll have to do something about what she says."

"What is he going to do?" If Bleak was that determined, they knew the girl wasn't afraid of taking off again if she felt threatened.

Ian shook his head. "He's not sure. Maggie's crazy about her. She's gone into baking mode. There were five different types of cookies out in the living room while we talked last night."

"And no one from the state is pushing to get her placed?" Angie felt bad for the girl. Torn between childhood and adulthood, she was in a no-man's-land.

"I guess since they know she's safe with Maggie and Allen, they're not pushing it. And, according to Allen, this aunt isn't pushing to have her returned. She told the social worker she just wanted to talk to Bleak. But then, when Allen talked to her, it was all about getting her back home."

"Weird. So, what's her real name?"

He laughed as he stood to refill his coffee. "Apparently it's Bleak. Magenta Bleak Hubbard. The community she grew up in is a little out there."

"How do you look at your new baby and call her Bleak?" Angie opened her notebook. "Anyway, don't answer that. I'm not sure I want to know her parents' mind-set. Do you want to know what I found out about the murders?"

She went through her conversations with Tara and the fact she'd seen the poisonous plant in her herb garden at the restaurant. She showed Ian a picture of the plant she pulled up on her phone. "See?"

"I didn't see that plant in the garden. And I looked at it pretty carefully. I was trying to see if there was a way for you to have one at the County Seat. But I think you'd have to buy the house across the alley from you and redo their backyard."

"I already have one expansion project going. I'm not sure I need another one. Besides, what would I do with the house?"

He shrugged. "It's just a thought. And you know property values are going to go up in River Vista soon. The urban sprawl of being Boise's bedroom community is coming sooner rather than later."

"Is the house even up for sale?" She had to admit, his reasoning was sound. But another house? Another mortgage?

"No. But you might want to take over some of Felicia's cookies and talk to the owner about securing first right of sale on the property, if she does decide to sell. I can introduce you. She attends church with us." He took her hand. "I can see the wheels turning in your head. Don't worry about it. Now, I think you should tell Allen about the plant thing."

"I know, but he won't call me."

As if she'd summoned him, her phone rang. Ian pushed the cell closer to her. "I think maybe he was just busy yesterday?"

Angie answered the call, which *was* from Sheriff Brown, and told him about Miquel's visit and talking to Tara. Then she brought up the plant. "I saw a plant like that in Tara's garden."

"You're absolutely sure? This woman is already making noises about suing for harassment. She says she has connections in the government that are going to make me, specifically, sorry for calling out my 'pet chef' to ask her inappropriate questions."

The implication that she'd gone over the line hung in the air. Then Angie remembered what Chris had told her. "Did she disclose that she was having an affair with the victim?"

Now it was Allen who fell quiet. Finally, he spoke. "No. I saw your text and just skimmed my notes from the first interview. She didn't mention knowing Nubbins except by reputation. Can you prove this, or is it a rumor? You chefs seem to love to gossip."

"Talk to Chris at The Library. He told me how she and Nubbins met for coffee once a week. And his friend works at the hotel where they had a standing reservation. If the room doesn't have a full kitchen unit, I think there's only one implication you can draw from that." She glanced over at Ian, who was grinning at her.

"Let me do some research on that theory. Even so, it doesn't mean she killed him."

After she hung up, she glanced up at the clock. It wasn't quite eight. If they left now, no one should be at the restaurant. She finished her coffee. "Drive me and I'll buy you breakfast."

"Drive you where? Or do I want to know?"

She checked Dom's food and water, then picked up her keys and tote. "You probably don't want to know. We're going to take a picture and send it to your uncle."

"So back into the lions' den? Are you sure your middle name isn't Danielle?"

She locked the door as they moved to the porch. "Nice Bible reference."

"I was wondering if you'd notice. You really should attend my adult class. You'd be surprised at all the things I know." He held the door to the truck open for her.

"Can't. You know Sunday mornings and late-night Saturdays don't mix." She hopped into the truck and put on her seat belt. When he came around the other side and started the engine, she added, "That's my excuse and I'm sticking to it."

"At least I know what to expect with you."

He turned up the music, and they didn't talk for a while. Angie watched mostly fields go by on the side of the road. Every once in a while, Ian would point out a hawk or a dog roaming the countryside. Finally, they were on the access road to the freeway. She pointed to the hotel that was on the other side of the road. "According to Chris, that's where Nubbins and Tara hung out."

"Far enough outside of Boise not to run into his wife, but right on the freeway for easy access. Makes sense." He merged into traffic and then looked at her. "I take it we're going to the Tea House?"

"Yep and I'm going to show you the plant. Your uncle is going to believe me. I don't know if she actually killed Chef Nubbins, but if she didn't, she at least has to explain why she has a toxic plant in her garden. Maybe he broke it off. Maybe he didn't want to see her anymore. Maybe he was going back to his wife, or worse, had found another lover. You never know."

"There's a lot of maybes in that scenario." He changed lanes, aiming toward the connector off-ramp.

"True, but it gives her motive and opportunity if even one of my maybes turns to fact." She glanced at her phone. Felicia had texted, asking when she'd be in today. She glanced at Ian. "Where do you want breakfast?"

"You're the food expert. I'll just drive." He turned up the music.

Angie glanced at her watch. They were less than fifteen minutes away from the teahouse, even if the traffic got worse. Then, if they went to the Omelet Shop on Broadway, they could be done and on their way back to the house by ten thirty, eleven at the latest. She texted "*before noon*" as her answer, and got back a quick "*K.*"

Slipping the phone back into her purse, she leaned back to enjoy the ride. Now the view was of retail strip malls and businesses. The rural feel had disappeared almost immediately when they drove into Meridian to get onto the freeway. Boise was getting bigger by the month. Which was great for business, but as a longtime resident of the area, it made her a little sad.

Ian swore under his breath as a red convertible swerved in front of him and he slammed on the brakes. He took a quick glance into the rearview and sighed. "People drive like idiots."

"Especially at fifty-five miles an hour. I bet no one but us is staying under the speed limit."

A touch of pink bloomed on Ian's cheeks. "Make that no one. I'm five miles over the limit as it is."

"Why, you bad boy." She dug in her purse. "Maybe I should call your uncle and tell him you're breaking the law."

"Maybe I should call my uncle and tell him what we did last month when we went to Santa Barbara for the weekend," he countered.

"No way. You tell him that, and there will be a shotgun wedding. I don't think he believes in premarital anything. Including kissing." She knew she was blushing as he navigated the downtown streets to the restaurant.

"We'll keep our secrets then." He pointed down the street. "The herb garden is on the other side of the corner. I'll pull up and park right there on the street and wait. You run and get the picture. If you run into anyone, you were just getting a feel for your own garden."

"Great cover." She hopped out of the truck with her phone. "Don't leave without me."

She sprinted across the parking lot and then climbed the steps to the garden, where the patio opened up seating for customers. She glanced at the window, estimated where they'd been sitting near the exterior wall, then turned back to the garden. The plant should be there, next to the wall of pavers that went up to the fountain and the patio. She scanned the area for the trumpet-shaped flower. She went closer and snapped several pictures. Then she ran back to the truck.

She strapped in and nodded to Ian.

When they were several blocks away, he pulled over to the side of the road in a residential area. "Did you get it? Let me see this bad boy plant."

She opened the camera roll and held out her phone. He took it and flipped through a few pictures. "I don't understand. I don't see anything."

"The plant was there on Monday. And it's gone today. The dirt's disturbed where it was. She didn't even bother to cover it up." Angie leaned on the door, watching Ian. "Does this mean she really did do it?"

Chapter 16

"We don't have any proof that the plant was even there," Ian said for the third time since they'd ordered breakfast.

Angie was digging into her chicken fried steak, trying to block out the disappointment she felt at not being able to prove to Sheriff Brown what she'd seen. "Just because we can't prove it doesn't mean it's not true."

"It makes it harder for Allen to do anything about it." He covered her hand. "Let him talk to the barista and the hotel. If there's proof, that's where he's going to find it."

"You're right. But I keep thinking all we needed was one picture. Maybe I shouldn't have Bleak come to the fair with us on Friday. Maybe it's not safe."

"No one is going to mess with you. According to Allen, they've upped the security at the event. Hired off-duty police officers rather than the temp guys they had last weekend. And someone's going to be at the area twenty-four seven." He finished his juice and glanced at his watch. "Are you about ready? I've got a meeting coming up."

"Sure, I feed you, then you leave. What's up with that?" Angie pushed the half-eaten plate away. "I guess I'm just not very hungry today. Let's go."

When he pulled the truck into the driveway after the quiet trip home, he grabbed her arm as she tried to get out. "Look, I'm sure he believes you about the plant. He wouldn't be looking into this affair rumor if he didn't."

"I know. I'm just tired of getting involved in these things. People lie. They hurt others. And I hate thinking that someone who cooks is like that. Cooking is a gift that you share with the world. Why would one of our own do this?" She closed her eyes. She was talking like a naïve girl rather than a mature woman. "I'm going to call Felicia and tell her I'll be in after I take Dom for a walk. He deserves some time. And it will make me feel a lot better."

He leaned over and kissed her. "Take care of yourself. Don't be taking any stray food samples from anyone."

"No polished apples from old women who look like they could be witches." She nodded. "Good advice. I'll be sure to stay away."

"I'll come by the restaurant tonight around closing. Will you eat dinner with me?" He ran a finger up her arm.

"I'll eat before we start service, but I'm sure I can squeeze out some time for you. Unless you want to come at four."

"I've got meetings up through seven. You eat. I'll come in and maybe you can share my dessert."

Angie nodded. "Sounds like a plan. I'll be looking for you. Tell Felicia to seat you at the back table so I can sneak out of the kitchen easier."

They said their good-byes and Angie went and unlocked the door, keeping Dom inside with her leg so Ian could back out of the driveway. She pushed her way inside, and Dom sat on his bed with a huff.

"Don't be getting an attitude. We're going for a walk, so give me five minutes and we'll be out of here." By the time she changed, checked her mail, and made a pit stop, it was closer to ten minutes. Dom still sat right at the door. Waiting. He knew her moods. He knew her words. He listened when she griped about work. He was the perfect boyfriend, except for the fact they were of two different species.

She filled the backpack, then leaned down to give him a hug. "I'm so glad I have you in my life."

An hour later, the walk done and her mood elevated, Angie arrived at the County Seat ready to face her day. Felicia was in her office, feet up on Angie's desk and a laptop perched on her legs. "Hey, how are you?"

"I'm better now. I was feeling a little stressed with everything that's going on, but Ian assures me that the fair organizers have upgraded the security around the Restaurant Wars area so no one should die on Friday." She sat in her chair and booted up her computer. "So, there's that."

"Sounds like a move in the right direction. I think it's ironic that the killer is using junk food as a delivery medium for the poison. What if someone had been on a diet? They wouldn't have eaten the nachos." Felicia glanced at the laptop. "Anyway, we're all set for next Sunday's class. And it's full. We could get so many more students if we had that room opened already, but I get that we need to take this slow."

"I just don't want to be underwater on the financing for the place." Angie opened the financial records their accountant had sent for approval earlier that week. "Want to go over the budget with me so we can get this back to Kim?"

"Sure. Going over what we actually brought in last month will help with the proposal, anyway. Are you thinking we'll take this to a bank for a loan?" Felicia closed her laptop and moved her chair around to sit near Angie so she could see the screen.

"Maybe. Or maybe we'll do it a piece at a time. Cash-flow the renovations. That way, we don't have to worry about paying back anything." The costs for the remodel had been high on her worry list. "Oh, and before he gets to you, Ian wants us to talk the neighbor into an option to purchase the house behind us so we can eventually have an herb garden."

"Mrs. Beverly lives there. She's in her sixties. She might not sell for years." Felicia glanced toward the back of the building. "What is Ian thinking?"

"I guess he's in the long-range planning mode." Angie went first to the reports that Kim had made as an overview of the business's financial net worth. "Me, I'm not sure what I'm doing tomorrow."

"That's not true, and you know it. But yeah, he's thinking long-term for the business—and for you." Felicia gave her a questioning look. "Are you sure he's not asking about something else?"

Angie shook her head. "Let's focus on the report, okay?"

After reviewing the monthly report, they looked at the budget. Angie compared the budget with their plan. "Food costs increased last month, but I was buying a lot of fresh vegetables that don't keep very well. This month, I'll be moving to more root vegetables that we can store extra from one week to another, so that should drop the costs back into normal range."

"We need to add more into payroll now that we've hired Bleak." Felicia was taking notes. "Will the fair event increase our payroll hours?"

"I don't think so. Except for the temp we hired for Hope's dishwasher duties." Angie glanced at the work schedule. "I already told Bleak she could come with us. Should I move her back to the restaurant this weekend to cover Hope?"

Felicia shook her head. "No. You should take her with you. From what I've heard, the girl hasn't had much of a childhood ever. She needs to know that having fun is part of life too. Not just work. Did you know she cooked for her entire family from the time she was seven?"

"Seriously?" Angie had felt bad that her parents hadn't wanted her back. Now she was wondering if Bleak was just lucky to be out of the family home. "No wonder she fits in so well here. She's a good worker."

"Yes, she is." Felicia checked her watch. "But there's more to life than just being a good worker. Speaking of, the team should start arriving soon. Anything else we need to adjust or talk about?"

"Do you know a guy named Jon Ansley from the area? His wife just died. He's a lawyer. Has a black labradoodle named Timber?"

"Well, now, that's pretty specific." Felicia ran her tongue over her teeth, a habit Angie had seen her do many times when she was thinking hard about something. "I don't think I've met any lawyers. A lot of my friends have husbands who are lawyers, but no one has died recently out of that group. Let me ask around. Why? Is something going on?"

Angie considered telling her the full story, but they didn't have time before they needed to start prep and get ready for service. "I ran into him and his dog at Centennial Park, and something just feels off about him."

"Like, 'could be our murderer' off?" Felicia flipped her notebook closed and put it on the table that served as her desk in the office. There was room for a second desk, but Felicia had wanted the table, saying that sitting was the new smoking for causing health problems.

"I don't see how. Unless he's stalking me, but that's a stretch. No, he just knew a little too much about me." She held a hand up to Estebe, who'd just walked into the office. "Just let me know what, if anything, you find out."

"Will do." Felicia turned and smiled at Estebe. "Thank you for the flowers. They're lovely."

"I'm glad you like them." He smiled back at her, and for a moment as their gazes met, Angie felt like she was watching a romantic movie. Then he turned back to Angie. "Can you come in and explain how you want this dish plated? We have a disagreement within the troops."

"I'll be right there." Angie sent the approved accounting documents back to Kim and added the next month's budget. She was great at keeping them in line and on track with spending. When she closed out the computer, she realized Felicia was still standing by her desk. "Sorry, was there something else?"

"No, I'm just thinking about your bad luck in meeting creeps out at the park. Maybe you should find another place to walk Dom."

"I like walking there." She stood and took her friend by the arm. "I'll be fine."

"You should take Mace."

"Dom's enough of a protector for me. Besides, nothing's going to happen at the park. There's people in and out of there all the time." She paused at the kitchen door and let Felicia go. "Let's have an amazing service tonight."

"Back at'cha."

When Angie opened the kitchen door, the smells of tomato bisque mixed with the lamb stew they were showcasing tonight hit her and made her smile. The kitchen was warm and inviting, and exactly where she wanted to be. She called out, "It's a great day for a great service."

"Yes, chef." The voices rang out. She had a full crew today. Estebe, Nancy, Matt, Hope, and even Bleak were working some sort of prep. She'd imagined a life like this from her first days at culinary school. She didn't find it in California, but since she'd come home, it had been a joy to work with these people.

Estebe waved her over to where he stood with Nancy and Matt. "So, you have two choices..."

* * * *

Friday morning, she sat drinking coffee, thinking about her schedule. She had to be at the fairgrounds by ten. Hope was picking up Bleak and would meet her there. She had about three hours to tighten the main dish idea she and Estebe had developed on Wednesday. She grabbed the ingredients and started setting up for the trial, writing down the recipe and adjustments as she went.

She was just finishing when a knock came to the door. Erica Potter stood on the porch, a basket with empty plastic containers and several small zucchinis in her hands.

"Erica, come on in. You can be my taste tester." She took the basket from her and set it on the table. "How are things going?"

"Getting ready for classes next week. Grans had a ton of doctor appointments this month." Erica reached down to give Dom some love. "So I've been busy."

"Is she all right?" Concern for her elderly neighbor made her pause and search Erica's face for clues.

"Just checkups. She's fine. Although my folks are coming to get her in September and she'll be there until May. The winter months are expanding this year. They want to take her on a cruise in October."

"That will be fun." Angie handed her a plate with the new creation on top. "Try this. So, are you excited about staying at the house this year to finish your classes?"

"You know it. I'll be the lady of the house until Grans comes back, so don't forget to come over and see me." She set the plate down without taking a bite. "And I may have a visitor every once in a while, so don't freak out or call Grans, okay?"

"You mean you'll have gentlemen callers?" Angie put the back of her hand to her head and faked a faint. "I'm not sure I can deal with such wantonness."

"Not sure that's a word, but yeah, my boyfriend will be visiting." She grinned as she took a bite. "This is really good. I thought it would be different."

"Well, hopefully the crowd will like it. I'd like to win one of these contests." Angie sat at the table next to her.

Erica jumped up. "Speaking of school, my study group is getting together to see what books we need for classes. I've got to get down to the bookstore."

After Erica left, Angie cleaned up the kitchen and then sat with Dom for a few minutes. "I should be home early tonight. The competition is over at six. I'll drop off Bleak and then come right home instead of stopping at the restaurant. Then we can watch television."

Apparently, Dom thought that was a great plan and pounded his tail on the wood floor to show his approval. She packed up what she needed in the SUV and left for Boise.

Since it was early, she got parking close to the main gate. She had to show a pass at the front to get in, then she made her way through the wandering crowds to the exhibition site. When she got to the Restaurant Wars gate, a security guard was arguing with Hope and Bleak.

"What's going on?" Angie stepped in front of the line of others waiting. "What's wrong?"

"He won't let us in," Hope said, crossing her arms. "He's being a jerk."

"He won't let *me* in," Bleak corrected. "I told Hope to go inside and I'd wait for you to come and fix this."

"If she isn't on the list, I can't let her in," the guard said, his arms crossed, mimicking Hope's stance and meeting her glare. "I'm doing my job."

"Do it a little faster," someone behind Angie shouted, and the guard turned a little pink.

"Please step aside and let me deal with the rest of the people who are on the list."

Hope shook her head. "I'm not moving."

"Actually, you are." Angie put her hand on Hope's shoulder and turned her away from the guard. She shoved an envelope in her hands. "You take Bleak over to the ticket booth and buy both of you a weekend ride pass. There's enough cash in there for both bands and a little extra for food and drinks. Meet me back here and I'll have this fixed by the time you get back."

Hope glared at the guard but moved toward Bleak and the ticket office. "I can't believe how mean some people are."

The guard held up his clipboard. "She wasn't on the list."

Angie stepped in front of him. "That's my fault. I didn't change my list of assistants. Can I do that with you? I'm Angie Turner, owner of the County Seat."

"No additions to the list unless they come from the administrative office. Sorry." He waved the person behind Angie to step forward.

"Sorry." Angie stepped in between them again. "So, where's the administrative office?"

The guard sighed and pulled out a map of the fairgrounds. He pointed to a white square. "Right here, behind the small animal tent."

"If Hope and Bleak come back before I do, let them know I'll be here as soon as possible." She started walking in the direction the guard had pointed.

"I'm not a message board."

When she turned back, some of her anger must have shown on her face. She saw the guard step back two small steps.

"But I'll be glad to tell them." He turned back to the guy who had been next in line. "Name?"

"That was impressive." Miquel stood watching her and slow-clapping.

"Not now. I've got stuff to take care of."

He dropped into step next to her. "That guy you were talking to outside your restaurant?"

"You were watching me?" She turned her head, but didn't stop walking. She needed to get Bleak approved, then head back to the trailer.

"You were standing right outside the window. What? Do you think you're invisible?" He jogged around a kid swaying a way-too-large ice cream cone in his direction. "Anyway, listen. I just saw him. He works here at the fair. In the concession stands. Not the local ones, but the ones in the carnival area? I was playing skee ball and saw him go into a stand to restock the cotton candy."

"Okay." Now Angie did stop and pull him to the side of the walkway, where they wouldn't be run over by people passing by. "What does that have to do with anything?"

"Don't you think it was weird he was all the way out in River Vista? If he's with the carnival, would he even have a car?"

"Again, I'm not sure why you're concerned." She had so much to do, but Miquel looked intent on telling her something. Something she should have been picking up on in his comments.

"Angie. The guy was at my restaurant the day before. I think he's checking us out." Miquel paled a little as he glanced around. "You don't think he's the one going after the chefs, do you?"

She pointed to the administrative office, which she could see from where they stood. "Look, I've got to get one of my team members on the list for today. You go tell the security guard what you just told me."

"Are you crazy? They'll think I'm trying to get attention off of me. You know they think I killed Nubbins." He shook his head. "I'm sorry I told you. I thought you'd help."

Angie watched as he took off down the walkway and disappeared into the crowd. She had things to do. "What a lunatic."

A woman walking by her pulled her child closer and hurried away.

"Great, now I'm the lady who talks to herself." She went up the stairs to the administration office to start the work to get Bleak on the list.

Chapter 17

When she got back to the security guard, he waved her inside. "The office called and approved your new team member. And just in time. They both sat there and stared at me for ten minutes before the office called."

"Sorry about the bother," Angie apologized. "I know you were just doing your job."

"Yeah, but the worst thing is they each brought back one of those fresh corn dogs from the stand near the gate." He looked sheepish. "I love those things. I was trying not to drool while they were giving me the evil eye."

Angie laughed and made her way to the trailer. Bleak and Hope sat at the outside table. Hope looked up when she stepped on the stairs. "Be warned, Estebe's in there and is in a rotten mood. He told us to stay out until he got things set up correctly."

Angie opened the door and peeked inside. Estebe was setting up the kitchen. Music poured out from a small player he must have brought with him. "Hey, what's going on?"

"I have all the food packed into the trailer and ready for our prep to start when they give us the green light. Now, I'm just cleaning and setting up the trailer so we have someplace good to work from." He didn't look at her.

"What's wrong?" Angie sank into a chair near the door.

"Nothing."

She let him pout for a few more minutes. Finally, her silence wore into him.

"I'm just wondering if I have gotten myself into a bad situation." He finally set down the bottled cleaner and rag and met Angie's eyes. "You know your friend better than anyone. Is she capable of a long-term relationship?"

Angie groaned inside. She knew if the couple had issues, it would affect the County Seat, but she didn't think it would be this quickly. "I'm not the one to ask. Have you talked to her about how you feel?"

"She talks about plans for the future. Plans that don't include staying here in Idaho. Which, by extension, don't include me." He leaned against the counter. "Am I a fool to hope?"

"So, you're saying you haven't talked to her. Tell her how you feel. Tell her that you're looking for something possibly long-term. I don't think she's ever had someone in her life who offered that possibility. Maybe she doesn't think it's on the table."

He stared at her for a long time. "You are wiser than your years. I hadn't thought of that."

"Again, I'm the wrong one to be talking to about this. Take her out on Monday when we don't have service and this thing is finally over. Tell her that you want her to dream about a future together. See what she says." Angie prayed that she wasn't sending him to get his walking papers from Felicia, but it was better he be hurt now than later. Especially if Felicia was just having fun.

"I will follow your advice. Now it's time to cook." He went back to cleaning.

Angie took a bottle of water out of the cooler. "Now it's time to wait for them to tell us we can cook."

"We need to wait for Matt. I sent him to get better potatoes. I didn't like the ones from the store." Estebe glanced at his watch. "He should be here in twenty minutes."

"And the event starts in thirty. Do you need me for anything?" She glanced around the trailer, which looked cleaner than it had when she first stepped inside.

"No. And thank you. I was being overly thoughtful and let my concern spill out into my working life. I will be more controlled in the future."

Angie walked over and put a hand on his arm, so he'd turn and look at her. "That's not what we do here. If you have something that's bothering you, personal or work-related, we're here for you. I'm here for you. I know you'd do the same for me, because you have."

"You have a kind heart, Angie Turner. Ian is a lucky guy." Estebe took a deep breath. "I am fine, and we will win this section. I am sure."

"I'm going back outside to check on the girls. Then, when Matt gets here with the last of the supplies, let's do a quick rundown of the dish. I think you're right. This one's a winner." She headed out the door.

"We cook with heart," he called after her. "We need a T-shirt."

Outside, Angie sat on the stairs. "Hope, you know your role, Estebe will run it through for you. Matt's dropping off the last of the supplies in a few minutes, then we'll start as soon as they let us. It's a challenging dish, but they're going to love it."

Bleak raised her hand. "What am I supposed to do? Hope says you can only have three people in the trailer."

"You are our runner. Once every half hour, I need you to stop in and check on us. If we need food or water, I want you to be the only one that gets it for us. No getting free apples from a friendly witch on the fairgrounds." She handed her an envelope. "That should be enough money for whatever we ask for, but if you run out, just tell me."

"So the rest of the time I just sit here?" Bleak glanced at her backpack.

Angie guessed she'd brought several books along with her. "No need. Go see the exhibition hall. I love the quilts, but there's all kinds of stuff in there. Go on rides, play games, eat junk food, just make sure you're back every thirty minutes. Do you have a watch?"

Bleak shook her head.

Angie took off hers and handed it to her. "You set your timer here. It will vibrate when the alarm goes off. Every time you leave here, set it for another thirty minutes. When we're done, either I can take you home or you and Hope can stay and she can take you home."

"She's staying overnight at my folks' house. Sheriff Brown already approved it." Hope grinned. "First thing in the morning, we're doing a mani-pedi thing at the house. My mom and sister are setting it up. And Dad's ordering pizza for when we get home tonight."

"Sounds like fun." Out of the corner of her eye, she saw the man who had been at the restaurant the other night. "I've got to check something out. I'll be right back."

She marched straight over to the fence where he was standing, watching another trailer. "I didn't expect to see you here."

Her words must have confused him, because when he turned to look at her, it didn't seem like he even knew who she was. "Oh, Angie from the County Seat. Sorry, I didn't recognize you out of your chef whites."

"You know my name, what's yours?"

The man shrugged. Today his red hair was tied back in a ponytail and he had on a T-shirt with the word *Galveston* in huge block letters. The guy must travel a lot. "Most of the crew call me Red, but my real name is Ted. I guess they think it's a joke." He glanced around at the gathering crowds. "You play hard today."

"It's not really playing." She nodded to the carnival opening. "You work for the carnival, don't you?"

His grin was slow. "It's my current employment. I think people define others way too much on what they do to put food on the table, don't you?"

"Angie?" A woman's voice behind her made her turn and find Barb Travis walking toward her. When she turned back to Ted, he'd disappeared into the crowd. Angie scanned the people milling around and found him moving toward the carnival area.

This was the guy that Miquel was afraid of. The one she'd told him to report. Maybe she should point him out to the guard? And say what? That he'd come to her restaurant? That he knew her name?

"Angie?" Barb stood next to her now. She looked at her face, then scanned the crowd for someone she might know. "Are you all right? Are you looking for someone?"

"I'm fine. What are you doing here? I didn't peg you for a fair type." Angie turned to Barb and took in her jeans and Jack Daniel's tank that showed off her toned arms. "You look great."

"I look great for a fifty-year-old woman." Barb glanced around the area. "I wanted to see what all the fuss was about with this Restaurant Wars thing. You're getting a lot of good buzz in *The Statesman*. In fact, you're one of the front-runners to win."

"I'm just hoping it brings in more customers to the County Seat."

Barb laughed. "From what I've seen, you're doing just fine in that area. And my bar receipts are going up to show it. People either come in early to get a drink before their reservation at your place or afterward. I guess being a dive country bar next to a high-end restaurant isn't a bad thing. I wasn't sure about the kind of people you'd bring in."

Seriously? Barb had been worried about her customers? "I'm glad we can support each other in bringing in more people."

"I don't think my crew is going to your place, so I'm the winner here." Barb patted her arm. "Anyway, fight hard today. And it's nice what you're doing for that girl. I tried to get her to tell me where she lived, but I guess I scared her off. Your Ian, he's good with scared things."

Angie watched the woman make her way through the crowd and wondered if she'd been one of the scared things Barb had referenced. She turned to the trailer and almost ran right into another woman standing behind her.

"Sorry, I was waiting for you to be done with your conversation. I'm Sheila Roberts from the Sandpiper?" The younger blonde had her hair pulled back into a ponytail and wore jean shorts and a tank. She held out a flyer. "Mrs. Nubbins wanted all the restaurants to know that they and their crew are welcome at the celebration of David's life tonight."

Angie took the flyer. "Seven? Isn't that late for a funeral?"

"It's not really a funeral, but more like a wake. The actual funeral is on Saturday. Mrs. Nubbins wanted to make sure as many of you who were here the day..." Sheila paused, swallowed, then changed her words, "the first day of the contest could be there. The Sandpiper is closed this weekend, so we'll have an open bar and food available. Don't worry about bringing anything. We're making tons of food. I think she's invited the entire Treasure Valley."

"Thank you for the invitation. I'd come and pay my respects, but I didn't bring any dress-up clothes." Angie glanced at the jeans and tank she'd worn to work in.

"Oh, I'm supposed to point that out too. Dress code is kitchen casual. She'd rather people show up in what they wore to cook in than not show up." Sheila pointed to the flyer. "See, she says that right there. I guess she knows chefs pretty well, huh?"

Actually, Angie mused, Mrs. Nubbins knew human behavior around death rituals really well too. Maybe Estebe would come with her. "She's covered all the bases, so I guess I'll be there."

"Great." For the first time since she'd started talking, Sheila smiled. "He would have liked knowing you were coming. He'd talked about the County Seat since it opened. How brave you were for being in River Vista and not setting up in town. He even ate there once, incognito. He said your chicken and dumplings made him miss his mother."

"How sweet." Angie wondered if Felicia had recognized the disguised chef. She'd have to ask her. "I'm touched that he even knew about us."

"He loved researching all the local restaurants. He said if you didn't know your competition, you got stale and then went down. He was focused like that." Now tears filled Sheila's eyes. "I still can't believe he's gone, and I found him in the trailer. It's like a bad dream."

"Did the cops tell you what happened? Heart attack, right?"

Sheila's eyes watered. "No. He was given poisoned cotton candy. Can you believe it? Someone sprinkled some sort of powder on the top. You know how the fluff melts in your hands, especially on hot days? Well, he got a huge dose of this poison. And his heart, it just wasn't up to fighting off the overload."

"That's so strange. I mean, it's crazy anyone would want to kill him. Did he have a fight with someone recently?" Sheriff Brown had been less than forthcoming on the details of the chef's death.

"No. Everyone loved him. Mrs. Nubbins said that he was going through a kind of rebirth and had made amends for all kinds of things with her just this last month." Sheila slapped a hand over her mouth. "I probably shouldn't have said that. They're a great couple, it's just, well, David could be very attractive to women. He had to keep telling everyone he was married and to stop trying." She glanced around and lowered her voice. "I think maybe sometimes he didn't say no."

"That must have been hard on her."

Sheila nodded. "She was crying and everything when she told me. Of course, she'd also been drinking, but who could blame her with her husband dying."

Angie saw Ann Cole climbing up to the podium. "Looks like the contest is about to start. Thank you for the invitation, and let Mrs. Nubbins know that the County Seat will be there. Should we send flowers?"

"No, it's on the flyer. She wants donations to go to the culinary program at Boise State." Sheila saw the chef from the Black Angus standing in front of his trailer. "I've got to go. There are so many people to invite."

Estebe was standing outside the trailer, watching her as she walked toward him. "What is wrong?"

"You read me too well." Angie shook off the unease she'd felt after the conversation with Sheila. "Do you and Felicia have plans tonight?"

He shook his head. "Why?"

"How would you like to be my date for a wake for Chef Nubbins tonight?" She handed him the flyer.

He read it, nodded, and handed it back to her. "I am guessing we are not there just to pay our respects?"

Angie shrugged as Ann Cole started her announcements. "If we happen to find out more about his death and maybe who killed him, that would only be a coincidence."

"You are very sly."

They listened as Ann went over her canned welcome to Garden City and how happy she and the other elected officials were that people were coming to their campaign booths located just inside the exhibition hall main entrance. Then she repeated all the same rules and assignments for the contest. Maybe there were other people here who didn't attend the other two events, but Angie noticed that most of the crowds' eyes were glazing over.

When she banged the cymbals one of the local marching bands had lent her, they moved to the back of the trailer. "Okay, Bleak, timer on. Thirty minutes and I expect to see you back here."

Bleak nodded and set Angie's watch. She held it up for Angie to see. "I'll be back on time. I'm going to go see the rabbits first."

"Make sure you hydrate," Angie called after Bleak. She held her hand up, letting Angie know she'd heard.

"Good call, Mom." Hope grinned and hopped into the trailer. "Where do you want me, Estebe?"

Angie might be the head chef, but Hope treated Estebe as if he was her boss. The guy had earned her respect by the way he'd taken her under his wing and taught her in the kitchen. Hope definitely wasn't treated like just a dishwasher. "Sue me for worrying. Let's get this going. I know we're going to win."

Their dish was based on the chick-on-a-stick idea, but this chick wasn't just chicken. It was a portable chicken-and-dumplings recipe. "*Just like Sunday dinner at Grandma's*" had been their menu descriptor. Angie just hoped it was inventive enough. She'd had spaghetti to go in NYC when she'd visited last year, a dish plated into a paper cone for ease of eating and walking.

As they started the prep, Angie thought about the smile she'd seen on Bleak's face when she'd taken off for the small animal barn. She was totally different from the closed-off, defensive girl she'd met just a few days ago. She might not have blood family here, but she was finding out what Angie had learned so many years ago. Family came in a lot of different baskets.

Chapter 18

Service had gone well that afternoon. The dumplings had been sturdy enough to stay on the stick, yet they still tasted light and fluffy. The chicken was tender and flavorful. Angie and Estebe were sitting outside at the table as Hope and Bleak finished cleaning the trailer. Angie finished off a bottle of water. "Did you see anyone else's dish?"

"I heard that Bien Viveres did a taco dish using fish. But I didn't actually see anyone else's work." Estebe grunted. "Like that's innovative. Everyone has fish tacos on the menu."

"You never know what's going to strike the right chord in the judges." Angie rolled her shoulders. She'd be glad when tomorrow was over. "As soon as they are done with the trailer, we'll go grab something to eat, my treat."

"Okay." Estebe thrummed his fingers on the table. "Tell me what you're hoping to find tonight?"

"I guess a reason that someone would target Nubbins specifically. I don't want to think this is all random. Random means chaos. I like order better." Angie rubbed her left shoulder, which had started to twitch under Estebe's watchful eye.

"You believe his girlfriend or his wife did this."

Angie knew it wasn't a question. "This one or another one. Sheila said he had problems with groupies. I can't see the wife hosting this huge wake to honor her husband if she was the one who actually sent him to the ferryman."

Estebe's lips twitched into a small smile. "It wouldn't be the first time a grieving widow turned out to be the one who set up her situation. But we will know more tonight when we meet her."

Angie closed her eyes. All she wanted to do was go home and fall into her claw-foot tub with a bottle of wine.

"Something is bothering me about your theory, though."

Angie's eyes blinked open. "What did I miss?"

"Chef Nubbins wasn't the only one attacked. If this was personal and about him, no one else, except someone in his circle, would have been hurt. Brandon Cook isn't even a chef, right?"

"Actually, he *is* a chef. He works in the statehouse for the governor. He just doesn't run a business like the rest of us." Angie's head hurt. Every time she thought she had a lead, someone, like Estebe, would burst her bubble. "But not a lot of people know that. Sydney's the chef everyone knows. And from what I know, Brandon wasn't attached to Nubbins in any way."

"Which means..."

Angie stood when Bleak came out of the trailer with Hope right behind her. "Which means I'm barking up the wrong tree. Let's go eat. I want to get rid of this headache."

"Woo-hoo. Where are we going?" Hope bounced as she waited for the answer.

"Don't get your hopes up. It's all fair food." She glanced at Estebe. "Any favorites?"

"I've heard the fish fry over at the Catholic booth is rad." He elbowed Hope. "I said that right, didn't I!"

"Rad isn't really popular now, so don't get your ego all big about it. You still have a long way to go to be comfortable with slang," Hope teased. She laughed at the confusion showing on Angie's face. "I'm teaching him how to talk normal. He's just so stuffy."

"You will think I'm stuffy when you come back to piles of dishes because I let Bleak cook on the line." Narrowing his gaze made him look determined.

Hope giggled. "You wouldn't do that. I've seen you clean a stove a second time because you didn't think Matt did a good enough job. Face it, you're a clean freak."

"I could be persuaded." He locked the trailer. "Ladies, after you."

Bleak and Hope moved off together toward the fish fry. Angie fell into step with Estebe. When they were far enough ahead they wouldn't overhear, Angie turned her head toward him. "I'm glad they're getting along. Bleak needed a friend closer to her age. I know that Hope's five years ahead, but she's a great role model."

"Bleak has an old soul. There is more childhood joy in Hope than I've seen in Bleak. I hope she learns to laugh soon." He smiled at her. "You are a good judge of people."

"I am a sucker for a good story." Angie pulled her phone out of her pocket. "Hold on, it's Felicia. I'll meet you all at the booth. And keep your receipt if you have to pay before I get there and I'll pay you back. Two-piece dinner for me with fries and coleslaw."

"I will get the children fed." He pointed to the phone. "Tell her I said hello."

Angie smiled, then turned off the walkway and tucked into a corner of the outside of a couple of booths. "Hey, Felicia, what's up?"

"Just checking in. Have they said anything about tomorrow's limitations? I'm thinking I'm going to spin some ice cream."

"Nothing yet. But we are on a dinner break as they deliberate. Then we should know about six. Want me to call you then?" Angie could hear the noise from the restaurant in the background. Service had just started.

"I'll be working the hostess station. Trish called in sick tonight, so I'm one person down. If you hadn't taken Bleak, I could have put her on the entrance."

Angie watched the swarm of people walking in front of her. All ages from grandmas to babies. Everyone loved the state fair. "It's good for her to have new experiences."

"She is an employee. You remember that, right?" Felicia teased. "And I hear you're taking my boyfriend out tonight."

"Oh? He's your boyfriend?"

Felicia laughed. "Something like that. Where are you guys going?"

"A wake for Chef Nubbins. His wife's putting it on and wants the group who was here when he died to come." Angie shivered in the hot sun. "It's kind of weird, but she sent Sheila around with flyers for everyone."

"And you're going to see if you can find out anything about why he might be dead?"

"You're a suspicious type. Maybe I just want the County Seat to be present and pay our respects. Especially since you'll be in the middle of service." Angie knew Felicia wouldn't buy the crap she was selling, but she liked to practice her excuse.

"Okay, I'll leave you to your sleuthing. Just wanted to let you know we're fine here. Nancy has everyone in the kitchen working hard to prove that they are just as good without you and Estebe as when you are there. I think you've got some competitive staff."

"You got that right. I'll call you on the way home and give you an update." Angie said good-bye and moved quickly to the booth, where the rest of the team probably were already eating. She wouldn't have a lot of time to eat before they were expected back at the Restaurant Wars event.

The girls were chattering and Estebe looking at something on his phone when she got to the table. Her fish and chips sat waiting for her along with a bottle of water. "Felicia says hi and that she misses you."

"You made up that last part." Estebe smiled, putting his phone away. "She is busy with the restaurant. She doesn't have time to miss anyone."

"Whatever." She glanced over at Hope. "Are you two going to the carnival tonight?"

"Most definitely. I didn't get to ride much last weekend due to my prone position, but I loaded up on water all day. The only thing that will keep me from doing all the rides are the lines." Hope and Bleak high-fived each other.

"And the trips to the bathroom," Angie added.

Estebe chuckled, but Hope and Bleak were already planning their attack to get the most out of the time they had at the fair.

"We should be done with the contest in just a few minutes after we get back."

Estebe shook his head. "The woman's speeches get longer and longer. Tomorrow she will have to talk from dusk to dawn to fit all the praise for her leadership into the discussion."

As they finished dinner, Angie saw a text from Ian. *What are you doing after the fair? Want me to come over?*

She texted back. *Sorry, I've got plans tonight. Come over for coffee early tomorrow. I have to be at the fairgrounds at ten.*

She put the phone back in her jeans and stood. "Let's go, kids. I want to get this over with. Maybe we'll get lucky and not be in the top three."

Angie's luck failed when the County Seat was announced as the day's winner. Since the Sandpiper had won the first day but had left the contest due to "unfortunate circumstances," they'd chosen a third restaurant based on overall votes that would be competing tomorrow. The County Seat, Copper Creek, and Bien Viveres. Rider James and the Black Angus were out of the competition. So, if he was the one killing to narrow the field, he'd narrowed himself right out of the running.

Tara stepped over after the announcements. Reaching out her hand, she said, "Congrats. I hope you win tomorrow."

"Really?" Angie knew by the look on Tara's face that wasn't what she'd expected.

"Yes, really. Look, you have a bad habit of investigating things. It's no skin off my nose. David's wife knew about me. She called me last night to see how I was doing."

"Wow." Angie didn't know what was up with all these confessions, but Tara had surprised her twice.

Tara shrugged, glancing around. "She called to invite me to the wake tonight. Said I might be feeling uncomfortable, but since she knew that David and I were close, that I should come."

"That's generous." Angie knew she'd never be that open to being kind if she'd found out that her future husband had been straying. "So, are you going?"

"Are you kidding? This could be a setup. Or maybe the widow likes to play with people's heads. Either way, I'm out of the picture. I have been for months. Your barista friend didn't tell you that we haven't been at the coffee shop or the hotel in more than seven weeks. He called it off. He wanted to make things right with his wife. So, we were done." She snapped her fingers. "Over and out. He always just saw us as fun. Not as a real couple."

Angie could see the pain on Tara's face. "But you thought there might be a chance."

Nodding, Tara took a tissue out of her pocket. "Silly me. I thought when he told me he loved me that he actually meant it. Dating just keeps getting harder and harder. I'm going to be an old maid, if they even call people like me that name anymore."

"I'm sorry for your loss." Angie could see the pain in Tara's face. Angie heard several clicks of a camera, and she pulled Tara next to her. She leaned close and whispered in her ear. "Smile. People need to see that you're okay."

After Tara had left, Angie watched as Hope came around the trailer. Estebe's digital camera hung around her neck. Angie reached out a hand and Hope gave it to her.

"Why did you want her picture?"

"Just wanted to see if anyone recognizes her from being around here last Friday." She glanced around and found the security guard who had been on duty the first weekend. "Estebe, I'll be right back and we can go. I'll see you two tomorrow, right?"

Hope and Bleak nodded. "We'll be here right at ten."

"Be careful," Estebe called after them. To Angie, he pointed to the table by the trailer. "I'll be waiting there. You be careful too."

Angie stepped up to the guard. "Hey, can I ask you a question?"

He frowned at her, then nodded. "You're one of the chefs, right?"

"Angie Turner of the County Seat." She held up the camera and pointed to the digital screen. "Do you recognize her?"

"Of course, she's another one of the chefs." He narrowed his eyes. "Why are you asking? I assume you already know who she is since she's posing with you in the picture."

"Friday night, when we went to grab dinner, was she still in the trailer area?"

"I don't know. There were a lot of people in and out." His eyes went wide. "What, you think she killed that guy? She must be all of five foot five."

"You don't have to be tall to poison someone." Angie dropped her arm that held the camera. "Thanks for your time."

"I said I didn't know where she was, not that I didn't see people going in that trailer." He smirked at her. "But since you have no legal authority, I don't have to tell you anything. Have a nice day."

Angie watched as he spun around and left the area. The guy had an attitude. Maybe Sheriff Brown could take him down a few pegs. She picked up the phone and called.

By the time she'd made it back to the trailer, Estebe was pacing by the door. Her tote was on the table. "There you are. We're going to be late if we don't hurry. You can ride with me, and I'll drop you back at your car afterward."

"Is the trailer locked? Do you want me to hold on to this?" Angie held out the camera.

"I will put it in my car. I don't trust these trailers. Anyone with half a brain could bust into this lock with no problems. I like my camera." He handed her the tote. "Let's go."

The Sandpiper was ten minutes away from the fairgrounds, but with the large number of people coming in and out of the area, she figured they'd be lucky if they got there in twenty. Estebe, though, had other plans. He whipped his Hummer around traffic, going the opposite way and across the river.

"The Sandpiper is on Main Street," Angie said through gritted teeth.

"I know where it is," he said as he weaved between a classic Mustang and a jacked-up Dodge Ram truck. It was Friday night, and everyone seemed to be on the road to somewhere.

Angie grabbed the built-in handhold and closed her eyes as he ran up behind a tanker truck with a large cow painted on the side. When she didn't feel the crash, she opened one eye carefully and looked around. They were past the truck and now turning onto a road that she knew went to a golf course. "I don't think there's a bridge to cross the river here."

"There is a bridge a few blocks down." He took the turn, and she slid in her seat.

She decided it was better not to question his route, and by the time they pulled into the restaurant's parking lot, they were only a few minutes late. He turned to her and grinned. "My brothers and I used to caddy at that golf course. I know exactly where the faster routes are."

"Remind me not to ride with you next time." Angie climbed out of the Hummer, her legs shaking when she hit the ground.

He came around and took her arm. "What's life without a little danger?"

They walked into the restaurant and into a crowd. Everyone who was part of the culinary community was there. The dean from Hope's program at the university waved at her from across the room. She thought she recognized several of her professors as well. It appeared that Tara had stayed true to her word and hadn't come.

Sydney and Brandon Cook approached from the snack table. Sydney's plate was stacked high with appetizers. "Angie, I'm so glad to see you."

"Brandon, glad you're up and going. You gave us quite a scare last weekend." Estebe shook his hand.

As he released from the handshake, Brandon reached down to touch Sydney's expanding belly. Angie wondered if he even realized he'd done it. The move seemed instinctual. "I know. Sydney always said food was going to kill me, but we thought it was because of my perfectionism while I'm working. Who knew you couldn't accept food from strangers?"

"Is that what happened?" Angie took a glass of champagne from one of the passing waiters.

Both Brandon and Sydney laughed. "Honestly, we're still not sure. The only thing Brandon remembers eating is the nachos that were on the table outside the trailer. He thought I'd ordered them because he'd told me a few minutes earlier that he was starving. I'd actually forgotten about getting food because we'd just been announced as the day's winner. So I was busy."

"Too busy to feed the father of her child," Brandon added.

She turned to him and patted his face. "An expectant father who has two good legs and his own source of money to get his own food. Anyway, we didn't put it together until your local sheriff started asking me about where the food came from. Then, I talked to all my staff. No one remembers seeing anyone come with the nachos."

Brandon pointed over to one of the professors. "There's Tina. I told her that I'd bring you over to show off the alien growing in your body."

"He's really excited about the baby." Sydney pointed to a row of tables. "Make sure you try the shrimp veggie wraps. They're amazing."

Angie watched as they walked away. "So, the killer didn't focus on Sydney as head chef like he did for Chef Nubbins."

"Maybe he didn't realize that there might be others around who might eat the food?" Estebe led her to the tables. "Are you hungry? I could taste-test for you so you know what's safe to eat."

"I doubt anyone's using a wake to try to kill off all the chefs in Boise." She glanced up at Estebe. "Right?"

He set down the plate he'd just picked up again. "So much for eating. I'm glad I ate before we left the fair."

Angie nodded. "Me too. This is just too random. I know there has to be some reason someone would kill Nubbins and then try for Sydney."

"If they were even trying for Sydney," Estebe corrected.

"Well, if they were, I'm next on the winner list." Angie nodded over to a gathering near the kitchen. "I think the widow is over there. Let's make an appearance. Then let's go home. I'm too tired to play Nancy Drew tonight."

Chapter 19

She called Ian to talk as she was driving home. “I’m on my way home now. Thought you might have some time to burn.”

“I wondered what you had going on. Meeting after the contest?” Ian didn’t seem surprised that she’d called. She was just glad she hadn’t woken him. He was an early riser.

“No. Well, kind of. Estebe and I went to a wake for Chef Nubbins. His widow put it on for all the culinary professionals who had been at Restaurant Wars the day he died.” She turned off the freeway and onto a highway that would take her to her house. Soon she’d be out of town and on a two-lane road. “A lot of the university culinary professors were there too.”

“Sounds like a nice idea.” He paused. When she didn’t say anything, he pushed on. “But from what I’m hearing, you didn’t think it was such a nice idea.”

“I just don’t understand her, I mean, the widow’s intentions. According to Tara—who came by to congratulate me, by the way—Mrs. Nubbins knew about the affair. His assistant said the same thing.” She passed a large sedan that was crawling down the road. “To each his own, but if that was you in the coffin and I knew about an affair? I’d be mad as heck. I wouldn’t be throwing parties and inviting your girlfriend.”

“Good to know. Of course, I wouldn’t have put myself in Nubbins’s position anyway. Cheating isn’t just a sin, it’s a betrayal. If you don’t want to be with me, go, have fun. But not if you’re with me.”

Angie could hear the sound of the television in the background. “See? You get it. Why would she have thrown a party to celebrate someone like that?”

"Maybe his public persona was too important to her to damage it. I hear he's been working on a cookbook. She could finish it and make him a hero after death."

"That makes sense. She had to protect the chef from being seen as a bad person." Angie nodded, even though she was alone in the car. She yawned. "So, tell me about your day. I need a story so I don't fall asleep on the drive home."

Ian entertained her as she drove. When she pulled into the driveway, she sighed. "I've got to go feed Precious and Mabel before I go in. If I don't, I'll fall on the couch and be out."

"I ran over on my way back from seeing Mildred at Moss Farms. They've been fed, even Dom. Although I'm sure he's going to try to tell you different."

Angie was so glad Ian had a key to her house. "Thank you, again. I owe you a home-cooked meal. Early next week, okay?"

"Sounds good, since we missed our date this week."

She smiled at the dash. "We went out. We went to Tara's Tea House for dinner."

"To try to find a killer. I'm not sure that's really even on the list for possible date ideas." He chuckled. "Go to bed. I'll talk to you in the morning."

"You coming over?"

His answer surprised her. "Yeah, I thought I might just so I can see my girlfriend. It's been a while since we've just hung out."

"What time?" She would have to leave for Boise by nine to be on time for the last contest.

"Set your alarm for six. I'll bring doughnuts and fruit. You can make the coffee."

"I'll see you then. And this totally counts as a date, by the way." She glanced over at the Potter house. The outside light was on, but all the other lights were off. Erica must already be home. Early for a Friday night.

"Works for me. Sleep well and have happy dreams."

"You too." She hung up and headed to the house. Before she even thought of sleep, she needed to spend some time with the other guy in her life. Dom would be on her as soon as she walked in the door. For a Friday, she'd be home early. Maybe she'd surprise him.

He had heard the car because when she opened the kitchen door, he was waiting. His tail beat the floor in greeting as she set her tote down and relocked the door. "Nine on a Friday. Don't get used to this. Next week we go back to our normal late hours."

He barked as if to say he understood, but for tonight, he wanted snuggles on the couch. With popcorn if she didn't mind. Or at least that's what she thought he'd say if he could talk.

So that's what they did.

* * * *

The next morning, she was up before her alarm and sitting in the kitchen answering emails when Ian arrived with the doughnuts. He glanced at the pot, which was half empty. "You didn't sleep in."

"I couldn't. I was thinking about Felicia's plan to open up the new room, and I had some ideas I wanted to run by her. Then I just got lost in email." She closed her laptop and moved it to the side. "How was your week?"

"Mildred lost a milker and she wanted me to go through the applications she got before she hired someone new. I don't think she realizes that running a dairy is just like running her nonprofit." He got napkins out and set a maple bar in front of her.

"Or she just wants your attention." Angie shrugged. "You know she leaned on your expertise way too much during the time she took over the dairy. She should be paying you for your knowledge."

"You're right. I let her get away with too much. Mostly because she pulls the grief card over Gerald. But I'll be stronger." He made a movement with his arm showing his muscle. "Besides that? It was just normal busywork. Closing out the farmers' market for the season is always a crazy-busy time."

"You're doing the once-a-month thing for the next few months, right?" Angie needed the market to be open so she could pick up last-minute produce items for the restaurant.

"Don't freak out, yes, we'll be open. It might just be for you, but at least most of the tables will sell something that day." He leaned back with a sprinkles-covered doughnut. "So, how did yesterday go? You were so busy telling me about the wake you didn't mention the contest."

"I didn't tell you I won?" Angie held up her hands. "We took the contest with chicken and dumplings on a stick. It was brilliant and so, so good."

"Congrats. How did Bleak do?" He polished off the doughnut and let one hand drop to pet Dom, who'd moved to a seated position next to Ian's chair, hoping for some droppings.

"She did great. She did a sleepover at Hope's last night. I love that she's acting a little bit more like a kid. I know she needs to get back into school, but I'm hoping once she starts feeling safe here, she'll go back on her own." Angie took a bite of the maple bar. Flour, sugar, fat, and egg.

The treat didn't have much in nutritional value, but she loved it anyway. "I was happy for about five minutes. Then we went to the wake and I got depressed. Sydney and Brandon are so into this whole baby thing. I can't believe anyone would even try to hurt either one of them."

"It gets worse. Allen's convinced that the target wasn't Brandon, but actually was Sydney. If she'd eaten those nachos, who knows what might have happened."

They both were silent for a while, thinking of the averted disaster. "If that's true, whoever is doing this is an awful person."

"Even if it's not true, the guy killed Nubbins. Just that one death makes them screwed up."

Angie grabbed a second doughnut. This one was blueberry cake. "I don't want to think about it anymore. Felicia is coming with me today to do a dessert. I haven't even had time to ask her what she's planning."

"Apples are just starting now. An apple turnover would be portable and yummy." He took a second doughnut. Dom beat his tail on the floor reminding Ian he was still there, waiting for a crumb to drop. "You should go eat your dog food. Drooling isn't a good look for you."

"And it gets my floor dirty." Angie snapped her fingers to get Dom's attention, then pointed to the bed. "Go lie down and stop coveting Ian's doughnut."

Ian watched him turn and stomp to the bed. He made three circles before settling down in the oversized dog bed. "I think the first part of that order is easier to follow than the second. Your dog has a gluttony problem."

"My dog has a sweets problem," Angie corrected him. She glanced at the clock. She still had time. "What's on your plan today?"

As Ian ran through his schedule, Angie thought of her own busy day. She'd be on her feet for hours at the contest, but she really wanted to take Dom for a walk before she left for town.

"So, do you want me to meet you tonight at the fair? This will be the last chance we'll have to explore. And they have a great band playing over at the racetrack." Ian sipped his coffee. "I'll buy you a corn dog."

"It's crazy but I love those things. The cornmeal covering is always so crunchy. And the mustard, yum." She glanced at Dom. He wouldn't be expecting her until late anyway, since it was Saturday and a normal workday for him. "Why not?"

"Not the rousing answer I'd hoped for, but I'll take it." Ian stood and leaned down to kiss her. "I need to go. I'm meeting with a farmer who might be joining us next year in the marketing coop."

"Yeah, I need to get ready as well." At her words, Dom lifted his head from his bed, watching her. She nodded. "Yes, we have time for a short walk."

"Be careful." He glanced at his watch. "Text me when you're on your way to Boise."

She laughed as she followed him to the door. "There's nothing wrong with walking through Celebration Park on a Saturday morning. It's going to be filled with hikers and families today."

"And somehow you keep running into the most interesting people there." He squeezed her arm. "I know, I worry too much. But I kind of like having someone to think about during the day."

Angie thought about Ian's words as she drove to the park. As she'd expected, even though it wasn't quite 8 a.m., the parking lot had several spots already taken. Some were hiking the cliff trail. Today, she wanted to meander through the flatter trail that ran the length of the park. Besides, there was a loop there she could take and still be home in time to shower and change before heading into Boise and the last day of the Restaurant Wars contest.

They were on their way back from Message Rock where early day travelers left messages to family following behind, when she saw the dog. Timber, the man had called him. They were ahead of them on the trail and close to the parking lot. Angie wouldn't catch them before they got into their car and left. But at least it explained why she'd seen him at Mrs. Potters' place. Maybe he lived closer than she'd thought. It wasn't unusual for people to drop in and talk, especially if they were related to someone. Besides, Erica hadn't seemed worried about the guy. He'd seemed normal when Angie had talked to him.

Yet as they arrived at the parking lot, she still glanced around to see if Timber and Jon were still around. Ian's words echoed in her head, and she repeated them aloud. "You meet such interesting people at the park."

Dom sat at the back door, waiting for Angie to open it so he could climb inside. He stared at her, apparently curious about who they'd met as they hadn't stopped to talk to anyone the entire trip.

"Don't mind me, boy. I'm just thinking out loud." She opened the back door to the SUV.

Back home, she checked Dom's food and water, then got ready. Next week she'd be back to her normal routine, and boy, was she looking forward to it.

The phone rang when she was in the car. She pressed the hands-free button to answer it. "Hey, Felicia, I'm on my way."

"Hey, winner, congrats. And I'm glad you lived through the night. Did you get sick at all?"

"No, but I don't know about the others. Estebe was fine when he dropped me at my car last night. And if something had happened to Bleak or Hope, I think we would have heard about it." Now Angie felt bad that she hadn't reached out to the others this morning.

"They're fine. I talked to Estebe earlier. And I just called Hope and told her to meet us at the grocery store next to the fairgrounds. I want them to be part of the shopping for today's event too."

"I'll be there in about forty minutes. Or do you want me to go right to the trailer and start setting up?" Maybe she hadn't had time to walk Dom this morning. She was always trying to fit in one more thing and misjudging her time.

"Come shopping with us. I want to run this dessert idea by you in case you have some last-minute changes." She paused, then continued. "How are you really? Estebe said you were a little bummed out after talking to Sydney and Brandon last night?"

"I just freaked out a little thinking that someone would be so cruel." Angie thought about the pang in her chest when she saw the two of them together, their lives ahead of them. "Sometimes I just don't understand people."

"You understand people fine. There are just some that are totally screwed up. Whoever killed Chef Nubbins and poisoned Brandon isn't a normal person. That's why you don't understand them. You're way too nice sometimes."

"I'm way too focused on my little world sometimes," Angie corrected. "Anyway, I'm glad we're working together today. Ian and I are going to play at the fair after this is done today. Want to hang out with us?"

"Sounds like a plan. Although Ian might not like me horning in on your date."

Angie smiled, thinking about all the times she, Felicia, and Todd, their ex-partner and Angie's ex-boyfriend, had hung out after events. "You're part of my life. My tribe. Ian gets that."

"You make our friendship sound like a cult." Felicia laughed, the sound tinkling over the speakers in the car. "Of course, with our work family added in there, maybe we are a little like a cult. One that worships food."

"Excellent food," Angie corrected. She had another call coming in. It was Ian and she'd forgotten to text him. "Hey, I've got to take this. See you in a few."

She connected with Ian. "Sorry, I forgot."

"I figured. I had some time while he was talking to his wife about the program, so I stepped out to the car to get a flyer and call you. I take it you're in the car?"

"Yep. Felicia and I were chatting about today's event. I'm meeting her at the store. Okay if she hangs with us tonight?"

"I'll have two beautiful women on my arm. What could be wrong with that?" He covered the phone. "Looks like we have an answer. I'll see you later. Good luck today."

"Good luck to you too." Angie turned up the music and pushed everything else out of her head. Today was about the cooking. No stress, no worry. Just cooking and feeding people. Those were the best times.

When she pulled up at the store, she found Hope, Bleak, and Felicia standing outside by Hope's little car. Bleak kept pointing toward the road. Angie parked and hurried over. "What's going on?"

"Bleak says…" Felicia started, but Bleak cut her off.

"That was Martha. I know it was." She pointed to a line of cars heading up the hill toward Cole Road and the west side of Boise. "In that VW Bus. That's her car. She's here to get me."

"Who's Martha?" Angie followed the vehicle with her gaze until they couldn't see it anymore. It had already been too far away to get a plate number. She couldn't even tell if they were Idaho plates, or Utah.

"Martha's my aunt. My father's sister. She didn't want me to come here. I shouldn't have trusted her. But she seemed like she cared about me. Like she didn't want me to have to…" Bleak swallowed. "I need to keep moving."

"No way in heck. We're going to call Sheriff Brown and have him check into this. Right now? You're under his house and his protection. If you don't want to go home, we'll figure something out." Angie glanced at Felicia, who had her arm around Bleak. "Why don't you two go inside and start our shopping. I'll talk to Hope, then I'll call the sheriff. There's no way that bus is getting close without one of us seeing it."

Felicia nodded and turned Bleak toward the store. "We've got some fun stuff happening today. If you don't want to leave the trailer, we'll get permission for you to stay inside with us. You can switch places with Hope and find out why she's so crazy about cooking."

Hope watched the girl as they walked off. "She got upset as soon as we turned onto Chinden from the freeway. Said someone was following us. We got here and that green bus followed us into the parking lot. When Felicia got out of her car to meet us, the woman took off. I think Bleak's right. That bus was following us."

"Don't let her out of your sight today. We're going to figure out if this aunt is really here and if she can just take Bleak with her. I don't think Sheriff Brown is going to let that happen." Angie gave Hope a hug. "You did great."

"I kept thinking what would Estebe do, but then that didn't work, because he's big and strong and he'd probably flip over the car." Hope let her lips curve into a smile. "Then I wondered what would you do and that's when I saw Felicia. I pulled into a parking spot and told Bleak to stay inside. Felicia scared her off. I think she was trying to get Bleak alone."

"So let's not let her be alone. You go inside and help with the shopping." Angie dialed Sheriff Brown's number as she watched the hill, making sure the woman didn't make a U-turn and come back. "Allen, this is Angie."

"What have you gotten yourself into now?" Allen's terse response made her chuckle.

"Where are you? At the fairgrounds?"

"Just arriving now. Don't tell me your trailer was torn up because you won?"

Angie hadn't thought of that. "I hope not. Actually, we're over at the grocery store. We think someone is following Bleak. Her aunt."

"The father said he was washing his hands of her. Why would her aunt come to find her?" The sheriff's tone wasn't dismissive, but instead, thoughtful, like he was trying to piece together a puzzle.

"I'm not sure, but I know there's more to the story of why she left than she's telling us. She said she confided in this aunt and told her about her plans to come to Boise. Maybe there's something more than just a bad childhood going on here."

The line was silent. "That was my initial thought too. These cults are known to marry off their daughters early. Maybe that's what Bleak's running from."

Pain crushed her heart. "Then we have to keep her here."

"I'm working on it." He sighed. "Of course, it's Saturday and I'm not going to be able to get any formal court documents before Monday. What's Ian doing today?"

"He was talking to a farmer earlier, why?"

"Keep an eye out on her. I'm going to call him and ask him to play bodyguard for the day until I can take her home. I don't like her around all those people by herself. People are abducted from big events like this all the time."

Chapter 20

"Seriously, I don't need a babysitter." Bleak glared at Angie like it was her fault Ian was going to be following her. "Maybe it wasn't even Martha. Maybe I was just seeing things."

Ian had shown up less than an hour after Angie had hung up with Sheriff Brown. Which told Angie how serious Allen had taken the threat.

"Then you'll have a handsome man at your beck and call all day until Allen comes to get you. I haven't seen all the fair yet. I keep meaning to get over here, but I'm always working. Would you mind showing me around? And if you wouldn't mind, I'd love to ride some of the rides. The last time I was here, my date was a little bit of a wimp around the rides." Ian pushed up the English accent just for Bleak's amusement.

"You wanted to go on the zipper. I hate anything that flips me upside down as part of the 'fun'," Angie explained.

Bleak laughed and Angie could see she was relaxing a little. "I guess I could hang out with you for a while. Just don't cry when we're on the rides. It's so embarrassing."

"We'll see who cries first." Ian lifted his closed fists under his eyes and twisted, like he was bawling. Then he dropped his arms. "That's as close as I'm going to get. You, on the other hand, you look a little frightened already, and we haven't even left the trailer."

"Oh, buddy, you're so on." Bleak grinned, but Angie could still see the worry in her eyes. The kid had moxie. She was going to pretend nothing was wrong as long as she could. "I guess if you insist, you're going to see what rides are supposed to be like."

Angie stopped Ian as he started to follow Bleak out of the trailer. "Keep her close, okay?"

"Don't you worry. You just get in there and cook amazing food." He kissed her, then focused on Bleak. "You want some food first? I'm starving."

"You're going to regret that," Angie said as she watched them walk away. She turned back to Hope and Felicia. "Or maybe not. Ian has an iron stomach."

Hope sank into a chair. "I really am praying this is a false alarm. She seemed so happy last night. She was even talking about letting Maggie check her into school next week. She asked what kids wore to school here. I'm going to go through my closet and see if I have some things that will fit her. She's so tiny."

"You're a good kid." Angie squeezed Hope's shoulder. "If there is a problem, Sheriff Brown will fix it. He's invested in keeping Bleak safe."

"Maggie told Bleak that they never had kids but they'd both wanted several. I guess she just couldn't get pregnant." Hope looked up. "I probably shouldn't have told you that."

"We're not going to spread rumors about the sheriff and his wife," Felicia assured her. "So let's get things unpacked and ready for prep time. Getting all those apples ready is going to take some time."

Felicia had decided on a caramel apple crumble. Simple, but full of flavor. It would be easy to carry in a small paper basket like the ones that loaded hot dogs came in, but you could also sit and enjoy the dish. Angie headed to the door. "I'll go outside and see where the judges are. We should be starting any minute."

When she stepped outside, she saw Sheriff Brown heading her way. When he came close, she shut the trailer door and moved to the table, motioning him to follow. "What's going on?"

"Where's Bleak? Did Ian get here yet?" He glanced around as if the two of them would be just around the corner.

"He's here. He took Bleak to get some food and to go have some fun. She needs to relax if she's seeing things like her aunt around every corner." Angie watched his face, hoping to see the answer she wanted. Instead, he stayed serious. Too serious. "Crap, her aunt is in the area, isn't she?"

"We don't know that. I just know that the officer I sent out to the compound verified that she wasn't there. Everyone's claiming not to know where she is, but her vehicle, a 1972 green VW van isn't at the compound either." He took his hat off and ran a hand through his thinning hair. "Maggie's scared for the kid."

"We'll just keep an eye out for her. I've got plenty of people who will take shifts being with her if you need more people."

He studied her. "That's kind of you. You've already bonded with the girl, haven't you?"

Angie smiled. "It happens when you cook together. She's part of our crew now. Hope's probably the closest person to her. I know she's older, but Bleak appears to be an old soul. I think they could truly be friends."

"I think you're right." He stood, checking his watch. "I've got to get back to the task force. They're bringing in Tara to question her this morning."

"I don't think Tara killed Chef Nubbins. According to her, they'd already broken their thing off." She stood and followed him to the edge of the counter. "She was even invited to the wake last night."

"About that, I heard you went. Didn't you think that maybe it wasn't the best idea? Especially since by winning yesterday's section, you're probably in the killer's crosshairs right now anyway?" He froze her with his gaze.

"Estebe was with me, and neither one of us ate anything. I could see the headlines in *The Statesman* this morning. Entire culinary community killed at wake for poisoned chef." She glanced around at the two other trailers in the lot. "I can tell you that I'm not coming back for next year's contest. This has been way too stressful for what should be lazy August days."

"You got that right. Although the fair is always a high-crime time, usually it's just kids breaking into all those shiny cars in the parking lot." He tipped his hat. "Good luck today and keep your eyes open for trouble. I don't think this is over yet."

Angie watched as he strolled out of the area. She thought he was right about one thing. She didn't think it was over yet either. Which was another reason she didn't believe that Tara was the killer. Either way, it was a good thing her restaurant hadn't made the finals. Tara would be too busy with the task force to focus on what to serve one hundred people. And, if she wasn't in the contest anymore, the killings couldn't have been about winning if she was the killer.

She closed her eyes. She was going around and around with this. She needed to clear her mind and think about the apple crumble. What could they do to make it stand out? Sydney was an excellent pastry chef, so Angie knew her dish would be outstanding. And Miquel had a solid pastry chef at Bien Viveres as well. The odds were about even that any of the three remaining contestants could win this thing. She just wanted it done and over with.

Feedback from the mic had her eyes flying open. She watched as the three judges along with another person climbed onto the wooden platform they'd built to bring the judges a little higher so people could see them. Ann Cole walked with a striking redhead up to the microphone.

"Looks like we got done just in time," Felicia said. Angie turned to see Hope coming out of the trailer to meet them.

"Who's that with Ann Cole?" Angie gestured toward the stage.

Felicia frowned. "You don't know? I thought you and Estebe would have met her yesterday."

When Angie shook her head, Felicia pointed. "That's Carol Nubbins. The widow?"

Angie studied the woman. At the event last night, she'd had her head wrapped in a black scarf. Now, her red hair was bouncing around her shoulders. She hadn't been wearing makeup either. The woman on the stage was drop-dead gorgeous. David Nubbins had been an idiot.

As Ann Cole tapped on the microphone to get everyone's attention, Mrs. Nubbins stood behind her, making eye contact and waving to several people in the audience. She glanced right over Felicia and Angie, not even pausing to see if she knew either women. Ann turned the microphone over to her and she smiled.

"Good morning, everyone. I just wanted to thank you all for attending the wake last night. David would have been so emotional knowing how much he meant to the culinary community here. I've been told by the Boise State Culinary Department that a scholarship fund has been set up to take donations in David's name. If you want to make a difference and support the future of the restaurant business, please consider giving."

She stepped away from the microphone and smiled at Ann. "With that lovely announcement, let's get this contest going. Today's winner won't be announced until noon tomorrow, so make sure you're here for the award presentation. Chefs, let's get those desserts going. We'll be serving at exactly 1 p.m., and voting closes at three. That should give you all enough time to choose your favorite dessert."

This time a man standing behind her blew an air horn, and the chefs scrambled back to their trailers to start working. Felicia was on her left as they walked back to the trailer. "I can't believe they're stringing this out for another day. I thought I'd have tomorrow to relax."

"We don't have to miss service if we don't want to. We could go in and work." Felicia climbed the steps to the kitchen. Hope was already at the sink, running water to wash the apples.

"I have a date tonight. You can do what you want, but you're more than welcome to hang out with us, like we'd planned."

"Angie Turner, I've never known you to turn down an opportunity to work. What has gotten into you?"

Angie shrugged and picked up a paring knife to start peeling the skin off the apples. "I'm being nice to Estebe. He likes to be in charge sometimes."

"That's for sure." Felicia laughed and turned on the stereo. "Then I'll be your wing girl tonight. As long as you don't think of me as a third wheel."

"Never. Now, let's get this dish done. The people aren't going to feed themselves now, are they?"

They were about halfway through prep when a knock came at the door and Bleak and Ian came bounding inside. Ian took a big whiff. "Hey guys, how's the food coming? It smells amazing."

"We're doing great. How's the fun times at the fair?" Angie didn't have to ask, really. Instead of the worried, almost-in-tears girl who had left with Ian a few hours ago, Bleak looked like she could float on air. Her face was bright red, though, from the heat. "Grab some water bottles. I don't want to have to pack any of this back home."

Ian grabbed two out of the fridge and threw one at Bleak. "We've exhausted the rides so we're going into the exhibition hall so we can see if there's any good free stuff left to grab."

"And you'll be inside out of the heat," Angie added.

He shrugged. "There's that too. What time are you serving?"

"One thirty. So be back here about one and you can help hand out bowls to people. That front window is way too tall for kids to reach."

"Sounds like a plan." He looked at Bleak. "You ready, kid?"

"Unless you need more time to cool off. Being old and all," Bleak shot back.

Ian shook his head and glanced at Angie. "The abuse I have to put up with."

"Whatever. Come on, old man. I want to get some fudge." Bleak moved to the door.

"Hope, step outside with Bleak a second. I want to talk to Ian." Angie glanced at Hope, who scurried after Bleak. "We'll be quick."

When the door closed, he focused on her. "So, it's not an idle threat."

"Bleak's aunt is nowhere to be found, but she told people she was coming here to get her." Angie touched his arm. "Be careful, but keep a really good eye out for her. The aunt can't know she's at the fair, but just in touch."

"I think she knows. Bleak told me she called her aunt from Allen's house and told her all about what was going on here. She thought her aunt was being supportive." He stepped toward the door. "I don't like her alone out there. Even with Hope."

Angie let him go, and soon, Hope came back inside. She paused at the sink to wash her hands. "Bleak already knew her aunt was here. She was just putting up a good face so she wouldn't look like a baby."

"She's a strong girl," Felicia said. "No one should have to decide that living in an alley is better than being home."

With that, they got back to work. But Angie's mind didn't leave Bleak's situation through the entire prep time. When they were ready to start serving, she opened the door and scanned the crowd. No Ian. No Bleak.

Felicia put a hand on her arm. "Don't freak out. They probably just got tied up with something and lost track of time. You know how hard it is to get somewhere with all these crowds. They could be right outside the gate, waiting to be let inside."

"You're right. Let's get this party started. Felicia, Hope, you two plate, and I'll go outside and hand out the dishes. When Ian and Bleak arrive, I'll come back inside."

"Sounds like a plan." Felicia grabbed the bowl of cream she'd just whipped and moved it to the table near the window.

Angie slipped outside and into the crowd. The number of people who were there seemed larger than yesterday. She didn't see the guard at the entrance. Had they stopped checking people before they came inside the event grounds? She ducked and weaved through the crowd, stopping at the large window at the front of their trailer. People were already lined up, waiting for them to start serving.

Angie smiled and handed out the first bowl. "This is our take on a caramel apple crisp. The County Seat uses locally grown products as much as possible in our creations, so the apples you're eating came from Emmett."

She kept talking about the County Seat and her philosophy of food as she handed out bowl after bowl of the treat. It smelled great, and about thirty minutes in, she realized she was starving. As soon as they were done with service, she was beelining to the corn dog stand. She'd just reached up to grab another couple of treats when a man reached up behind her and took both bowls.

"Go back in. Bleak and I can handle this now." Ian stood in front of her and handed the bowls to the next two people waiting in line. He smiled at the women in front of him. "The County Seat is a farm-to-table restaurant located in a small town south of here called River Vista. Have you been there?"

"We've been to the town, but not to the restaurant. Where are you from? Are you the chef there?"

Angie thought the woman actually batted her eyes at Ian.

"No, ma'am. That's my girlfriend's job. I'm from the area originally, but grew up in England. If you will excuse me, there are a lot of hungry people in line." He turned back to Bleak and waved Angie back to the trailer. "We're handling this. Go back inside and help Felicia and Hope. Bleak, grab me two more. You get them from the trailer, and I'll hand them out."

Within ten minutes, the routine of adding two more people to the process had their line totally worked through. They had a few stragglers here and there, but Angie thought they might just have served most of the one hundred people who had bought wristbands for the event.

"Just ten more minutes and we're done." Felicia rolled her shoulders. "I swear, this is more stressful than a full service at the restaurant."

"I agree. It's because the service is all condensed." She leaned against the wall and watched the people milling by the trailer. Ian was talking with an older gentleman about apple orchards from what Angie could overhear. She glanced around but didn't see Bleak. She stepped closer to the window.

"What's wrong?" Felicia scanned the area. "Do you see something?"

"It's what I don't see that bothers me. Where's Bleak?" She called to Ian. "Ian, where's..."

"She's there." Felicia pointed to the middle of the crowd. Bleak was talking to an older woman dressed in a long denim skirt and a peasant blouse. Her hair was wrapped around her head in braids. The two seemed to be arguing about something, and Angie saw Bleak try to step away. The woman grabbed her arm, pulled something out of her tote, then slammed it into Bleak's forearm. The girl went down like she'd been shot.

"Ian, stop her." She pointed to the crowd then started out the door. "Show him where she is. I'm going after them."

She pushed through the crowd without a sound. She tried to aim in front of where the woman would have Bleak now, especially since the girl wasn't able to struggle. Then she saw Bleak's shirt. The woman had her standing, walking her out of the area. They'd just been stopped by the guard at the front gate.

"I can call emergency services, and they can get her some assistance," Angie heard him say as he reached out to get his microphone.

This time she saw the black stun gun in the woman's hand. The guard started shaking, then fell on the ground.

"That won't be necessary," the woman said as she stepped over him and dragged Bleak with her. Angie had one shot before the pair got into the stream of people heading to the exit. She judged the distance, then dove into the woman. She knocked her down onto the ground.

They were all in a heap on the grass.

"Leave us alone. You don't understand. If Bleak doesn't fulfill the contract, Amie will have to step up. She's too young." The woman dug in her tote, but Angie saw the stun gun had fallen out in the struggle.

Angie pushed Bleak away from them. The girl was still out of it as Angie stepped between her and the woman who appeared to be her aunt. "You're not taking her. No matter what your reason is. She's not going back."

"You don't know what you're doing." The woman dove for the stun gun, and Angie crossed the few feet between them and stepped on her arm. The woman screamed and jerked back, but she didn't throw Angie's stance off. But she didn't expect the aunt to fling her other arm toward Angie's knees and toss her on the ground. They both reached for the stun gun, but a male hand reached down and picked it up.

"This isn't the way to come visiting your niece. And she was just telling all of us what a good person you are. I guess you had her fooled." Ian picked up the stun gun and tossed it to Felicia, who was now standing next to him watching. "Hold this while I tie this one up?"

Ian pulled the woman to her feet. Angie rolled over toward Bleak and checked to see if she was breathing.

A golf cart rolled up to the site. The security guard from the first night called out to the growing crowd around them. "Move aside, folks, let me in. Looks like we have an issue here."

Angie waved him over. "This girl needs an ambulance. That looney tune used a stun gun on her."

The security guard glanced at Ian, who had Bleak's aunt in a hold with her arms behind her back.

Ian smiled at the guard. "Todd, you don't have any handcuffs or restraints, do you?"

Todd picked up his walkie-talkie and called for an ambulance, using his other hand to give Ian the handcuffs off his belt. Then he knelt beside Angie and checked Bleak's pulse. "You people seem to always be in the wrong place at the wrong time."

"Tell me about it." Angie brushed Bleak's hair away from her face. "Is she going to be okay?"

"Her heart rate is steady. Are you sure she just stunned her?" He glanced up at Angie. "Typically, people don't pass out from being stunned."

"I saw her pull something out of her tote." Angie stood and went over to where the woman's purse sat on the ground. She dumped it out on the grass.

"Hey, that's my property." The woman—Bleak had called her Martha, Angie remembered—tried to pull away from Ian.

"We won't steal anything from you. Not like you tried to take Bleak from us." Ian pulled her back, away from the purse.

"Bleak isn't yours. She's my family," Martha growled.

Angie pointed to a syringe on the ground. "What did you shoot into her? Into your family member?"

Martha shrugged. "Just some go-to-sleep juice. It's an easy fix when you need someone to be quiet."

Angie wanted to scream. The fact that Bleak was as normal as she was had to be a testimony to the girl's determination. She definitely didn't get it from her family. She made eye contact with the guard. "The ambulance needs to hurry."

"Don't worry, they'll be here soon. It's just hard to get through all these people." He stood and began to try to disperse the audience watching the scene they were causing. "Nothing to see here, folks. Check out your evening news if you want the full scoop."

Felicia knelt next to Angie. She pointed out other things on the ground. "Duct tape, rope, more drugs. Man, the woman came prepared."

"With a stun gun to fight us off. Who does that?" Angie took the stun gun from Felicia and tucked it in her jacket pocket. She'd hand it over to the police, if they ever got here. Maybe the guard hadn't adequately expressed the urgency of the situation. But he had been successful in moving the people away. She glanced around at the slowly dispersing crowd. "And where is the ambulance?"

"Relax, mama bear, I can see it coming down the walkway." Ian nodded to the left and all of a sudden, they were surrounded by five more golf carts and a full-sized ambulance van. Emergency personnel poured out of the vehicles and moved in on the group.

"Ian, what do you have there?" Sheriff Brown went right to his nephew. "Tell me this is Martha Lancaster. I'd like to sleep a little better tonight than I thought I was going to with her loose."

"According to her Utah driver's license"—the security guard picked up the wallet and handed it to the sheriff—"that's her name. And this was all in her purse. I witnessed Ms. Turner dumping it out on the ground."

Sheriff Brown looked at the license, then at Angie. "There a reason you dumped her belongings on the grass?"

"Yes, we assumed she'd stunned Bleak, but then, Terry here said that a stun gun wouldn't make someone unconscious. So, we needed to know what she gave her. She said it was some sort of narcotic."

"Well, from her employee ID card, it looks like she should know. She's a CNA at a nursing home in George, Utah." Sheriff Brown turned back to the woman. "Looks like you're going to need to come with me."

"I'm going to sue all of you. There won't be a restaurant when I'm done with you. And I'm suing the fair for letting these people manhandle me. I was just taking my niece home," Martha blustered as two deputies took her and put her in one of the golf carts. "Where are you taking me?"

"Take her to the security trailer. We need to make sure what jurisdiction should be prosecuting her attempted kidnapping and assault." He walked away from the screaming Martha and then took Angie's arm and pulled her away from Bleak. "Let the EMTs do their job. She's in good hands now."

"I can't believe I watched her just try to walk out with her. I told Felicia to call you. Or I thought I did. It's all jumbled up. I probably shouldn't have tackled her, but I couldn't let her just take Bleak like that. I mean, if Bleak wanted to go, I'd drive her back home. But she shouldn't be forced to go, right?" Angie knew she was babbling.

Ian came to her side and tried to move her away. "Come sit in the trailer. Let them do their work."

"I had to save her. You know?" Angie leaned into him and then let him lead her back to the trailer. When they got there, he opened the door and sat her in a chair. He got her a bottle of water, then knelt down to look at her.

"Are you sure you're okay? You're not hurt, right?"

Angie sipped the water. "No. I'm just shaken up. Do me a favor and go check on Bleak. Send Felicia with her in the ambulance. She shouldn't be alone."

"I've already called Maggie. She's meeting them at St. Luke's, but I agree, someone should go with her. I'm going to send Hope home, but I'm pretty sure she'll ignore me and go to the hospital too." Ian picked a piece of straw out of Angie's hair. "You did awesome out there."

"You helped." Angie shuddered, remembering reaching for the stun gun and trying to beat Martha to it. "If you hadn't shown up then and she'd gotten the stun gun, Bleak would be gone."

"Let's just say it was a team effort." He glanced out the window at the empty event area. "Looks like we missed the announcement of today's winner. I'll try to find out who won."

Angie shook her head. "Don't bother. I'm not even curious. Just go make sure Felicia stays with Bleak. I'd hate to learn there's another relative just waiting to snatch her at the hospital. Or run the van off the road and kidnap her there."

"Your mind runs in weird ways. If there is someone, Felicia might be hurt." He paused at the door.

"Felicia carries in her handbag. She always has." She laughed at his look of horror. "You thought she was all sweet and innocent, right? The girl has a conceal and carry license and spends at least one day a month target shooting. I'd trust my firstborn with her against a storm of baby kidnappers."

"The things you don't know about people." He nodded to the water. "Finish that and I'll take you out to dinner as soon as I get back from talking to her. Then we can go spell Felicia at the hospital. I think we both need a short break from crazy."

Her life seemed to focus on the crazy. At least since she'd been home from San Francisco. Who knew that the big city horrors she'd been warned of so many times by well-meaning friends before she left Idaho wouldn't occur until after she'd moved back home? People were crazy everywhere. Maybe Idaho was just a smaller area so you ran into them more frequently.

She was considering this line of thought when a knock came at the trailer door. Either Ian had been really fast and had locked the door when he'd left, or she was about to get a lecture from Ann Cole about not being available when the awards were given out. She hoped it was Ian, but she had a bad feeling that she was in trouble.

She swung open the door. And immediately a man forced his hand on her mouth and pushed her back inside, closing the door with his foot. "Scream and I'll make this quick."

Angie looked into blue eyes that reflected a glee at his threat. She had no doubt that he'd follow through. She felt the point of a blade at her stomach. She stayed still and nodded her understanding. The man in front of her had been the man who had scared Miquel. The carny who had been visiting the restaurants.

He dropped his hand off her mouth. "You seemed like a bright girl. I'm just sorry I'm going to have to take you out."

"Why were you at the County Seat? Why are you attacking chefs?" Angie's throat felt bone-dry, and she wanted to cough but thought if she moved even an inch, the knife might make its way into her body.

"Aren't you the curious one? You don't ask why I'm killing you. Or even beg for your life. Although we might get to that later." His gaze dropped to her chest, and he licked his bottom lip.

The movement made Angie shudder. She swallowed again. "So, are you going to tell me?"

"Why should I? Why should I waste the precious time we have together?" He leaned into her. "You smell wonderful. All cinnamon and sugar and a little bit of fear."

She tried not to move. "Humor me then."

"You are a determined one. I like my women like that. Maybe I'll just take you with me. The carnival is closing up and leaving tomorrow anyway. We could be two states away before anyone even misses you. And my sister can just deal with it." He licked her neck.

The smell of his breath, heavy on the whiskey, made her tremble. She was going to die. Today, tomorrow, next month, whenever he was done with her. It didn't matter, it was going to happen. All she could do was hope that it would be fast. She glanced around the trailer hoping that Felicia had been too distracted with Bleak's abduction to put away all of her knives. Maybe there was something she could fight with. And going down fighting was better than just letting it happen. She was having a very bad day. She just prayed it wasn't her last.

She saw the door move a bit in the wind. He hadn't closed it when he'd kicked it. It had banged open again. Ian stood outside the door, his face red and finger to his mouth. He held up a phone and then pointed away from the trailer. Translation, she hoped, was that he was going to call for help. If it had been Felicia, she would have just told Angie to drop and she would have shot him.

Angie felt in her pocket. She still had the stun gun she'd taken from Felicia when she'd dropped it by Bleak. She shook her head, hoping that Ian wouldn't walk away because she thought she'd only have one chance at this.

Tackling Martha had been the dumbest thing she'd ever done. In just a few seconds, it would be the second dumbest.

The man pushed away from her. The grin on his face made her gut drop. He might kill her, but he had other things on his mind now.

"Yeah, you taste really good. She's just going to have to wait a bit for your demise." He set the knife down and shrugged out of his jacket.

"Who's your sister?" Angie didn't wait for an answer. She stood, planted her feet, and raised the stun gun. She hoped this version didn't have some sort of safety she had to mess with. If it did, she was probably dead. And Ian with her.

She pulled the trigger.

Chapter 21

The man fell toward her and as she jumped back away from him, Ian burst into the trailer.

Ian stared at the man on the floor. "What in the world did you do?"

Angie took his phone and pointed to the man still jerking from the shock. "You probably should tie him up or something. Is this Sheriff Brown?"

"What is going on over there?" The phone vibrated with his voice.

"I did what I needed to do. Oh, by the way, I forgot to give anyone Martha's stun gun. So, it's going to have been used again. How far away are you?"

The door swung open, and she had her answer. Sheriff Brown stood in the doorway, filling up the small trailer area. He handed Ian his handcuffs. "We were coming to deal with this."

"The guy had a knife to my gut. I think I would have been in the hospital on a surgery table in the best scenario if I'd waited. He's pretty crazy." Angie nodded to the door. "Do you mind if I go sit outside at the table? I think I might need to throw up now."

Sheriff Brown moved away from the door, and Angie aimed for it. Her vision was off. She hadn't been hurt, so why was she feeling so woozy? He grabbed her arm. "Hold on a moment. What's on your neck?"

She reached up, but he held back her hand. "Ian, grab me a wet paper towel and a baggie if we have one in here."

Angie giggled. "Bottom drawer. He left his cooties on me."

"He left a lot more than cooties." Sheriff Brown eased her down the stairs and onto the chair. He took the items from Ian. "Tanner? Get in there and get that guy under custody. He's poisoned her."

"I don't feel poisoned. I feel happy." Angie stretched her neck out to the left so the sheriff could clean the powder off her skin. "And tired, really, really tired."

"Ned, call for an ambulance. We'll meet them at the front gate so she doesn't have to wait." He tucked the paper towels into the bag. "Let's get her on the golf cart, and we'll head over to the front gate. Tell them to hurry."

Ian moved in front of his uncle and picked Angie up into his arms. "I'll carry her. You drive."

"I can walk, you know," Angie protested, but honestly, she wasn't sure she really could. Her head was pounding now, and the light seemed really bright. She closed her eyes and leaned into Ian. "You smell really good. Not like that other man. He smelled wrong. Like he was too angry for a long time."

"Shhh, now. We're going to take a quick run to the hospital." Ian slipped into the back seat of the golf cart and checked to make sure she was tucked in beside him. "Go, Allen, I think it's getting worse."

"I just got a text. The ambulance will be waiting for us. They had been called out on a heatstroke incident but the kid refused treatment." Sheriff Brown started the engine. "Let's get her out of here."

They weaved through traffic, taking the golf cart as fast as it would go, which seemed like forever to Ian. When they reached the gate, the EMTs took her off his lap and put her on a gurney. Ian followed them. "I could have walked her here faster."

"Not with all those people. They would have knocked her out of your arms." Allen slapped Ian on the back. "Go with her. Give me your keys, and I'll have someone drive your truck over to the hospital. Do you remember where you're parked?"

"Row EE near a light pole." He nodded to his uncle. "Thank you. I'll let you know what they say."

"I've got a few things here to clean up, then I'll be over there. Maggie's already there with Bleak, so check in with your aunt too, okay?" His phone rang, and he nodded to Ian as he walked away from the ambulance. "Sheriff Brown."

The EMTs had already loaded the gurney with Angie into the van. One of the guys held open the back door. "You ready?"

Ian climbed inside and started praying.

* * * *

Angie's eyes hurt as she blinked them open to see where she was. She remembered little about what had happened after they'd finished service. Something about Bleak. Something about Chef Nubbins. Her attacker's face filled her mind. She tried to sit up. To get away.

"Hey there, calm down." Ian's face filled her view. She took a deep breath and smelled his cologne. She was safe. He wasn't here. He hadn't killed them.

"I stunned him." Her eyes widened as she remembered what had happened. "Oh, no, I stunned him. Is he dead?"

"Not dead yet. But if I ever get the chance to talk to him about how he treats my girlfriend, he might be." He smiled at her. "He is in jail and will stay there. He admitted that he was ordered to take you out, but then he stopped talking when they asked him who did the ordering."

"His sister. He said she was in charge. Of course, he's crazy. I could see it in his eyes. For all we know, he could be taking his orders from one of the chickens in the poultry barn." She reached up to her aching head. "I don't understand. Why am I in the hospital? Did he hurt me?"

"Apparently he used some sort of topical drug on your neck. Allen saw it when he took you out and wiped it off. If he hadn't, the doctors say you would have had quite an interesting afternoon." He took his hand in hers. "But you're here and you're safe now."

"He said he had to kill me. But he had decided to play with me for a while. He was going to take me out of town." She rubbed her temple with her free hand. "He sounded smug about it. Like he'd done it before."

"Allen thought he'd put poison in the drug stuff, but they tested it and thought it was just the drug. He was probably using it to get you to his car." Ian squeezed her hand. "Don't worry about it. It's over now."

"For me. It's over for me. The sister might be doing something like this to someone else. Maybe if you run his fingerprints you can find out who he is. He told me his name was Ted." She brushed off his hand and struggled to sit up.

Ian handed her the bed adjustment. "Here, but you're not getting up, so don't try anything."

"Glad to see you're putting your foot down." Sheriff Brown came into the room. "Ms. Turner, you have to be the most unlucky person I know. Even when you're not investigating, the idiots can't help putting you into their crosshairs. You're going to get seriously hurt one of these days."

"I didn't do anything. I was sitting, waiting for Ian to come back, and I heard a knock on my trailer door. I wanted to go to the hospital to be with Bleak." She looked around the room. "Not be stuck here in my own room and bed. Someone needs to feed Dom and the others. I don't think I'll be home tonight."

"I already called and talked to Mrs. Potter. She's having Erica go over before dinner tonight. And she knows where you keep your extra key." Ian looked up at Sheriff Brown. "Any word on the guy who did this?"

"His name's Ted." Angie rubbed her eyes.

"He's not talking, but his prints came back and we know who he is. Funny thing, he used to be a chef. Had his own restaurant and everything in Shreveport. Lost it in a flood. He'd let his insurance expire and then, wham, natural disaster. Some people just don't learn. And his name's not Ted." The sheriff glanced at his watch. "Maggie's taking Bleak home in a few minutes. Once she woke up, she was fine. The ER is busy enough without us hanging around. Are you going to be all right?"

She glanced at Ian, who was sitting next to her. "Looks like I'm going to be fine. Sorry about stunning him. I'm not going to be in trouble, am I?"

"Looked to me like self-defense. He was holding you against your will, correct?" Sheriff Brown adjusted his hat. "We don't put people in jail when they're just trying to save themselves. Although, if I thought it would teach you a lesson and keep you safe, I might try it."

"Hey now, I was being good. I was sitting in my trailer, waiting for Ian to get back. I didn't ask for a crazy guy to come knocking at my door." She repeated her story. She knew he was kidding, sort of, but still, she wanted to make her case.

"And yet, they always do. We need to figure out why these people are attracted to you in the first place. You either have the worst luck, or you're pushing out bad karma into the world." Sheriff Brown held up his hand. "No explanations needed. I'm just going to have to keep expecting things like this to happen to you. Honestly, I know you did the right thing in both cases today, but you're scaring me just a little."

"Thanks, Allen. We appreciate all you do." Ian stood and walked his uncle to the door.

Sheriff Brown turned and looked back at Angie. "She's your problem now. Try to stay out of trouble. I hope to have this case closed soon. We still need to figure out who and where his sister is located. From what I heard of his rantings, she's got to be the brains of this outfit."

Angie watched as Ian and Sheriff Brown walked out into the hallway. In just a few minutes, he was back inside her room, pouring her some ice water. "You may be dehydrated."

"So, you think I put myself in danger too?" she asked.

Ian set the glass down on the table and moved it closer to her. "I think sometimes you take risks that make my heart hurt. I just want you to be safe. Sometimes what you do doesn't keep you safe. What if you'd missed when you'd tried to tackle Martha? What if you'd missed trying to stun this guy? You're taking chances."

"If I hadn't stunned him, he would have tried to take me out of the trailer. You would have tried to stop him and might have gotten hurt. I don't want you to get hurt because of me," Angie explained her reasoning. "Besides, from what you've said, I might not have had a second chance the way he drugged me."

"I'm not going to get into this argument. You're safe now, that's all that matters." He closed his eyes and took a deep breath. "You scare me sometimes. And today, you scared me twice."

She knew how he felt. She'd thought she was dead. That the man would mess with her for a while, then kill her. She tried one more time to explain her side. "If I hadn't known what he was planning, I wouldn't have tried to get away."

"Don't second-guess yourself." He leaned forward, hands on his knees. "As much as it pains me to say it, you did what you needed to do."

They were quiet for a minute. Ian picked up the remote, then set it down. "Something's bothering me, though."

"Why I had the stun gun?"

He shook his head. "We'd just gone through chaos, I can see you forgetting to hand it over to the authorities."

"Then what?" Angie's head was hurting. Whatever Ted had tried to drug her with hadn't reacted well with her system. Or maybe she had some kind of drug hangover? She hadn't had any experience with illegals. This could just be a side effect.

"He looked familiar. I know we saw him at the fairgrounds our first night, but he looks like someone. I just can't put my finger on it. His eyes, they remind me of someone."

Angie sighed and leaned her head back on the pillow. "I know. I had the same feeling when I was talking to him. Like it was on the tip of my tongue, but then, poof, it was gone."

"Maybe if we both stop thinking about it, we'll remember." He picked up the remote. "They're letting you go home tonight. We're just waiting on your doctor to check you one more time. Then I'll drive you home."

"What about my car?"

"Estebe and Felicia are heading over there before service to pick it up. It will be waiting at home when we get there." He turned on the television, then flipped through the channels until he found a chef cooking some sort of beef. "You just relax. You've had a busy day fighting crime, Super Chef."

She smiled at the nickname. "I love this recipe. I was going to change it up and see if the crew wanted to make it next summer when our tomatoes are fresh."

He picked up the remote. "You've seen this before? Do you want me to change the channel?"

"No. I like watching reruns. It's more relaxing when you know how the recipe is going to turn out." She reached for his hand.

"Not many people turn a cooking show into a fiction story. You're a strange girl, Angie Turner."

She squeezed his hand. "And that's why you love me, right?"

"Definitely."

By the time they pulled into the driveway, it was almost nine. Angie had tried to talk Ian into stopping by the County Seat. She hadn't been in the place for a couple of days, and she was feeling restless. He'd driven on past, not even slowing down when she'd pointed out an on-street parking spot.

When she almost fell out of the truck getting out at home, she'd knew he'd been right. She was so tired. Ian hurried to her side and walked with her to the porch. "You want some soup or something to eat?"

She studied him. "I don't have any instant ramen or canned pasta to heat up."

"You do have soup in the freezer, and I know perfectly well how to warm up soup on the stove." He didn't let her stop in the kitchen, but instead, led her to the couch and handed her the remote. "Dom, watch her and keep her from doing anything."

Dom woofed in answer. But Angie thought it was just a greeting rather than an answer to Ian's command. "You weren't expecting us so soon, were you, boy?"

Dom sniffed her hands and her bare forearms. She wondered if it was the hospital smell or if somehow he could smell the residuals from the drugs she'd been given. He gave out a small woof, apparently confident that she was all in one piece and okay. Then he laid his head on her lap.

"Television it is, then. Let's see what's on now." They hadn't watched Saturday night shows since she'd opened the restaurant. "Look, it's Guy. We love his shows."

She settled into the couch and with Dom next to her, quickly fell asleep.

The smell of spicy tomato soup woke her a while later. Ian stood next to the couch, a tray in hand. "I love that soup. Keeping the tomatoes in bigger pieces rather than straining it and adding onions and peppers made it almost like a beanless chili recipe."

"You're good. Of course, you did make it, but your freezer is filled with all kinds of soups. You don't have to cook for years, from what I saw." He set the tray on the coffee table and sat down next to her.

Dom must have moved over to his bed near the fireplace sometime while she'd been asleep. She broke open a roll and spread butter on it. "I wouldn't say years, but yeah, I have a good supply. I probably need to slow down since Mrs. Potter isn't in residence next door year-round now."

"I can take some home and put it in my freezer, if you want. I'm always looking for quick meals for lunch and dinners." He grinned. "Besides, when your girlfriend is a chef, you're not supposed to know how to cook. I'm fine living on leftovers and scraps from the restaurant."

"You sound like you're eating out of the trash cans." Angie laughed as she turned down the volume on the television. "All you have to do is show up at the restaurant and Felicia will seat you at the bar. We'll make you dinner."

"I don't like to bother you at work." He sipped his soup. "This is so much better than canned."

"I should hope so." She leaned back and watched him eat for a minute. "Did you hear from Allen?"

"I did. He's at the station with the DA figuring out what charges to file. Bleak's home with Maggie. They're watching some fashion contest." He squeezed her hand. "She's fine. And she's made a formal request to be removed from her home. I guess her aunt Martha was correct. Her folks had promised her in marriage to some forty-year-old guy in the cult. I can't believe that still happens in this day and age."

"At least she's safe." Angie curled her legs underneath her. "If I fall asleep, wake me up before you leave."

"What, you don't think I can carry you upstairs?" He nodded to the soup bowl. "Do you want more?"

"I'm good." And for the first time in days, she actually believed in her own words.

Chapter 22

When Angie awoke Sunday morning, Dom was already gone from the bedroom. "Thank God for doggie doors," she muttered as she made her way into the bathroom to get ready for her day.

By the time she got out of the shower, she smelled bacon cooking. Quickly dressing, she wondered who was in her kitchen cooking. She paused at the doorway and smiled. The better question would have been who *wasn't* in her kitchen this morning.

Ian was sitting at the table in the same clothes he'd worn yesterday. Apparently, he'd stayed over on the couch last night, even though she'd assured him before she went to bed that she was fine. Estebe was at the stove frying the bacon, and Felicia was coming in the door with Dom on her heels.

"Precious and Mabel are fed. I swear, that goat has such a huge personality. It was like she was asking where Angie was and why I was feeding her," Felicia announced to the room, then laughed when she saw Angie at the same time Dom realized she was at the doorway and trotted over to say good morning. "Good morning, sunshine. I was going to give you a few more minutes to sleep while Estebe finishes up breakfast."

"What are you guys doing here?" Angie walked over and gave Ian a kiss.

"Ian called and said he needed clothes from his apartment and asked if I would drop them off before heading into town for the Restaurant Wars announcement. I talked to Estebe, and we decided to come over and have breakfast together. Especially since you single-handedly caught the killer yesterday." She grabbed a slice of bacon, then slipped into one of the kitchen chairs. "Tell me all about it."

"Coffee first. And I didn't single-handedly catch him. I just defended myself when he came after me." She went over and pour a cup. "There's a big difference. One I'm sure Sheriff Brown will be lecturing me on as soon as he thinks I'm well enough to be yelled at."

"Allen won't yell at you." Ian glanced at her over the rim of his coffee cup. "Much."

"Besides, I'm sure Angie doesn't want to go over such a traumatic experience before she has eaten." Estebe put a plate in front of her. Hash browns with cubed potatoes, onions, peppers, and sausage covered half the plate. A couple of eggs over easy with three slices of bacon filled the other side. "We should have brought bread. You don't have any."

"Yes, I do." Angie nodded to the fridge. "I keep it in there because it's homemade. I don't want it to go bad so fast. There's a sourdough loaf and rosemary focaccia."

Felicia jumped up. "I'll make you toast. Sourdough?"

"Please." She didn't pick up her fork. "I'll wait for you all."

"Don't wait, your food will get cold. Ian, you're next. How do you like your eggs?" Estebe moved back to the stove while he was waiting on the answer.

It took less than ten minutes, and everyone was finally seated at the table eating. Felicia looked up at Angie, then wiped her mouth. "I totally forgot to tell you."

"The County Seat burned down last night." Angie really couldn't handle any more bad news.

"What? No, the restaurant is fine. Although we were totally booked, including the bar seats, last night. Everyone wanted to talk to you about what happened. It was great for business." Felicia shrugged off Estebe's look of surprise. "Anyway, we won yesterday's competition. Even before you went all hero-mode to stop a child abduction and apprehend a murderer. Totally based on our food. We won a second segment."

"Not a surprise here. That must have been why he targeted me. Which means he knows who wins before it's announced." Angie spread strawberry jam on her toast. "He wasn't one of the judges, we know that."

"But maybe he was related to one of the judges." Ian nodded, thoughtful. "I get where you're going with this. Maybe his sister was on the panel."

Angie shook her head. "Ann Cole's the only female on the judging panel. And according to her bio at the City Hall website, she's an only child. So, unless she lied, she can't be our man's sister. Ian, your uncle said they already knew who it was. Do we have a name?"

"Jamie Jeremiah Johnson." Ian picked up a slice of bacon. "I'd kill, too, if I had to live with a name like that. It sounds like a race car driver's, not a chef's."

"So, let's see what Google has to say about Triple J." Angie took her empty plate to the sink and ran water over it. Then she grabbed the laptop she kept in a kitchen desk. She let the computer boot up while she poured another cup of coffee.

"I'm pretty sure Allen's search engines are way more powerful and he hasn't found anything on the guy." Ian finished off his plate and mirrored Angie's movements, sitting down with fresh coffee. Angie knew he typically liked tea more, but she guessed he was needing the caffeine hit.

"Sometimes easy works better," Angie said, ignoring the jab at her primitive investigation skills. "Here we go. Ten pages of results. A lot about some fire at his restaurant. So he wasn't lying about that. He had been a chef."

The room got quiet as she skimmed the news reports.

"According to this, the reporter tried to contact him on the five-year anniversary of the fire where five people died, by the way, but couldn't find him. Off the grid, totally." Angie met Ian's gaze. "So, he must have hit rock bottom and joined the carnival. That way, he could make everyone pay for what he's doing. I bet if we track his carnival's stops for the last five years, we'd find several missing or dead girls."

"Looks like Allen has a slam dunk." Ian let out a breath. "I was worried that the guy might actually get out on bail. If that had happened, you'd be spending some quality time across the pond with my mother until he was back behind bars."

"That's so sweet." Angie's eyes widened as she took in Ian's threat. "But honey, I have a business to run. I'm needed here."

"Not if someone's trying to kill you, you're not." Felicia sipped her orange juice. "We've built a perfectly adequate staff so that you could be gone for a while and not have it affect the business."

"So glad you consider me 'adequate'." Estebe tugged at Felicia's hair. "But at the cost of my pride, she's right. If you had to go, we would hold up the restaurant. And you know there's such a thing as Skype, right? You might bring us some new exciting dishes from your exile."

"From England?" Ian shook his head. "I think you haven't traveled much. We're kind of Plain Janes in the food department."

"I thought that was a generality?" Estebe leaned forward, and the three of them continued their discussion on the value of English cuisine.

Angie kept digging. Finally, she found what she was looking for. An old picture of Jamie with two women. An older woman with a pinched face. Angie couldn't tell if the clothes were as dark as they seemed in the black-and-white newspaper photo, but from the cut and style, she assumed they were. All three were being awarded ribbons from the county fair in North Carolina. His mother, Edna Johnson, had won the pickling contest; the sister, Jane, the baked breads division; and Jamie, who was only fourteen with high wader pants and a choppy home-done haircut, the cookie division. Angie bet that he was taunted mercilessly when he started high school. Had all serial killers had bullies in high school who made their lives miserable? She turned the laptop around. "His sister's name is Jane."

"And he has to have the worst haircut in North Carolina history. What is he there, twelve?" Felicia leaned in to see the picture closer.

"Fourteen. Which would make him just about to start high school. This couldn't have been easy for him when he got around the jocks." Angie shook her head. "I am not feeling sorry for him. He was going to do horrible things to me. He told me so."

"Just because you understand the wolf, doesn't mean he won't bite." Estebe looked at the clock. "If we're going to be on time for the ceremony, we need to get Angie's kitchen cleaned up."

"I can do it when I get home." She went back to the list of hits and looked for more information.

"I will not leave a house with a kitchen I dirtied. You just sit there and research. Maybe you'll find out where this Ruth went to after high school." Estebe got up and started cleaning out the sink.

"Can I use your shower?" Ian stood and picked up the tote that Dom had been using as a headrest.

"Of course." She squeezed Ian's hand as he walked by. "Estebe, you know I have a dishwasher."

"Hand-washing dishes is relaxing. There have been a lot of not-so-relaxing things happening lately. I will choose relaxing for today." He kissed Felicia on the cheek as she came up and started helping.

"Fine, don't mind me. It's just my house." Angie didn't feel as testy as her words seemed to portray. Besides, they didn't listen to her anyway. She focused on the computer, writing down bits and pieces to hand over to Sheriff Brown. Of course, he probably had professional investigators doing the same thing, but this gave her comfort. She really wanted to be doing something. Yesterday had scared her, and she didn't want to feel like a victim anymore.

By the time everyone was ready, she didn't have much to report. She put all the towns and high schools and names into an email and sent it to Sheriff Brown's account. She'd done what she could. Now it was time to go market her business.

She didn't like this part of owning a business. To be seen at specific events just to show off the restaurant and hopefully bring in new customers. She glanced at her capris and tank and decided it was upscale enough just in case they did win. And as a bonus, she hadn't spilled anything on the front of her while she'd been eating.

They took three cars since Ian was heading over to his aunt and uncle's house after church. Felicia and Estebe had ridden together, and he promised he'd get her home. So that left Angie driving alone to the event. She didn't mind. She could turn up the volume on the stereo or sing along with songs she loved. Being alone was a bonus since it hadn't happened much lately.

They pulled into the fairgrounds at the same time and the teenager directing travel set them up one next to the other. Now all they had to remember was that they were on the Elephant Row, slots 200 through 202. Felicia grinned as she came out of Estebe's Hummer and met Angie. "An elephant never forgets, so this is a good sign."

"I'm not sure it works that way," Angie countered, but Felicia wasn't listening. She waited in the middle of the parking lot in front of the cars.

Waving, she giggled. "Let's go! It's the last day of the fair."

"She really gets into this, doesn't she?" Ian fell in step behind Angie, tucking his keys into his front pockets.

"Felicia loves a party." Angie smiled as they followed Estebe and Felicia and made their way to the main gate. "When we're done with this, I'm heading home. Precious needs some playtime, and Dom needs a walk."

"Just be careful out there at Celebration. It's a long way from anywhere."

"Stop being an overprotective boyfriend. Geez, it's like someone tried to abduct and possibly murder me yesterday." She took his arm.

"Sure, laugh it up, but I was scared. And I'll be scared until you call me and tell me you're back home again, safe and sound." He held up their passes, and after a bored glance at them, the teenage guard waved them inside. "I guess they're ready for the fair to be over too."

"It can be a little much—all the heat and food and party atmosphere. I'm sure I came home crying on more than on occasion to visit the fair when I was a kid." She rolled her shoulders. "Seriously, I am out of here. No rides, no animal barns."

"No corn dogs?" Ian pointed to the booth ahead of them. All week the line had been at least ten deep. Today, there was no one waiting. It was early, but still.

"Don't get crazy." Angie took off at a trot. "Do you want one?"

"We just had breakfast."

Angie turned back, confused. "So that's a no?"

"Get me one. Lots of mustard." He pulled out his wallet and set a twenty on the counter before she could pull money out of her pockets. "I'm buying."

"Okay, then. But this so doesn't count as date night." She leaned into his shoulder, waiting.

The girl behind the counter laughed. "You two are so cute. I don't know why, but so many couples fight at the fair. Isn't this supposed to be the happiest place on earth?"

"I think that's Disney World," Angie corrected, her mouth watering as the girl slathered mustard on the freshly cooked dog. She held out a hand, but Ian got there first.

"I pay, I get first dog. Especially since this isn't a date." He took a deep breath. "I so want to dig in, but I know it's too hot and will burn my mouth."

"That's the best part." Angie leaned on the counter watching her corn dog frying. "So, spill—were any of the couples Idaho-famous?"

"Like the actors who live in Sun Valley?" The girl shook her head. "No such luck. But the dead chef and his wife came by on Friday night. They were fighting."

"Chef Nubbins?" Angie took the corn dog from the girl.

"That's the one. Man, I wouldn't have been surprised if she'd killed the guy. It just goes to show that you don't know how much time you have on this earth. You have to treat everyone like it's their last day."

"Well said." Ian took the change she handed back and then left a few dollar bills on the counter for a tip.

"I bet she's going to wish she wasn't such a witch to him when he called her Janey June." The girl laughed. "You should have seen the fire light up in her eyes. She was red hot."

As they walked away, Ian paused and took Angie to the side of the pathway where there was a bench. "I want to make sure you're okay before we go in. And no eating anything that I don't hand you."

"Triple J is in a jail cell. Maybe we should call him quadruple J now." Angie took a bite of the corn dog. The tang of the mustard with the heat of the corn covering made her eyes water. "Wait, did we know that Mrs. Nubbins's name was Janey June?"

Ian shook his head, focused on the corn dog. “I thought it was June. She introduced herself that way last night. Just June.”

“Then maybe Janey June is a family name. Like Jamie Jeremiah.” She thought about the two people. They both had red hair. Was that enough to call foul with siblings? “Call your uncle and ask him if they have Triple J’s family information yet.”

“You can’t be thinking…” Ian pulled his phone out.

Angie interrupted him. “That’s exactly what I’m thinking. She did a quick turnaround in forgiving him for the affair with Tara. Framing her for his murder would be the icing on the cake.”

“Yeah, but what would Jamie get out of it?” He dialed a number.

Angie sighed. “That’s the question, isn’t it?”

Chapter 23

They didn't have long to wait. At the end of Ann Cole's presentation of the winner of Restaurant War to Sydney Cook, Sheriff Brown came into the audience and stood by Angie. "This thing is quite the show, isn't it?"

"Sydney deserves to win. She cooked some amazing food during this whole thing. And she did it while building a person inside her tummy." Angie waved at her friend, cheering as the audience started clapping.

"I was actually talking about the whole murder thing."

Angie whipped around so fast she got a little dizzy. "Are you serious? You figured it out?"

He shook his head. "No, you figured it out. Janey June Johnson is Jamie's sister. And for the last twenty years, she has been David Nubbins's wife. She planned this whole show."

"But why try to poison Sydney?" Angie glanced up at her friend who was still on the podium talking to everyone. And, she saw now, Mrs. Nubbins was up on the stage too. Two police officers were flanking the stairwells on both side of the stage. Janey June was oblivious to their presence, chatting with a tall, handsome man to her right. When she saw the police officers, there was nowhere for her to go.

As they led her down the stairs, she paused by Angie. "If my stupid brother had been thinking rationally, this would have ended a whole different way."

"If your brother had been rational, you couldn't have talked him into taking out your problem." Angie stared into the woman's cold eyes. There was no goodness there at all. No sadness. No guilt. Just anger.

"Get her out of here," Sheriff Brown ordered the men. "You did Mirandize her when you put the cuffs on, right? I'd hate for this confession to get thrown out."

Janey June Nubbins rolled her eyes. "Like I'll spend even a night in jail. Money buys a lot of things, including bail."

As they walked away, Angie felt Ian's arm around her. "I'm going home. I've had enough of the fair for one year. Maybe even longer than that."

* * * *

Monday morning when she woke up, she smelled the coffee and bacon and wondered who was in her kitchen cooking. Again. She could get used to this. She took her time getting ready and even put on a little tinted lip gloss. She could do with a date Monday.

When she got downstairs, Ian was sitting at the table with Mrs. Potter and Erica. They were all sipping coffee and eating doughnuts that Ian must have brought from town.

Angie went straight for the coffee cups. As she poured the life-giving liquid into her cups, she realized the people at the table had grown silent. Maybe she was still dreaming. She took a sip of the coffee, and her eyes widened just a bit. Nope, she was definitely awake. "If you'd told me there was a party going on in here, I would have come down sooner."

She sat at the table, but still no one spoke. "Okay, guys, this is getting a little creepy. Am I dreaming? Did someone die? Oh, no, is Felicia okay?"

"Everyone's fine. Mrs. Potter just has something disturbing to tell you." Ian reached over and took Angie's hand.

"It's okay, I figured you'd leave sooner or later." Angie took a doughnut out of the box. "So, when are you moving? This fall?"

"You knew he was going to try to buy the ranch? Don't tell me you already sold?" Mrs. Potter looked angry.

"Wait. Who's buying the ranch? What did I sell?" She looked around the table in confusion.

"That guy you asked me about who visited Grans? He made her a really good offer for the house and the land. Top end of the scale, from what I can see." Erica glanced around the kitchen. "I'll miss this place. You made it feel so homey."

"Jon Ansley offered you money for your farm? Why? We're out in the boonies. Are you wanting to sell?"

"He said they're bringing in a soy processing plant. They bought up that veterinarian's fields last year. I figured I don't want to live here with all that going on." Mrs. Potter rubbed the table that had been Angie's Nona's kitchen table too. "There are just so many memories in these houses. I can't bear to think of them torn down."

"No one's tearing my house down. I can't tell you what to do, but I'm fighting this. I don't think they can put the plant up without community support, and I'll make sure there isn't any. Not one drop." Angie finished off her doughnut and went for a second. She was at war, and she needed the calories.

"That's my girl." Ian beamed at her, pulling out a notebook she kept in her kitchen desk. "So now, let's figure out how to stop this guy. Tell me everything he said. Let's figure out where we need to start."

And for the next few hours, they planned and plotted and did the work to save their homes. At the end of the day, as Erica helped Mrs. Potter back across the road, she stood on her porch watching. The sun was setting, and the evening felt perfect. There was no way some guy was going to take this all away from her for something as simple as money.

She'd find a way to stop this from happening. She had to. Too many people were counting on her.

Dear Readers:

I learned to cook early. When my friends were using canned tomato soup for a sauce for spaghetti, we had to make our own sauce with fresh veggies and home canned tomatoes. Even when money was short, we always had food available, but it was what we'd call whole foods today. Fresh, frozen and home canned vegetables. Meat frozen in the chest freezer in the mud room. Mom would buy bread at the outlet store where we'd also get fruit pies which got popped in the freezer as well. Hamburger Helper never sat on my mom's pantry shelves.

Mom's meal planning was pretty basic. Meat and potatoes with a loaf of bread and butter on the table. A big salad and a vegetable. Plain Jane meals, but when I think back, they were always filling and tasty.

When I started my own life and got married (the first time), that's the only way I knew how to cook. Homestyle. I've tried prepackaged meals and they just don't taste the same. And typically, it's just as quick for me to whip up something in the kitchen rather than wait for delivery.

I do love weekday meals that don't take forever to make, yet taste like you slaved away in the kitchen. Especially since I spend a lot of time here, on the computer with you all. This recipe is one of those meals. My version of Shepherd's Pie. To save even more time you can use the refrigerated mashed potatoes found at most groceries. Or to make it lower in carbs, use mashed cauliflower.

Enjoy,
Lynn

Shepherd's Pie

Heat oven to 400 degrees.

Topping

4 large russet potatoes

Peel and boil until soft then drain and mash with the following:

1/4 cube butter
1/4 cup milk
1/2 cup sour cream
Salt/pepper to taste

Meat Mixture

1 chopped onion
1 tsp garlic (or two crushed cloves)
1/2 tsp thyme

Fry over medium heat for five minutes
Then add and brown:

1 1/2 pounds of ground beef

When beef crumbles, add a 12oz bag of frozen mixed veggies.

Cook for five minutes, then add two Tbsp of flour. Stir so it coats the hamburger. Then add:

2/3 cup of beef broth

Cook down for five minutes – then put meat mixture in shallow baking pan.

Spread mashed potatoes over the top of the meat mixture and put in the oven for 20 minutes.

So, so good and filling for a chilly winter night. The cowboy gave it his seal of approval.

Eat well.

Love Lynn Cahoon?

Don't miss any of her outstanding

mystery series

The Farm-to-Fork Mysteries

The Tourist Trap Mysteries

and

The Cat Latimer Mysteries

Available now.

Printed in the United States
by Baker & Taylor Publisher Services